The SONGS of MAGIC Trilogy

"An engaging fairy-tale adventure."

—*School Library Journal* (*A Darkening of Dragons*)

"Patrick's clever, compelling story is set apart by the incredibly rich history and mythology of its world. It is by turns dark and funny, and the interspecies friendships ring warm and true."

—*Booklist* (*A Darkening of Dragons*)

"Nonstop action and plot twists keep readers on their toes."

—*Kirkus Reviews* (*A Vanishing of Griffins*)

Stories in The Songs of Magic Series

A Darkening of Dragons
A Vanishing of Griffins
A Thundering of Monsters

In a world of dragons, song-spells, Pipers, and battles, three accidental heroes found themselves thrown into an epic quest which began in *A Darkening of Dragons* and continued in *A Vanishing of Griffins*.

✶ ✶ ✶

Now, although they've been separated, Patch, Wren, and Barver continue their hunt for the evil Piper of Hamelyn in a final thunderous adventure.

A Thundering of Monsters

The Story So Far

Ten years years after the **Hamelyn Piper** stole the children of Hamelyn Town—making sure his own twin brother was punished in his place—the evil Piper escaped justice and went into hiding. **The Pipers' Council**—the highest authority for Pipers—launched their **Great Pursuit** to track him down.

Patch Brightwater is a trainee Piper who has proved his courage time and again. **Barver Knopferkerkle** is a draco-griff—part griffin, part dragon. **Wren Cobble** used to be cursed into the shape of a rat, but her curse has been lifted by the Sorcerer **Underath** in gratitude for our heroes' help in saving the life of his only friend, the griffin **Alkeran**. Wren now hopes to learn the art of shape-shifting. But Patch and Wren have discovered the Hamelyn Piper's hiding place—calling himself the **Black Knight**, he wears a suit of armor made of the magical substance **obsidiac**. All he needs is an ancient amulet to complete the armor, and he'll be immortal.

Time is running out!

Helping our heroes thwart the villain's plans are **Alia Corrigan** and **Tobias Palafox**, members of **the Eight**—the brave group who hunted the Hamelyn Piper all those years before.

Thinking they can catch the Hamelyn Piper by surprise, Tobias sets out to raise an army to help. Alia, seeking the aid of dragons, takes Patch, Wren, and Barver to **Skamos**—the only city where dragons and humans live side by side. When the city is destroyed by the dragon **General Kasterkan**, they have no choice but to flee and find help from griffins instead.

But when they meet with the small army of Battle Pipers and soldiers that Tobias has raised, the tables are turned! They discover that the Hamelyn Piper commands a vast army of mercenaries; our heroes are outnumbered and face annihilation!

Wren is captured by the evil Piper! Thanks to her courage, however, the others escape using the magical

Leap Device, which lets them travel great distances, only to find themselves trapped in a mysterious land—where they discover Barver's father, long thought dead. They realize they're imprisoned in an unknown Sorcerer's **Bestiary**—a magical zoo.

That only leaves **Rundel Stone**, famous officer of the Custodian Pipers, and his apprentice **Erner Whitlock**, who are heading to **Tiviscan Castle**, home of the Pipers' Council. They're desperate for the Council's help, yet are uncertain if they can trust them—mindful of a prophecy that suggests the Council could betray them all.

★ ★ ★

Can Patch and his friends escape their strange prison? Will Wren survive the terrible wrath of the Hamelyn Piper? Can Rundel and Erner find help at Tiviscan, or does only betrayal await them?

And can the Hamelyn Piper be stopped before he finds the amulet he seeks—and becomes impossible to defeat?

A Thundering of Monsters

BOOK THREE OF **SONGS OF MAGIC**

S.A. PATRICK

PEACHTREE
ATLANTA

Published by
PEACHTREE PUBLISHING COMPANY INC.
1700 Chattahoochee Avenue
Atlanta, Georgia 30318-2112
PeachtreeBooks.com

Text © 2022 by S. A. Patrick
Cover and inside illustrations by George Ermos
Title typography by Leo Nickolls

First trade paperback edition published in 2025

First published as *A Thunder of Monsters* in Great Britain in 2022 by Usborne Ltd., Usborne House, 83–85 Saffron Hill, London EC1N 8RT, England. *www.usborne.com*.

First United States version published in 2024 by Peachtree Publishing Company Inc.

All rights reserved. No part of this publication may be reproduced, stored in a retrieval system, or transmitted in any form or by any means—electronic, mechanical, photocopy, recording, or any other—except for brief quotations in printed reviews, without the prior permission of the publisher.

Composition by Lily Steele
Imported by Jonah Heller

Printed and bound in January 2025 at Sheridan, Chelsea, MI, USA.
10 9 8 7 6 5 4 3 2 1 (hardcover)
10 9 8 7 6 5 4 3 2 1 (trade paperback)
HC ISBN: 978-1-68263-584-1
PB ISBN: 978-1-68263-789-0

Library of Congress Cataloging-in-Publication Data

Names: Patrick, S. A., author.
Title: A thundering of monsters / S.A. Patrick.
Description: First edition. | Atlanta : Peachtree Publishing, 2024. | Series: Songs of magic ; Book 3 | Audience: Ages 8-12. | Audience: Grades 4-6. | Summary: Patch Brightwater, dracogriff Barver, and an army of Pipers find themselves stranded on a mysterious island while their shapeshifting friend Wren is held captive, but the three friends work to reunite and prevent the Piper of Hamelyn from achieving immortality and thwart a sinister plot.
Identifiers: LCCN 2023041390 | ISBN 9781682635841 (hardcover) | ISBN 9781682635858 (ebook)
Subjects: CYAC: Magic—Fiction. | Dragons—Fiction. | Friendship—Fiction. | Adventure and adventurers—Fiction. | Characters in literature—Fiction. | Fantasy. | LCGFT: Fantasy fiction. | Novels.
Classification: LCC PZ7.1.P3789 Th 2024 | DDC [Fic]—dc23
LC record available at https://lccn.loc.gov/2023041390

EU Authorized Representative: HackettFlynn Ltd, 36 Cloch Choirneal, Balrothery, Co. Dublin, K32 C942, Ireland. EU@walkerpublishinggroup.com

THIS IS FOR LAURA—ALTHOUGH, REALLY, EVERYTHING IS. WITH ALL MY LOVE

1
The Lost Army
Patch & Barver

Patch Brightwater sat near the cliff's edge, watching the sun rise over an unknown sea. From a cord around his neck hung the cross-eyed owl, Wren's favorite Fox and Owls playing piece. Every morning since they'd arrived in this mysterious place, he'd done the same thing: look out to sea and think of Wren.

This was the third morning.

Nearby was the cave where Barver slept. Patch missed his dracogriff friend during the night, of course, but it was right that Barver spend time with his father. Patch made sure to send him off in the evenings, reassuring Barver that he'd be perfectly fine here in the camp.

In truth, he wasn't fine. He didn't feel *unsafe*, though. Alia was there, and Tobias; both were formidable Pipers, and Alia had the added bonus of being a powerful Sorcerer. There was also the small army they'd brought with them, with forty Battle Pipers and two hundred and thirty soldiers—as well as the three griffins who'd helped them in their doomed quest to track down the Hamelyn Piper, two of whom were still seriously wounded.

So, no, he didn't feel unsafe, but he did feel miserable, and strangely *alone*.

Last night, Patch had noticed Merta Strife, one of the griffins, sitting awake by the fire near where the two injured griffins lay sleeping. He went over to join her.

"You can't sleep?" he said.

Merta shook her head and nodded to the slumbering griffins, Cramber and Wintel. "Cramber is healing well, Tobias tells me," she said. "But until he regains consciousness, his life remains in the balance."

Cramber was laid stretched out with one wing tied to his side, allowing the dressings on his chest wound to be changed without having to move him. Wintel was beside him, curled up with her head under her wing. Cramber's breathing was ragged; Wintel's was regular and peaceful, but she'd taken a severe blow to the head.

"How's Wintel doing?" asked Patch.

"She spends most of her time asleep," said Merta. "When she wakes, she's confused and can't see anything but a blur. The next few days will be key to how well she recovers."

Patch thought back.

They'd been so sure of their plan.

The Hamelyn Piper had been vulnerable, they'd thought—hiding out in the forests of the Ortings with a small group of his own soldiers. They'd known he'd created a suit of magical armor, one that would make him an even more powerful Piper than before; they'd known that he was looking for an ancient amulet that would grant him immortality.

Even so, they'd believed they would easily outmatch him with the army they'd brought. At last they would bring the evil Piper to justice!

Instead, it had been the Hamelyn Piper who had outmatched *them*, ambushing them in Gossamer Valley with a huge army of mercenaries. They'd not stood a chance.

"Wintel was so brave," said Patch. "You all were."

"We did what had to be done," said Merta. She gave Patch a kindly smile. "But it's Wren we all owe our lives to."

Patch clutched the cross-eyed owl, feeling tears prick at his eyes. *Wren*. She'd come up with the only plan capable of saving them. A plan that meant sacrificing herself, but which allowed their entire army to escape certain destruction, magically transported to this unknown place.

Unable to speak, Patch simply nodded.

He felt like everyone in the camp had said it, or something like it, in the last few days. Every Piper, every soldier, seeing Patch's heartbroken face, would put a hand on his shoulder and say, "*She will always be remembered.*"

And he wanted to scream at them to *shut up*. Because they all thought the same thing—even Alia and Tobias and Merta too. That Wren was gone forever.

Dead.

And that was why he felt so alone at night, once Barver had gone to his father's cave—because Barver was the only other person who hadn't given up hope.

So here sat Patch, looking at the sunrise and waiting for his friend to wake up. At last he heard the sounds of movement from the cave, and a few seconds later Barver sat down beside him.

"Morning," said Barver.

"Morning," said Patch.

"Can I?" asked Barver.

Patch nodded. He took the precious owl from around his neck and set it in Barver's hand; Barver held it tightly. They sat in silence and, together, thought of Wren.

Hoping.

The smell of smoke, and of meat cooking, made Patch realize he was hungry. They headed back toward camp.

"Did your dad say much last night?" asked Patch as they walked. Barver's father had been a prisoner here for over twelve years, utterly alone, not even knowing why he'd been captured. The sudden arrival of others, and of his own son especially, had seemed so strange to him that he didn't think it was real most of the time.

Barver smiled. "He talked and talked as usual, like he had a decade's worth of words to get out, yet I didn't mind. Just hearing his voice is a gift I never thought I'd get again. His eyes shone when I told him about my adventures—although there's a lot to tell! I had to cover the Hamelyn Piper and the quest of the Eight before I could even *start*, because when he was captured none of that had happened yet." His smile faded. "He made little sense most of the time, though," he said. "He claims he's never seen a single ship, or even a bird, out to sea. He warned me that sometimes dense mist rolls in and 'everything changes.' He wouldn't explain what that meant, but the idea seems to really upset him. If we're going to find a way out of here, we need anything he can tell us, though until he starts making sense I'm not sure how useful it is."

"Did you sleep at all?" said Patch.

"No," said Barver. "I came out as soon as he nodded off. I'll get some sleep later." He sighed. "It's so strange, talking to him. One moment he seems like my dad, and the next he's distant, talking aloud to himself or speaking like a child. Although I still haven't told him about Mum. When he asks about her, I just tell him she's well and missing him." He looked at Patch with sorrowful eyes. "I don't know if he could take it, knowing she died. Or that we'd fallen out beforehand."

As they walked through the sycamores, the smell of cooking grew stronger, and now they could hear the sound of axes on wood. Of all the oddities in this curious prison, the strangest surely had to be the way the vegetation regrew overnight. Much of the plant life was edible—wild carrots, derdily tubers, apples, and berries. Yet whatever they picked, the bushes were laden with fruit again by morning; whatever they dug up, a replacement appeared by sunrise. Even the trees, their trunks cut down for firewood (or for the various projects Alia had thought up) would regrow as if an axe had never touched them.

It was the same, they suspected, with the rabbits and pigeons, the only animals they'd found so far—their numbers seemed the same each morning, however many they'd caught the day before.

The camp was spread over several glades in the trees. In one, the horses grazed, each hitched to a ground pole. The Battle Pipers and soldiers camped in a second glade, at the edge of which the injured griffins were tended, Merta keeping a watchful eye.

The other glade in use was where Alia's "projects" were taking shape. Closest to the cliffs, and to the cave of Barver's father, this was the one that Patch and Barver reached first. Even though the morning was young, there was already plenty of activity here.

Alia spotted them and waved. She stood in the center of the glade while soldiers worked around her. Yesterday, they'd been gathering and preparing logs; today, they were tying those logs together.

"It's taking shape," said Barver when they reached Alia. "Whatever it is."

"*They* are taking shape," Alia said, and Patch realized there were three separate groups, lashing wood together with what looked like milkweed stems. "Two rafts and a scaffold. A resourceful lot, these soldiers of Kintner! Most of their equipment was left behind in the camp at Gossamer Valley. Luckily some of the horses were saddled with equipment packs when we *leaped*, so we have four axes and a variety of knives."

"Why do we need rafts?" asked Patch.

"And what do you mean by a *scaffold*?" added Barver. The rafts were easy to spot—a basic rectangle of lashed wood at their core—but the third construction was harder to work out, various sizes of log tied together into triangles several feet across, which were being fastened together into something much longer.

"You'll see what that's for later," said Alia. "First, though . . . any improvement with your father?"

"It's hard to tell," said Barver. "Although he does appreciate having *cooked* food for the first time since he's been imprisoned here."

Patch sniffed the air. The smell of roasting pigeon was making his stomach gurgle. "Speaking of which . . ."

Alia came with them, and Barver pressed her for an explanation of her rafts and scaffold.

"We have to do everything we can to escape from this prison," she told them. "The world must be warned of the Hamelyn Piper and his army! But how to escape? We know this is a Bestiary, a magical zoo. It seems to be split into enclosures. *This* enclosure is bounded mostly by cliffs, and the only way out is the large meadow beyond the sycamores. Past the meadow lie the bone trees. When the griffin Alkeran was also a prisoner here, he must have been in his own enclosure, far enough away that your father never heard him cry out. We have no idea how big this prison is!"

"Indeed," said Barver. "Everything about it seems wrong. There's a hill in the distance, but the air shimmers and I can't tell how far away or even how *high* it is. If we attempt to fly above the height of the trees, we fall unconscious. And as for the creatures that live in the bone trees . . ."

Patch shivered, remembering the horse that had panicked soon after they'd found themselves here, all of them disoriented by their magical *leap*. The poor animal had bolted across the meadow and into the tall trees that looked horribly like leg bones. As soon as it had gone out of sight, it had been attacked by something—its screams had filled the air before suddenly being silenced.

"Exactly," said Alia. "That's our neighboring enclosure, I believe. Many creatures with magical value are dangerous, but whatever lives in those bone trees seems particularly nasty. Your father said they sometimes hunt in the meadow, didn't he? Yet they never venture into *this* enclosure."

"Yes," said Barver. "They only hunt in the meadow on the darkest nights. Dad said he'd never actually laid eyes on one—that if you heard the *sounds* they made, you'd not want to see them either..."

Alia nodded gravely. "Well, if they're as unpleasant as they seem, then something must *prevent* them from coming here. I think those carved posts that run along the edge of the sycamores mark out the enclosure and act as a barrier."

Patch thought of the strange posts with just simple rope between them. "A barrier?" he said. "It wouldn't stop *anything*, let alone such vicious creatures."

"They're clearly magical," said Alia. "I imagine similar posts and ropes mark out all the enclosures in the Bestiary.

They didn't stop *us* from crossing them, so perhaps they're specific to the creatures being kept imprisoned."

"My father is *chained*," said Barver. "He can't travel far from his cave. Why be so cruel, if a magical barrier would stop him from leaving anyway?"

"A good point," said Alia. "But there's plenty of magic that only works for simple beasts. Those posts might be unable to trap an imprisoned griffin, yet they could still keep the creatures of the bone trees at bay. Now, to find a way out of here, we have the option of marching through those bone trees and fighting our way past the horrors lurking there. And then to the next enclosure, and the next, for however long the Bestiary continues! But a better plan may be to reach the sea and go by raft around the coast."

Patch was puzzled. "At the bottom of the cliffs? Where the sea crashes into the rocks?" He couldn't help picturing those rafts reduced to tiny splinters.

"You just need to get a bit of distance from the rocks first," said Barver. "I could fly a raft down there for you, I know I could!"

Alia was already shaking her head. Right from the start Barver had suggested he fly out to sea and get help that way, but Alia had forbidden it and made him swear not to try. "I told you, Barver," she said. "Whatever spell causes unconsciousness as you fly *up*, it's possible the same would happen when you flew away from the cliff, even if it was only a short distance. And there'd be no way to save you!"

"I'm sure I could carry a raft down safely!" he protested.

"I don't doubt your ability, Barver, but there's no need to take the risk," she said. "That's what the scaffold is for, you see—we push that out over the cliff edge and lower the raft down away from the rocks."

At camp, there was a steady supply of pigeon and rabbit being provided by the camp cooks. Barver asked them to put some aside for his dad, for later.

They sat on the grass as they ate and could hear the sound of Tobias playing his Healing Songs for the injured griffins. Patch would take a turn playing soon. He was proud of how good he'd become in such a short time. Not long ago, his skill at Healing Songs had been rather limited. While he'd been training at Tiviscan, his teachers had spotted that Battle Songs were one of his strengths and had often focused on that. Yet Healing was far preferable, Patch thought, and with Tobias as a teacher he'd discovered he had a knack for that too.

"When do you think your scaffold will be ready?" he asked Alia.

"Tomorrow, I hope," she said. "Although we'll have some other excitement this afternoon. Some of the soldiers are intending to *climb* down the cliffs!"

Barver frowned. "That would be even slower than escaping by raft," he said.

"They have a very important goal," said Alia. "We know you black out if you go too high *up* . . . What if the same thing happens when you go too low *down*?"

"That would spoil the raft idea," said Patch.

"Quite," said Alia. "By climbing down the cliff, we'll find out if the rafts can work. My fingers are very tightly crossed! Otherwise, we'd have no choice but to face the creatures in the bone trees and then to move from enclosure to enclosure—confronting whatever terrible beasts we come across. Not a pleasant thought."

It wasn't long before Tobias finished his Songs and joined them, just as Patch ate the last of his pigeon.

"Good morning," said Tobias. He eyed Patch's food. "I suppose I should go and get myself something to eat. Even if it's rabbit and pigeon . . . *again*."

"It's not that bad," said Patch. "They try their best."

"Just imagine what I could do with the right ingredients," said Tobias. "I keep thinking of the hedge-beet onions I bought. The vinegar makes those onions so much sweeter . . ." He had a faraway look in his eyes. "I'd had two barrels delivered and they're just going to waste in Ural Casimir's pantry. Such a terrible shame!"

"Not for me," said Barver, grinning. Patch grinned too—when Barver had eaten those onions before, he'd burped out a torrent of fire. "Hedge-beet plays havoc with my guts. If I'd been a dragon it would have been even worse, believe me."

"Yes, sorry," said Tobias. "I should be grateful we have food at all, I suppose."

"How are the patients?" asked Alia.

"Steady improvement," Tobias replied. "It's your turn to play for them, Patch. Focus your Song on Cramber this morning and keep his breathing steady. Wintel is out of danger, but Cramber could slip back if we're not careful."

Patch nodded and stood. Barver stood too—still rather battered after his encounter with the Hamelyn Piper in the battle of Gossamer Valley, he always curled up nearby when Patch played his Healing Songs, gaining some benefit as he caught up on his sleep.

"Oh, wake me when the cliff climbing starts!" Barver said to Alia before he and Patch headed to where the griffins slept. "I don't want to miss it!"

2
IN THE CAMP OF THE BLACK KNIGHT
Wren

Wren knew she was going to die.

The first time she realized it had been on the hills overlooking Gossamer Valley, moments after she'd seen Patch and Barver disappear into the shimmering ripple of the Leap Device's magic, taking her friends to safety.

She'd not been able to stop herself from grinning at the sight. Seconds before, the great explosive spheres had been launched from the many enemy catapults on the hilltops, converging on Tobias's meager army in the valley. Once the Leap Device had done its work, whipping her friends out of harm's way, those projectiles had detonated together in a gigantic explosion that had almost knocked the Black Knight—the Hamelyn Piper himself!—off his feet.

Wren had been sure he would kill her then and there; cheated at the point of victory, his rage seemed overwhelming. Instead, he'd hit her across the face, splitting her lip wide open. Wren had kept grinning. It was hard not to, knowing that her friends had escaped.

The days since had seemed like months. Manacled at the center of camp, she'd been fed very little. Her stomach was starting to hurt from it now, and she felt weak from lack of water. She'd not seen much of the Hamelyn Piper, not up close at any rate, but enough to notice that the piece of armor she'd stolen—the solid chunk of pure obsidiac that had allowed Alia to take their army to safety—had been replaced by steel.

His anger must be incandescent, she thought. She dreaded the inevitable moment when the Hamelyn Piper would come calling.

Four guards watched her at all times. They considered it beneath them, guarding a young girl just because their leader said she was dangerous. She was no threat at all, they thought, and Wren was happy to let them think it.

She'd tried to stay awake on the first night so she could practice the exercises she'd learned from her book on shapeshifting. Thankfully, she'd left the book with Alia—the first thing they'd done when they chained her up was to search her. If they'd found that book and thought she could shapeshift, they would have kept an even closer eye on her.

So Wren had played the role of pitiful girl as best she could, whimpering and shivering. She'd kept her tears just loud enough for them to hear. She'd pleaded with the guards to give her a blanket, a request that was met with laughter, but it had been worth a try. Even though the night was mild, a blanket would have hidden any changes she brought about if her shape-shifting exercises bore fruit.

She'd practiced picturing the form she wished to take, in as much detail as she could. That part was easy. She'd spent long enough as a rat to know everything about them. Even so, nothing had come of her efforts.

When morning arrived, the Hamelyn Piper's army struck camp and moved deeper into the forests of the Ortings. Wren was led by a chain fixed to her manacles. Whenever she stumbled and fell, the soldiers would kick her. At dusk, the army set up camp again. Another four soldiers took their turn to guard her. A meager gulp of water and a crust of moldy bread was her only meal.

That night, she practiced for an hour before exhaustion swooped down and took her. She hadn't managed to make anything happen—not even a whisker, let alone a tail. Again, the army moved on in the daylight.

She listened carefully to what the soldiers around her said, hoping to hear news of her friends and their escape. There were mutterings and complaints about the long daytime marches, and sometimes the talk turned to what had happened in Gossamer Valley, but nothing she didn't already know.

She thought of Rundel Stone and his apprentice, Erner Whitlock. They'd set out for Tiviscan, intending to discover if the Pipers' Council could truly be trusted. So much had happened since then! Skamos, the only city where dragons and humans had lived side by side, had been destroyed by a merciless dragon army, while the plan to capture the Hamelyn Piper had ended in the disaster of Gossamer Valley.

Wren knew it wouldn't be long before Alia got word back to Tiviscan Castle about the Hamelyn Piper and his vast army of hired mercenaries. And then, surely, the Pipers' Council would have to act.

Another night was spent camped; another day on the move. Still no word of her friends; still no success with her exercises. She thought back to the whisker that had appeared on her face in Ural Casimir's home. She thought of the tail that had taken her by surprise in Skamos, after eating spicy food. How did she ever expect to be able to shape-shift her entire body, if she couldn't even achieve the things she'd done by mistake?

There was another problem, one that would only get worse. Her thirst and hunger were making it harder for her to think straight. That night, she struggled to even *remember* her exercises. Actually *accomplishing* anything seemed farther away than ever.

The guards were crueler than they'd been up until now. They gave her no water at all and showed her handfuls of bread but then threw it to the ground, just out of reach. Their laughter filled her ears, and the tears that came were very real. The night was crueler too, turning much colder. Her hands were numb, her shivers uncontrollable, her pleas for a blanket ignored. Sleep wouldn't have come even if she'd sought it, but she had her exercises to do, if she could only rid herself of the rage she felt toward the soldiers guarding her!

And then it happened. A tail appeared, uncomfortable under her clothing for the few minutes it was there, but a triumph nonetheless.

Why now? she thought. At first she wondered if her *anger* was the secret, but then she had it—the anger had brought out a stubbornness that her underfed and dehydrated mind had been lacking.

Luckily, if there was one thing Wren Cobble had always been good at, it was being *stubborn*. The joy of her success proved enough to let her sleep, in spite of the cold.

When she woke, it was to a bright morning and more mocking laughter from the guards.

"Hungry, girl?" called one, seeing her wake. "Best be quick, you have competition!"

Where the guards had thrown the bread the night before, there was now a group of seven crows tussling over the crusts and crumbs. The guards thought it was hilarious, but Wren ignored them. Instead, she focused entirely on watching the birds: their feathers, their wings, their feet and beaks. She tried to burn the images into her memory and give her something other than rat flesh to concentrate on in her exercises later.

Her plan, such as it was, involved becoming a rat again, finding places to hide, and scampering through the shadows unseen until she could safely take human form. Whether she could get far enough away was her greatest worry. Rats could hardly cover any distance in a day. Humans on foot weren't that much better.

Watching the crows, though, gave her an idea. What if she could become a *bird*?

After all, now that she'd had her first success, why not be more ambitious? In a day, a bird could cross a whole *country* . . .

3
Master and Apprentice
Erner & Rundel

By the time Rundel Stone and Erner Whitlock reached Tiviscan Castle, Wren was already in the clutches of the Hamelyn Piper.

They had come to Tiviscan to determine where the loyalties of the Pipers' Council truly lay. If they were satisfied that the Council could be trusted, they would tell them of the plan that Tobias and Alia had hatched to locate the Hamelyn Piper and bring him to justice.

There was no way they could have known it, but they were already too late.

Their ride to Tiviscan had been at a faster pace than Erner was happy with—not for himself, but for his master. Rundel Stone was still recovering from being poisoned, and long days of horse riding were likely to set him back.

Rundel, though, dismissed the concerns of his apprentice, even insisting on riding through the night on this last stage of their journey.

Erner watched his master carefully and grew increasingly anxious at how tired Rundel was becoming. It was a great relief when, soon after dawn, Tiviscan Castle appeared ahead of them, high on the cliffs overlooking thick forest.

The Castle looked magnificent as always, although a few areas of stone were a slightly different shade of gray than the others. It had needed extensive repairs after the dragons besieged it, hurling the great rocks that had given them access to the dungeon cell of the Hamelyn Piper—or at least, the man *thought* at the time to be the Hamelyn Piper. Seeing it now, it was hard to imagine that there'd been any damage at all. The Castle looked impregnable.

Rundel Stone was clearly thinking the same thing. "They did a fine job of fixing the damage," he said.

"They did, Master," said Erner. He thought of Patch and Wren and the tales they'd told him on their travels together—of climbing out of their ruined cell and descending the cliff face to the bottom where they'd met Barver. Erner couldn't help wondering about the strange nature of fate: if the dragons hadn't caused all that damage in the first place, Patch would still be in those dungeons. And the Hamelyn Piper—the *real* Hamelyn Piper—could well be sitting in the

Castle itself, ruling over whatever parts of the world he'd managed to conquer.

Rundel and Erner wore the robes of the Custodian Elite, of course, and throughout their journey they had been well treated—the respect for Custodian Pipers was universal. The highest authority among Pipers was the Pipers' Council itself, yes, but while the Council could decide what the laws of Piping were, it was the role of the Custodian Elite to enforce those laws. More than that—Custodian Pipers represented justice and hope to the poor and downtrodden in the world. Only the most skilled Pipers were accepted into their ranks, using their abilities to help wherever they could.

The town of Tiviscan spread out from the walls of the Castle, toward the grassy plains beyond, and as Rundel and Erner rode through its streets there were plenty of greetings to be acknowledged from those townsfolk who were up and about at this early hour.

Here at Tiviscan, the face of Rundel Stone was known by all.

"Virtus Stone," they called, using Rundel's rank of "Virtus"—the highest of all ranks in the Custodian Elite. Rundel nodded back and did something Erner had never seen him do before in his dealings with the people of Tiviscan.

He *smiled* at them.

Erner could see in their faces a slight confusion, and he understood. Virtus Stone was a serious man with a serious face who lived a serious life. *The Cold Heart of Justice*, many called him. The last thing they expected was a smile. *Yet the smile was perfectly reasonable*, Erner thought. Rundel Stone had almost died, never to see his beloved Tiviscan again. For him to be here at all was miraculous, and if that didn't deserve a smile, what did?

In the town square, they stopped by the statue of Erbo Monash to let their horses have a well-deserved drink from the trough at its base. Erner dismounted and used the hand pump to top up the trough. As the horses drank eagerly, he looked up at the statue. Centuries before, Monash had founded the Pipers' Council and created the Custodian Elite—gathering the best of all Pipers, working to a code of honor for the good of all society. It caused Erner an almost physical pain to think that the Pipers' Council might not be trustworthy now.

In through the Castle Gates they rode, under the great double archways. They dismounted at the central Keep, near the eastern wall, where Rundel gave orders to a guard to stable their horses. "Is Lord Drevis back in Tiviscan yet?" he asked the guard.

"Not yet, Virtus Stone," the guard replied.

"A shame," said Rundel. He said it matter-of-factly, but Erner knew how much Rundel had been hoping that

Lord Drevis had returned. Drevis was leader of the Pipers' Council now, but ten years ago he had led the Eight in their hunt for the Hamelyn Piper. To Rundel Stone, there was no greater Piper in the world. Whatever corruption might have infected the Council, Lord Drevis was the only one they could trust without question. But when the Council had decided to launch their Great Pursuit, sending almost every member of the Custodian Elite on expeditions to hunt down the Hamelyn Piper once more, Lord Drevis had joined the first such expedition. He had been away from Tiviscan ever since.

"When the Council wakes," said Rundel, "tell them that Virtus Stone has returned, and that I expect them to convene a meeting of great urgency, no later than nine bells. In the meantime, I shall retire to my quarters."

"Yes, sir," said the guard, and led their horses away. Rundel looked at Erner. "We've done all we can for now," he said. "Now we must sleep, before exhaustion claims us."

The Custodian Quarters were at the western side of the Castle. As a Virtus Piper, Rundel's room was larger than most, with a decent amount of shelving and cabinets that he could, if he so wished, fill with knickknacks and ornaments to make the place feel friendly and warm.

Yet Rundel's room was mostly bare. His shelves contained copies of books that detailed the laws of Piping, as well as histories of Tiviscan and the Custodian Elite. There was nothing by way of keepsakes, nothing that had even a pinch of sentimentality.

The room weighed heavily on Erner's heart.

"How long has it been since we were last here?" Rundel said as they entered.

"We left the day after Patch Brightwater's trial," said Erner. "Four months back."

"Four months...," said Rundel. "It feels like years." He visibly sagged, leaning against his desk.

Erner insisted he get into his bed and rest. "I'll wake you in plenty of time for the Council," he said. Grumbling, Rundel took off his boots and coat and climbed into bed. He was asleep within moments, and Erner took the chance to lay a thick blanket over him.

He could do with sleep himself, but he wanted to visit the infirmary on the north wing first. There they had a small bathhouse that kept water heating from dawn to dusk, and Erner planned to ask them to keep one of the larger tubs free for his master.

Before he went anywhere, though, he opened a small closet next to Rundel's desk and took out a folded coat. The coat was deerskin and had belonged to Patch—taken from him when he was brought to Tiviscan and jailed. Patch's grandfather had made it for him, and Erner had promised to look after it; it had been here for safekeeping ever since. He unfolded it and hung it from a hook by the door.

He looked forward to returning it the next time they met.

Coming back from the infirmary, he passed by the notice board at the entrance to the Custodian Quarters. Neither he nor Rundel had paid it any attention on their arrival, but now he took the time to look over some of the notices pinned to it—a collection of local and worldwide decrees and pamphlets.

One of the pamphlets caught his eye, and he stared at it for a full minute before tearing it from its nail and hurrying to Rundel's room.

"Virtus!" he cried as he entered. "Master!"

Rundel was quick to wake, as all law enforcers tend to be. "What is it?"

Erner thrust the single sheet of paper into his hands. "Skamos was destroyed," he said.

Rundel read through the report. The details were sparse—a dragon army had forced the evacuation of the city of Skamos before destroying it "in moments with fearsome weapons." He raised an eyebrow. "It must be exaggeration," he said. "The rocks the dragons used on Tiviscan were effective, certainly, but damaging a castle is very different from destroying a city. The Council will no doubt have more information by now and will be planning their response."

He looked at Erner's worried face. "Patch Brightwater certainly has a habit of being in the wrong place at the wrong time," he said. "But the report states the city was evacuated beforehand, so we must assume they're all safe."

"We can't be sure of that," said Erner.

"Trust me," said Rundel. "The printers of such pamphlets wouldn't fail to mention casualties if there were any. They think it makes for a much better read if deaths are plentiful. With luck, some of the dragons of the city would have answered Alia's request for help, in which case even now they scour the forests of the Ortings, hunting down the Hamelyn Piper."

"I hope you're right," said Erner.

"Don't fret," said Rundel. "We'll hear encouraging news soon enough. For now, our task is unchanged! I gave Tobias and Alia my word not to tell the Pipers' Council about their plans until we're certain the Council can be trusted. I will tell them that Ural Casimir is dead, and I will tell them of my own brush with mortality, but news of the Black Knight must wait. If there's even the slightest chance that any of them are in league with the Hamelyn Piper, it would be disastrous." He shook his head. "Prophecies . . . ," he said. "Whether you act on them or ignore them, they're always trouble. I despise the things."

Erner said nothing. A prophecy was the reason for their caution now—one spoken by Alia in a magical trance on

Gemspar Mountain as she'd made the very first attempt to cure Wren's curse. The prophecy had been a warning of *betrayal* that had eventually cast suspicion on the Pipers' Council.

But the very same prophecy had already led to Erner being captured by mercenaries and held prisoner by pirates. It had almost cost him his life.

He despised prophecies just as much as Rundel did.

4
The Tentacle
Patch & Barver

A Piper's gift was a very rare thing. One of the most popular children's games was to play at being a Piper, and that was sometimes the way a child realized they had the gift—finding that they could create simple forms of magic merely by whistling. Their friends would look on with envy.

The magic was greatly enhanced when a Pipe was used. An ordinary instrument like a flute had the opposite effect, robbing a Song of all strength, but a Pipe was specially crafted to enhance a Piper's gift and transform those magical melodies into Songs of extraordinary power.

Now, as Patch played his Healing Song, he thought back to when he'd first discovered he had the gift. He would sit in the woods by his grandparents' home, whistling and seeing the effect it had on the wildlife as they drew near, intrigued and playful. His younger self would have been astounded by the things he could achieve with Song now, his skills honed by his time at Tiviscan.

He focused his Healing Song on Cramber, as Tobias had instructed. The other griffins—Wintel and Merta—slept as he played, as did Barver. For the first two days, the dressings around Cramber's midriff had been red with blood as his chest wound repeatedly tore open with his breathing. Now, the dressings were clean; as long as Cramber's breathing was kept controlled, the wound shouldn't tear again.

It was a challenge for Patch to maintain that slow, steady breathing with his Song. It required rapid finger work at times, and after an hour of playing he was worn out, but it was rewarding to see Cramber so serene.

There were two other Battle Pipers in their army who excelled at Healing Songs, and now one of them came to take over from Patch and to let him know that the attempt at climbing down the cliffs was about to begin.

Patch woke Barver, and together they returned to the glade where the rafts and scaffold were being built. All work had stopped, though. Everyone was leaving the glade and heading toward the nearest cliff edge. The pair followed and found thirty or so soldiers and a small group of Pipers lined up along the cliff, Alia and Tobias standing among them.

It was easy to spot who was intending to make the climb

itself—two men and three women stood with rope tied between them. The bulk of the rope was coiled on the ground nearby, its end tied firmly to the trunk of a sycamore. After a little more preparation, one of the Battle Pipers began to play a Song that was very familiar to Patch—the Song of the Climb. The greatest effect would be felt by the volunteer climbers, of course, granting the skills needed to move easily from handhold to handhold, but inevitably some of its influence touched all those standing near. Patch felt his hands almost *yearn* for rock to grip. He moved closer to the cliff edge and looked down to the sea. A drop like that would have scared him without the Song, but not now.

He thought back to when his dungeon cell in Tiviscan Castle had been breached. He and Wren had almost fallen to their deaths, but with the Song of the Climb he'd managed to climb down the cliffs under the Castle and find safety—his little rat friend clinging on for dear life.

The volunteers were soon ready. A small team took the strain of the rope at the top of the cliff—ready to give out slack or to haul the climbers back if necessary.

The first climber lowered herself over the edge and started to descend. "Tricky going!" she called. "The rock crumbles easily in places—be careful!"

Progress was slow, the climbers losing their footing often as the fragile rock gave way. Everyone watched in silence as they got lower and lower down the cliff. One of the team letting out the rope called out from time to time to mark the progress: "Forty feet! Fifty feet!"

The climbers reached halfway down the cliff without trouble, and Patch could feel the relief in those around him. They all knew what was at stake here—if the climbers had lost consciousness and had to be pulled back up, all their plans would be in ruins.

But the relief was short-lived.

The ground began to shake, so slightly that Patch thought he'd imagined it at first. Then the shaking grew.

"There!" shouted a soldier, pointing to the sea at the base of the cliff. Patch looked in horror as a vast area of water frothed up, and from it emerged a shape so huge that it took a moment before he could accept what he was seeing.

A *tentacle*, rising from the depths!

Patch stared as it reached ever higher. The narrowing tip of the terrifying shape was now as high as the cliff itself; the base of the monstrosity was sixty feet thick at least, and rock seemed to flake off as it moved, as if it had been buried in the stuff.

Cries came from the climbers to pull them up at once, as the shaking ground caused pieces of the cliff wall to give way. The lower two climbers lost their holds and slipped, hanging helpless as the great tentacle moved toward them. The rope team hauled as quickly as they could, but it was a race that could only have one winner. The tentacle reached for the climbers, wrapping itself around them one by one as they cried out in fear.

Suddenly Patch was aware of other soldiers running to the cliff near him—archers with their bows ready. They loosed a volley at the tentacle before they were ordered to stop. The arrows bounced harmlessly off the dense flesh. The only danger was to the poor climbers now in its grip.

"Stand clear!" came a cry, and Patch knew the voice at once—it was Alia, purple sparks flowing around her hands as she prepared to do whatever she could to save those brave lives. Everyone backed away from the clifftop, giving Alia the room she needed. The climbers were screaming now, waved around by the colossal tentacle—brought close enough to the clifftop that Patch could see the absolute terror in their eyes before the tentacle swung away again.

Patch felt the power build as Alia's concentration grew, a grim determination in her expression. The brightness of the purple sparks around her fingers intensified, and she leaned forward.

Here it comes, thought Patch—whatever Alia was planning, she was about to do it. And then he felt something else, some kind of *heat* in the air, and the grass itself seemed to glow with a ghostly white light that converged on Alia. She looked suddenly anxious, glancing around her as the glow rose at her feet like mist. With a *crack* like the breaking of a tree, the light leaped up and engulfed her. She collapsed to the ground. An instant later the light was gone.

Alia lay still.

The screams of the soldiers in the tentacle's grasp drew Patch's attention, the vast arm speeding near the clifftop again. This time it came even farther, coming *over* the grass, provoking shrieks from those who thought it was trying to capture more victims. Instead it slowed, almost *resting* on the ground at the top of the cliff. When it pulled away this time, the climbers were left behind—gasping for breath, shocked beyond measure.

But unharmed.

The tentacle began to slip beneath the waves, and within mere seconds it had gone completely. The rumble beneath their feet settled too.

Soldiers ran to the climbers and helped them come away from the edge. Alia got to her feet and stared out to sea, looking strangely lost. Patch and Barver hurried over to her, but they were beaten to it by Tobias.

"It seems the raft idea has hit a major snag . . . ," said Alia, despondent.

"Are you injured?" said Tobias, his anguish clear. "When the light engulfed you, I feared for your life."

Alia waved his concerns away. "That was a *warning*," she said. "The magic in this place doesn't take kindly to the interference of upstart Sorcerers, apparently, but if it had wanted me dead I'd be little more than ash by now. The next time I try something like that, I suspect it won't end so well." She looked to the weary climbers, who were hurrying to untie their ropes.

"I can still try to fly around the coast," said Barver. "I'm sure I could evade the tentacle, if I was quick."

"It was a warning to us all, Barver," she said. "That . . . *thing* could crush you in an instant. You're forbidden from risking it."

"But I—"

"*Forbidden!*" She stared out to sea. "I can't lose anyone else, Barver. I *can't*."

Patch's hand instinctively went to the cross-eyed owl. "She's right," he said. "Don't. Please."

But Barver wasn't giving in so easily. "Then let me fly straight out," he said. "And get help that way! If I'm swift enough, something that large wouldn't have a chance of catching me, and—"

"*No*, Barver!" shouted Alia. "Even if you didn't lose consciousness after a hundred yards and plummet to your doom, there's something else. If you'd been paying attention, you would have seen it when the arrows flew at that beast." She called over two of the archers. "Each of you, fire one arrow out to sea," she ordered. "The greatest distance you can manage."

The archers pulled back their bows and fired high. The

arrows soared, going beyond where the tentacle had been, and then:

They shattered in the air, stopped by an invisible barrier.

"You see?" said Alia. "There's no escape out there."

"Alkeran escaped!" said Barver. "He was injured and threw himself into the sea. And no great sea monster devoured him!"

Alia nodded. "That's true," she said. "Perhaps this place took pity on him and let him go." She pointed to the water, where the tentacle had submerged. "But did *that* look like a beast that would simply let us leave?"

"Then *what*?" said Barver. "What do we do next?"

But Barver already *knew* what, really. All of them did. They turned to look back inland, toward the meadow, and beyond.

"Next, we see what creatures are waiting among the bone trees," said Alia. "It's time to talk to your father again, Barver."

Barver took the pigeon and rabbit that the cooks had put aside and returned to his father's cave. This time Alia, Tobias, and Patch went with him, which was a first—Barver had asked that his father be left alone by the others, at least to begin with. After twelve years without company, Gaverry

Tenso—for that was his name—was deeply uneasy about the presence of so many new arrivals.

"Are you sure he'll be okay with us coming?" asked Patch as they approached.

"He needs to get used to it," said Barver. "Give me a moment to see if he's awake."

Barver went inside while the other three waited. Soon enough, Barver appeared again and gestured for them to enter.

"Forgive the mess," said a deep voice from shadows at the far side. The cave was dim, with only the natural light from the entrance. A hundred feet wide, it was high enough that Barver didn't even have to crouch. Around the edges of the cave were dozens of pieces of carved wood; wood offcuts and shavings were strewn across the bare-rock floor. The carvings, Barver had told Patch, had been his father's savior all these years. The griffin would cut down trees with his great claws and use the wood to create the carvings. Patch had been expecting rough-hewn things, but instead they were beautiful, ranging from sculptures of animals to abstract spheres with intricate swirling patterns etched into the surface. He marveled that such delicate work could be achieved with a griffin's huge claws.

Gaverry Tenso stepped forward with a nervous smile. Around his neck was a great metal collar attached to a heavy chain that looped on the floor. There was enough slack there, Barver had said, for him to get a few hundred feet from the cave, allowing him to hunt his food and reach a water spring.

He was significantly larger than Barver, his coloring black and green; his feathers didn't have the same luster that other griffins had, and those around his collar were ragged and sparse.

"You remember Patch?" said Barver. "You met him that first day."

Gaverry nodded. "Now that my son has told me all about your adventures together, it's good to see you again, Patch." He came closer and reached out his hands. It was the griffin way to shake two hands at once, so Patch reached out his own.

"And you," he said. Even though he was used to Barver, Gaverry's hands seemed huge; Patch was very aware of how sharp those claws must be. But the handshake was as gentle as the wood carvings were delicate.

"And these are Alia and Tobias," said Barver.

Gaverry smiled and shook hands with them both. "My son has been telling me about the Hamelyn Piper and the Eight. He told me both of you were among those great heroes, but that I'm not to bring it up because you don't like talking about it."

"He doesn't filter anything," said Barver. "You get used to it."

"Out of practice!" said Gaverry. "Sorry! My friends here never complain." He nodded to the carvings. "But I'm trying hard. I'll endeavor not to break wind while you're in here, as it might overpower you."

Barver raised an eyebrow. "I brought some food," he said, offering up the rabbits and pigeons.

Gaverry took them and had a deep sniff. "Wonderful!" he said. "Cooked food is such a joy! I envy my son, always having his own source of fire. The greatest benefit of being half-dragon, I'd say. Anyone want some?"

"We've eaten," said Alia. "This is all for you."

Gaverry sat and picked out a piece of rabbit, relishing it as Alia and Tobias told him of the day's events and their intent to venture into the bone trees.

"I did wonder what was happening," Gaverry told them. "I felt the ground shake and could hear your shouts and screams, but there are too many trees between here and there for me to see what was going on."

"Has it happened before?" asked Alia.

"The shaking ground, yes," he said. "But I've never seen a *tentacle* rise from the depths! It's quite impressive that you've annoyed this place so much, given how short a time you've been here."

"*Annoyed* it?" said Patch.

"He talks about it like it's a person," said Barver.

"It *is* a person, of sorts," said Gaverry. "It has moods,

certainly. As I'm sure you'll discover if you brave the trees beyond the meadow. What lives there is truly dreadful!"

"Is there anything you can tell us that might help?" said Tobias. "It could make all the difference."

Gaverry sighed and shook his head. "I've told Barver everything I know. Whatever creatures haunt those trees, they sometimes prowl the meadow to hunt. They leave no marks on the grass, so must not be heavy, lumbering things. They move quietly and quickly—all I ever heard was the terrible death cries of rabbits. Beyond that, I don't know. And I don't think I *want* to know."

Alia nodded. "Anything you can remember helps us," she said.

"I'll try my best," said Gaverry. He popped a whole pigeon into his mouth, smiling as he swallowed. "Barver told me of the magical device that brought you here. I wondered if I could see it?"

"Of course," said Alia. She reached to her pocket and produced it. "The Leap Device! I still carry it with me, even though we have nothing to power it." She passed it over—a small metal box with a clip on the side, and in that clip was one of Barver's feathers.

Gaverry turned it over and over in his hands. "A little thing, to work such wonders," he said.

"It was in the Caves of Casimir, Dad!" said Barver. He looked to Patch and whispered: "We got to that bit last night."

"Casimir?" said his father. He grinned at Alia and Tobias. "Oh, he was your friend, one of the Eight! The one who made the Iron Mask! Did he make this?"

"No," said Alia. "This was made by Lar-Sennen. A great Sorcerer from centuries ago."

"Oh, tell me all about him!" said Gaverry, eyes glistening with interest.

"He loves to hear stories," said Barver. "Could you . . . ?"

How could they refuse? "Ural Casimir held Lar-Sennen in the highest regard," said Tobias.

"More than that, Tobias!" tutted Alia. "To Ural, Lar-Sennen was the greatest hero in all of history, revered by Sorcerers across the world."

"What was so great about Lar-Sennen?" said Gaverry. "Just because someone is powerful doesn't mean they're *great*."

"I quite agree," said Alia. "But it was said that Lar-Sennen had compassion to match his powers. And talk about inventive! He had a busy mind. *Too* busy, some might say. He finally realized that if his inventions fell into the hands of his greatest enemy—a dark Sorcerer called Quarastus—they would be used for evil. He went to great lengths to hide them."

Gaverry nodded and handed back the Leap Device. "But it was *good* people who found this one," he said. "And that makes me glad!" After a moment, though, he frowned, and his voice took on a distant tone. "Even though they'll all be killed by what lives beyond the meadow." Everyone fell into awkward silence.

"What did I say about not filtering?" said Barver.

5
THE RIVER CROSSING
Wren

Wren's delight at creating a tail had left her in a bright mood that was hard to disguise. The cold weather that had come overnight had worsened, a chilly drizzle starting early and not letting up, yet Wren had a smile on her face. The soldiers guarding her became uneasy at her cheerfulness.

Late in the morning, word came through about moving on again.

"Just *one day*," said a guard, a quick-tempered man whose name Wren had picked up as Purdle. "That's all I ask! Just one day to let us get some proper rest! I'm right, aren't I? I said, *aren't I*, Kallen?"

Kallen was another of this set of guards, a woman who looked like she could punch granite into gravel without breaking a sweat. "You're right," she said. "Worse still, we're tasked to watch the brat until nightfall. That means wherever we're headed, we're walking alongside *her*. No cheating a ride on one of the carts this time." She looked at Wren with a cold eye, and the other guards gave her equally frosty looks.

It's going to be a long day, thought Wren.

There were, as far as she could make out, at least ten different mercenary groups in the Hamelyn Piper's army. As the camp was packed up—horses saddled, carts loaded—she took in as much as she could about her captors. When she escaped, Tiviscan would need all the inside information they could get.

She smiled as she realized that she was thinking of *when* she escaped, rather than *if*. For the first time, her certainty that she was going to die had been replaced by the hope that she would see her friends again.

The Hamelyn Piper rode his horse at the head of the army, and soon Wren and her guards joined the convoy. The guards walked two in front of her, two behind. Kallen was in front; she held the chain that Wren's manacles were attached to and wasn't averse to giving it a hard yank now and again to vent her irritation.

Wren caught glimpses of the other mercenary groups as they walked. They passed a collection of carts that were all canvas-covered, which she knew from the comments of previous guards to be the catapults that had launched the terrifying explosive projectiles at the army in Gossamer Valley.

The convoy took a winding path along a series of hills, and when Wren looked back she could see the sheer size of it stretched out along the route: long lines of carts, infantry, cavalry. Her heart sank. This was a truly formidable force.

Kallen yanked harder as they walked on. Wren's wrists were bleeding now where the manacles rubbed hardest.

By afternoon, the convoy reached a river. The crossing was wide, across flat water-smoothed rock. It didn't seem deep and would have made for an easy crossing if the river was slow and calm. But as they approached the bank, Wren could see those in front struggle at times, the water fast-flowing. Kallen and the guards cursed when they saw it, but they had no choice.

"Great," scoffed Kallen. "Wet feet were the only thing I was missing for a perfect day."

A sergeant standing by the bank glowered at her. "It's not deep, soldier. Quit griping and move along."

Wren looked downstream. The river narrowed and passed through larger rocks, deepening and growing angrier all at once. The carts ahead were heavy enough to have little trouble, and the horses didn't seem anxious, but each row of infantry linked arms for support. Sometimes a soldier went down and brought one or two more into the water, but they were up quickly. Those behind took even more care.

Kallen, Purdle, and her other guards laughed at how *ridiculous* it would be if the four of them linked arms as they crossed, but it was nervous laughter. Into the water they stepped—it was bitterly cold, and Wren immediately felt the power it had, eager to whip her footing from under her and plunge her down.

By the time they were halfway across, Purdle began to boast.

"Not so hard after all," he said, sounding out of breath. "That lot bungled it, didn't they?" He nodded up ahead to the infantry, a dozen of them sodden and sorry for themselves.

Then Purdle's foot slipped sideways and down he went. The water took him into Kallen's legs, and she was next to go. Instinctively, Kallen pulled on Wren's chain for support, yanking Wren forward hard enough to leave her facedown in the water.

But then the chain slipped from the guard's grasp, and Wren felt herself pulled by the current. To her horror, she realized the water was sweeping her downstream.

By the time the guards saw that their captive was in trouble, Wren was beyond reach, crying out in panic, the water dragging her over the smoothed rock as it deepened and sped up.

Suddenly Wren's feet weren't touching the bottom

anymore. As she went under the surface, an image came into her head—a *fish*. If only she'd had the time to perfect her skills, perhaps she could have turned herself into a fish and simply swum away. But all she'd ever managed was a rat's tail, and that would be no use to her now.

The water battered her against the larger rocks. She surfaced and took a great gulp of air, only to be dragged back down an instant later. Again and again, as she fought with all she had, she stole what air she could when the waters allowed it, though her strength was almost gone. She wasn't fighting now, just swept along, her consciousness fading, but she felt pain in her wrists as her manacles rubbed and pulled, and slowly she sensed herself rising, her arms being stretched up until they were directly above her—and at last her head came free of the river. She sucked in a great breath and opened her eyes, eager to see her rescuers. She was in the middle of the raging flow, but the water around her was calm. Her arms pointed up, and her shoulders ached, and above them was the chain, rigid and vertical, suspended in the air. There was nothing else there. She looked to the bank and saw a solitary horse. Beside the horse, its rider had dismounted. A rider in black armor that glinted in the sun.

The Hamelyn Piper had saved her.

She felt the chain above her twitch, then move—dragging her lower half through the water, the curious calm region staying with her as the torrent raged around it. The

Piper's lips moved as he played a Song, his brow furrowed in concentration. He needed no Pipe to play now, the armor *itself* amplifying what he whistled into Songs more powerful than any Pipe could create.

The chain didn't lift her above the rocks, it simply dragged her over the unforgiving jagged surfaces until she was on dry land. The Hamelyn Piper stopped his whistling. The chain fell, and she fell too, collapsing in a pitiful heap.

The Hamelyn Piper stepped toward her.

"You don't escape me so easily," he said, and then he nodded to the four soldiers who were thirty feet back from them both. As he mounted his horse and moved off, the soldiers forced Wren to stand, one of them taking her chain.

These four were her new guards, she realized, wondering if the Hamelyn Piper would take it out on Kallen and the others. She found she didn't care.

They stopped to set up camp only an hour later, much sooner than she expected—it was well before dark. Even so, when they hammered a stake into the ground and fastened her chain to it, the guards also lit a fire next to her and brought her a simple blanket. These guards said nothing, not even to each other, and Wren liked that too.

Eventually she stopped shivering. Eventually her clothes were dry, and the feeling came back to her fingers and toes. They brought her a simple meal, root vegetables and meat in a wooden bowl. It was heavenly. There was also a small piece of bread, but Wren put that safely in her pocket. She planned to attract the birds in the morning, if she could. She had *studying* to do.

But there would be no exercises now, not tonight. Tonight she would sleep.

Or so she thought.

Darkness fell, and the camp began to quiet. As Wren closed her eyes and wrapped the blanket around herself, she heard the approach of footsteps.

She opened her eyes. The four guards were leaving, dismissed by the newcomer, who sat down next to the fire.

Wren sat up, suddenly awake. Suddenly *afraid*.

"I think it's time we spoke, don't you?" said the Hamelyn Piper.

6
The Bone Trees
Patch & Barver

Patch and Barver watched from the boundary line as final preparations were made in the meadow.

If the army was to march into the bone trees, they had to know what they faced. So tonight, they would try to lure some of the creatures out into the meadow and observe them from behind the boundary. And even though Barver's father had been sure that the creatures couldn't cross that line, the soldiers had set to work cutting down trees, preparing wood for defensive barricades.

Now those barricades were ready. Darkness would be maintained until the creatures had emerged from the bone trees, and then the order would be given for archers to fire burning arrows and light up the meadow. The remaining archers would try to kill one of the animals, if that was even possible. *Seeing* the beasts was the first priority, but obtaining one for study was a close second.

Half a dozen soldiers were out there now, laying bait trails of rabbit and pigeon carcasses, leading from the bone trees to the barricades. The soldiers got as close as they dared to the ugly trees, with those bizarre leg-bone trunks; even from here, Patch could see how anxiously they watched for signs of movement within.

When the bait-laying was finished, everyone began to take their positions. Apart from a small group right at the front and a line of Pipers and archers a hundred feet back who would come to their aid if needed, everyone else had been ordered to stay well away, deep in the sycamores. That was where Patch headed now, and he assumed Barver was coming too. But then someone called Barver's name.

"That's me, then," said Barver. "I'd best get over there."

Patch stared at him. "What?"

"Alia wants me up front," said Barver. "I have the best night vision by far."

Patch scowled, but it made perfect sense. He gave Barver a hug and tried to ignore the feeling of dread that rose up inside him. "Good luck," he said.

Barver grinned. "I'll be very careful."

"That'd make a change," said Patch.

The darkness was complete and unnerving. The whole

camp was under orders to extinguish all fires and torches, and above them even the stars were hidden behind clouds.

Many minutes passed before Patch heard the first rabbit die. It seemed that the bait had succeeded in drawing the creatures out of the trees, but even so they weren't giving up on their live prey. Every few seconds there was another brief shriek from a different part of the meadow.

At last a shout came, and light brought the world back into view—the archers sparking their arrows and launching them into the air.

There were no panicked yells, no signs that anything had gone wrong; no indication that the creatures had attacked the soldiers at the barricades.

An all-clear signal was given, and torches were lit by the soldiers around him. Patch looked for Barver, listening to those who passed him, eager for news of what had been seen in the meadow. There was plenty of grumbling, but he couldn't make out much.

Finally, Barver came.

"Well?" said Patch. "What's out there?"

Barver took a deep breath. "We still don't know."

"How?" said Patch. "I could hear the rabbits as they were taken!"

"Whatever those things are, they're fast," said Barver. "Tobias gave the order, but by the time the meadow was lit there was nothing there, Patch. Nothing at all!"

"How is that possible?" said Patch. Besides Barver, there'd been a dozen well-trained eyes looking for any sign of the creatures, yet they saw nothing.

Barver shook his head. "I don't understand it," he said. "And worse, I don't *like* it, not one bit."

Patch shivered, but it was a moment before he realized that it wasn't just fear—the temperature really had dropped. He glanced through the sycamore trunks toward the meadow, where the light of the torches let him see the mist that was spreading.

Barver scowled. "The weather's turned," he said. "We should get you back to camp. Then I'll go see Dad and let him know how things went. He warned me about the sudden mists—they really upset him."

"You mentioned that," said Patch. "But you really have no idea *why* he gets so upset?"

"All he said is that everything changes. What he means by that, I have no idea."

They found out when the sun rose.

Patch had been too on edge to sleep when he'd returned to camp, so he'd taken a late shift playing Healing Songs for Cramber and Wintel. It was good to have something to take his mind off the fact that the mysterious creatures in the meadow had become even *more* mysterious. When his time was up, he found a spot next to a fire. The mist had thickened to fog, the damp air making sleep elusive, but it came at last. Barver woke him just before dawn and gestured silently for Patch to follow.

"It's too early," muttered Patch. "Let me sleep!" He closed his eyes.

But Barver kept nudging him until he sat up and scowled. Then Barver led the way.

There was no movement in the camp as they walked. A few soldiers were on watch, the rest of the army sleeping. The mist was thankfully gone, but a stiff breeze blew over the glade and Patch soon pined for the warmth of the fire.

As they reached the horses, Patch saw Merta walking ahead of them. "What's going on?" he said to Barver.

"Alia wants to speak to us," said Barver. "When I came out of my dad's cave I realized something was wrong with the *sky*! I started to hurry back to camp and saw Alia by the cliff where the tentacle had appeared. When I began to tell her what I'd noticed she shushed me and sent me to get you, Tobias, and Merta—who were both *much* easier to wake than you, by the way."

Patch frowned. "Something wrong with the *sky*? What do you mean?"

"You still haven't noticed?" said Barver.

Patch looked up. It was cloudy, the predawn twilight

brightening; the sun wouldn't be up for a few minutes yet. He couldn't see anything unusual.

Alia was standing at the clifftop when they reached her, looking out to sea. Tobias and Merta were already there. Alia looked tired, and Patch wondered if she'd slept at all.

"Good morning," she said. "I know this must feel . . . *strange*. But I wanted to tell you all first, those who've been on this journey the longest. Tobias will inform the army soon enough."

Tobias looked even grumpier than normal. "*What* will I inform them of, Alia?"

"Just a little longer, Tobias," she said. "I spent most of the night here, thinking about what happened in the meadow. From the moment we arrived in this strange place, I've been trying to identify it. A *Bestiary*, yes, but whose? And where? Of all the theories I've considered, there was one that seemed so *impossible* I dismissed it entirely. The events of last night made me think again, and as I saw the approach of dawn, I knew I had the proof I sought. Barver noticed it too. Can the rest of you see it now?" She pointed out to sea as the sun edged above the horizon.

Merta realized first. "*No!*" she said. "It can't be . . ."

A moment later, Tobias's eyes widened. "I don't believe it . . . ," he said.

It was a few more seconds before it finally hit Patch: every morning since they'd arrived here, he'd sat at the cliff by Gaverry's cave and had watched the sun come up. But this morning, there was a difference.

The sun was rising in the *wrong place*.

"Dawn has *moved*," said Alia. "By eighty degrees at least, I reckon. Now it could be that the sun *itself* has shifted and the very nature of the heavens has been drastically altered, but I think that's a little far-fetched, don't you agree? Which leaves us with just one other possibility!" She turned away from the sun and faced them all. "The only explanation is that this *land* has moved. This *island*, to be precise. Because I finally know where we are."

7
Rundel Stone, Gentleman Thief
Erner & Rundel

Rundel and Erner presented themselves at the Keep gate shortly before nine bells. Erner kept yawning; Rundel glared at him to stop, but it was hard. He was exhausted after only two hours of sleep. A bath, fresh clothes, and a bowl of mutton stew had helped, but it wasn't going to be an easy day.

Rundel led the way up the central steps of the Keep to the Council chamber's ornate door. They went inside and sat in the seats in the middle of the empty chamber. The rows of seating around the walls loomed above them, and Erner thought back to the trial of Patch Brightwater, when those seats had groaned with the weight of onlookers.

At the toll of nine bells, the door in the far wall opened and the Pipers' Council entered: Lord Pewter, Lord Winkless, Lord Cobb, and Lady Rumsey—only Lord Drevis was absent. The Pipers' Council had always been five strong, its members selected from any of the branches of Piping.

Erner watched them approach, wondering if it was really possible that these four respected Pipers were capable of betrayal, as the prophecy predicted.

Lord Pewter had always been a favorite of Erner during his training. All of the Council members gave at least *some* courses to trainee Pipers, as was tradition, but Lord Pewter in particular was a friendly and patient teacher. Supposedly he'd been one of the most talented Arable Pipers of his day, but old age had taken a toll; he was by far the oldest member of the Council, and arthritis in his hands prevented him from Piping anymore.

Next to Lord Pewter was Lord Winkless. His specialty was the history of Piping, and he knew more about the nature and theory of Song than anyone else alive. He was also popular among the trainees, and one lesson in particular was never forgotten—a demonstration of how various materials were prepared for glazing Pipes. This involved a furnace and plenty of small explosions, and was immensely entertaining. There was also a slight sense of *danger*, as Lord Winkless always came across as rather absent-minded. Erner found it hard to believe that he could ever be *organized* enough to betray anyone.

Lady Rumsey and Lord Cobb, though, were altogether different beasts. Both were Battle Pipers with a long history of service. Trainee Pipers found them terrifying, because they would dole out severe punishments for minor offenses and become enraged if you couldn't answer their questions. But even though he didn't *like* them, Erner had always considered them principled and honorable. *The prophecy*, he thought, *has to be wrong*. Somehow.

All four Council members seemed a little disgruntled. Once they'd taken their seats, Lord Cobb began the meeting. "Virtus Stone!" he said. "Couldn't we have waited until lunch? It feels somewhat uncivilized to be doing this so early..." He yawned, and it took all of Erner's willpower to stop himself from yawning too.

"We've heard little from you lately, Rundel," said Lady Rumsey. "I must admit I'd quite lost track of where you were, or why."

"I was last here for the Brightwater trial," said Rundel.

"Has it been so long?" said Lord Pewter. "All the drama you've missed!"

"Drama *indeed*," said Rundel, nodding. "The dragon siege, the Castle damaged, the Hamelyn Piper supposedly dead—then showing up again in Tiviscan, attempting to take control of the minds of the best Pipers in the world!"

"Say what you will about the villain," said Lord Winkless. "He shows ambition."

"And that very lad Brightwater being the one to throw his plans into chaos and disaster!" said Lady Rumsey. "Who'd have thought it?"

"The boy has proved his worth, certainly," said Rundel. "I underestimated him."

Lord Cobb scoffed. "The boy was lucky, that's all. He had a friend who was part dragon, part griffin—now *he* was the one who destroyed that dreaded Pipe Organ. Deserved some kind of medal, I thought, but before we could organize it Brightwater had left and the half-dragon had gone too. Didn't even get his name."

His name is Barver, thought Erner, but he said nothing, nor did Rundel; even though the Council didn't know it, this was the start of their *interrogation*. The proper way to interrogate someone was to find out everything they knew while revealing as little as possible yourself. As far as the Council was aware, Rundel had not seen Patch since the day of the trial and had never even *met* Barver.

"I was hoping for news of Lord Drevis," said Rundel. "I understand he's venturing on the Great Pursuit of the Hamelyn Piper?"

"Yes," said Lord Winkless. "He left on one of the earliest expeditions, I believe."

"You *believe*?" said Rundel. "Surely you know where he is?"

The members of the Council shared uneasy glances. "Lord Drevis was secretive about it," said Lord Pewter.

"He organized several such expeditions to leave at the same time, and we simply don't know which one he accompanied. Have you returned to aid in the Great Pursuit, Rundel?"

"Sadly not," said Rundel. "I've come to bring terrible news. Ural Casimir is dead. *Murdered.*"

The Council was shocked.

"No . . . ," said Lady Rumsey. "One of the Eight, murdered? What happened?"

"He was bludgeoned in his own home," said Rundel.

Lord Pewter seemed most shocked of all. "Has his death been properly investigated?" he asked. "After all, hardly anyone knew his true identity."

"I certainly didn't," said Lord Cobb, sounding almost offended.

"*None* of us did," said Lord Pewter. "Only Lord Drevis, Rundel, and the other surviving members of the Eight. But perhaps in the circumstances, revealing his identity would ensure justice is served?"

Rundel shook his head. "He wished it kept secret even after his death."

Lord Pewter frowned. Although he didn't know it, he'd been wrong about only the Eight being aware of Ural Casimir's true identity. Erner knew it too, as did Patch, Wren, and Barver.

Ural's real name had been Yemas de Frenn. Left a vast fortune at fifteen when his parents died, a pampered life of wealth had held no interest for him. His skill in Piping was his only passion. Wanting no special treatment, he took a false identity and trained at Tiviscan. As one of the Eight, though, he became famous—much to his irritation. Like Alia and Tobias, Ural Casimir had wanted none of the fame. Alia had become the Witch of Gemspar; Tobias had become a monk. As for Ural, he returned to the grand mansion that was his family home. Becoming Yemas de Frenn once more, he used his wealth to study Piping and sorcery in secret, adding to his enormous collection of magical books and artifacts in the Caves below his home. That collection would have been eyed enviously by many Sorcerers and thieves—and Ural wanted only his colleagues in the Eight to have it after his death. Hence his desire that his true identity stay a secret.

"There are still many aspects to the murder that can be investigated," said Rundel. "I ask permission to choose six Custodian Pipers from the Castle's garrison to help me. I would also like to speak to each of you in private, as part of my inquiries. If that's acceptable, of course."

"Certainly," said Lord Pewter. "I'm sure we all want to help in any way we can."

Lord Winkless, Lord Cobb, and Lady Rumsey gave begrudging nods.

"Good," said Rundel. "I'll call on you all later today. Oh, and one last thing. The Pipe Organ the Hamelyn Piper used . . . I understand the remains are being held securely in the Castle?"

"Indeed," said Lord Cobb.

"I'd like to check for myself that they're secure," said Rundel. "For my own peace of mind, as a member of the Eight. If the Hamelyn Piper managed to get hold of that obsidiac..."

"We're quite aware that its security is paramount," said Lord Cobb, bristling. "I took care of it myself, and I assure you there's nothing to worry about."

"Indulge me," said Rundel.

Cobb looked ready to explode; Erner noticed that the others had a glimmer of amusement in their eyes. Lord Cobb could often be a cantankerous and big-headed man. Seeing him taken down a peg or two was, Erner suspected, a rare but welcome sight.

"I see no reason why not," said Lord Winkless.

"If it would soothe your concerns, then absolutely," said Lady Rumsey.

Lord Pewter nodded to Lord Cobb. "I agree," he said. "See to it at once, yes?"

Lord Cobb took a deep breath. "Very well," he said. "No time like the present."

The remains of the Obsidiac Pipe Organ were locked in an ancient vault under the Keep. Lord Cobb led Rundel and Erner through a mazelike series of tunnels to an iron gate, then along a damp corridor that seemed to go on forever.

"When Lord Drevis returns, I intend to convince him to use the obsidiac to make our Battle Horns even more powerful," said Lord Cobb. "We should have done it when they were repaired after the dragon siege."

"Isn't that dangerous?" asked Erner. "What if they had a similar effect as the Organ? Something to rob people of their will?"

Cobb scoffed at the idea. "Unlikely," he said. "Besides, our defenses should be as powerful as we can possibly make them! You heard the news about Skamos, I presume?"

"We did," said Rundel. "Has the Council decided on their response yet?"

"A *strongly worded letter* has been sent to the Dragon Triumvirate," said Lord Cobb. The Triumvirate was made up of the leaders of the Dragon Territories—three monarchs who ruled as one. "We'll see what they have to say for themselves, although there are rumors . . ." He shook his head. "Which I shouldn't discuss without the agreement of the rest of the Council."

At the end of the corridor was a door of dark wood and iron, in front of which stood two Custodians.

Lord Cobb ordered them to stand aside and produced a key from his pocket. "This vault has long been used for forbidden and dangerous things," he said. He looked at Erner, widening his eyes. "Such stories I could tell you! There are haunted skulls—and knives that drip blood whenever the moon is full."

"Just two guards, though?" said Rundel. "I expected more protection."

Lord Cobb smiled. "There *is* more, Virtus Stone," he said. "*Much* more. The route to reach the vault is monitored in secret by guards in hidden chambers in the walls. Did you notice you were being watched?"

"No," admitted Rundel. Erner looked back along the corridor and thought he could just make out narrow slits in the stonework from which hidden guards could observe.

Lord Cobb's smile widened. "Each guard can instantly bring down a gate, hidden in the roof. And if you look at the floor..." They looked. The stones at the vault entrance were inlaid with a curious metal pattern. "If anyone leaving the vault crosses this marker carrying anything they didn't bring *in*, they won't get far!" He turned the key in the vault door. "Go inside and look," he said, offering his lit torch to Rundel.

Rundel and Erner entered. Within was a huge circular chamber, a hundred feet across. Around the walls were a series of locked chests—presumably containing various dangerous artifacts that had been kept here for many years. In the center, though, was a vast pile of black and brown fragments—the pieces of the Obsidiac Pipe Organ. The largest was a portion of cylinder four feet across and eight feet long, but most were only inches wide.

They walked around the pile, both of them fascinated. Rundel, deep in thought, took handfuls of the Pipe Organ's remains, letting them fall from his grip. At last he handed Erner the torch. "Stay here," he whispered. He picked out a hand-sized piece and returned to the vault door. "Now let's find out if you're right," he said to Lord Cobb. He held the piece up high and crossed the threshold of the vault.

At once, a clamor of bells filled the air; from the damp corridor came the thudding echo of heavy iron gates falling to the stone below.

Lord Cobb's smile was wider than ever. "You see?" he said. "Any attempt to remove items from the vault results in all the drop gates shutting. Bells alert the *entire Castle*!"

Rundel returned the smile. "Erner!" he called. "Put this back." He threw the piece of Pipe Organ through the vault entrance. Erner caught it and set it down on the pile.

"Are you satisfied with our precautions?" asked Cobb.

"I am," said Rundel. He gestured for Erner to come out.

"Wait," said Cobb, locking the vault door with Erner still inside. "Your apprentice will have to stay there until the mechanisms have been reset. You can't catch me out that easily!" It took ten minutes, but when the door was finally unlocked again, Erner crossed the threshold and no alarms sounded.

Lord Cobb smiled. "So you see, the Hamelyn Piper cannot steal his precious obsidiac," he gloated. "Not while I'm in charge!"

"That was easier than I expected," said Rundel. "Easier than I *feared*." He stood by his desk and emptied his pockets, depositing several handfuls of Pipe Organ fragments in a small heap. The Pipe Organ was made from wood, coated in a thick resin-bound layer of obsidiac flakes, but it seemed to Erner that these pieces contained very little wood and mainly obsidiac. Rundel had selected them carefully.

"Yes, Virtus," said Erner, feeling ill as he stared at the fragments. They had just committed the theft of dangerous magical substances from a supposedly impregnable vault. The fact that Rundel Stone himself had committed the crime didn't make it much better.

When Rundel had kneeled by the obsidiac in the vault, the pile had blocked Lord Cobb's view while Rundel put fragments into his pockets. Then, after openly taking a large piece across the threshold to trigger the alarm, he had thrown that piece to Erner, back across the threshold. As far as Cobb was aware, all the obsidiac was returned—he hadn't thought to check Rundel's pockets.

If Rundel reveals what we've done, Lord Cobb will be humiliated, thought Erner. But the purpose of the theft hadn't been to embarrass Lord Cobb—Rundel and Erner needed the obsidiac for very good reasons.

Those *good reasons* were now taken from the bag they'd brought from Ural Casimir's home. Three magical devices from the Caves of Casimir, devices that needed obsidiac to function—identified by Alia in *Thoughts of the Unlimited Dark*, the book that held the plans of the Black Knight's armor. Before they'd set off on their journey, Alia had translated the instructions for their use.

The first was a small cylinder of carved stone containing strange metal cogs. This was a device for detecting *magical persuasion*—it gave them a way to determine if someone's thoughts and deeds were being controlled through magical means, and to be sure that the members of the Council hadn't been turned into puppets of the Hamelyn Piper. Alia had been confident that it would work.

The second was a small stone pyramid with eyes carved on the sides. This was a device that supposedly indicated if someone was lying, although Alia had been much less sure of the translation; one aspect she *had* been sure of was that it quickly *used up* the obsidiac it was given, just as the Leap Device did. Discovering lies was an expensive trick.

The third device consisted of a pair of pendants. Alia had been even less certain of the translation for those, but if they worked as she suspected then Rundel and Erner would wear one each, and they could prove invaluable.

Rundel selected a small fragment and used a knife to separate the obsidiac from the wood. "The amount of work that went into this!" he said. "So much flaked obsidiac, it boggles the mind. It must have required the application of dozens of layers."

Erner nodded. Obsidiac was an incredibly hard substance and difficult to shape—the use of a grinding stone was really the only way, and was surely how the Black Knight's armor had been created. For Pipes, the most effective method was to use a glaze—flakes built up in layers with resin. Doing that on such a large scale for the Pipe Organ was, he had to admit, an impressive achievement.

Erner thought back to the unforgettable lesson Lord Winkless would give every year to the trainees, showing how various materials were prepared for use in Pipe glazing. He would take small pieces of glass or crystal and heat them in a furnace before dousing them in cold water, safely enclosed in an iron box called a Flaking Chamber.

The pieces would shatter into sharp fragments, the process repeated until all that was left were thin flakes.

Lord Winkless would start with substances that produced no more than a pop before working his way up to things like salt-glass and fincite, the resulting explosions never failing to make everyone jump. He would always end his lesson by bemoaning that he couldn't show them firsthand what happened with obsidiac, the use of which had been banned long ago. What he *could* show them, though, was an older Flaking Chamber from before the ban. He would open it up and let them see where the iron was visibly dented in places. The trainees had always gasped, thinking of obsidiac shards flying apart with such force.

"What device shall we try first?" Erner asked Rundel.

"The *lying* device, I think," said Rundel. He turned the pyramid upside down, opening a small flap in the base and putting the obsidiac inside, then took a seat at the desk. He pointed to the chair in front. "Sit."

Erner sat.

"Alia's translation states that I hold it in my hand, and it will tremble slightly when a lie is spoken," said Rundel. "So now I'll ask you things, and sometimes you must lie. Are you ready?"

"Yes," said Erner.

"Is your name Erner Whitlock?" said Rundel.

"Yes," said Erner.

"*True*," said Rundel. "At least, I felt nothing. Are you an apprentice in the Custodian Elite?"

"No," said Erner, squirming inside. Lying didn't come naturally, even when he was being ordered to do it.

Rundel smiled. "A slight tremble," he said. "Good. I'll try some I don't know. What is your favorite food?"

"Plum pie," said Erner.

"*Lie*," said Rundel. "Try again."

"Fresh bread with butter," said Erner.

"True," said Rundel. "Have you ever lied to me before today?"

"No," said Erner.

Rundel paused for a moment, then raised an eyebrow.

Erner winced. There *had* been the occasional time . . .

After a dozen more questions, Rundel stopped. He turned over the pyramid and took out the obsidiac within, which was now only half of its original size. "The lies wear it out," he said. "But it seems to work. Now we must get some sleep. We can question the Council members once they've had their lunch. By the day's end, we'll hopefully know if any of them are under the control of sinister magic. And if we decide they can be trusted, we'll tell them about the Black Knight and the army in Gossamer Valley."

"And if we can't trust them?" said Erner.

Rundel set the pyramid device on his desk, his expression solemn. "Then, Erner, we are on our own, and in terrible danger."

8
The Island
Patch & Barver

Tobias, Patch, Barver, and Merta all stood near the cliff edge, looking warily at Alia. Behind her, the sun had risen fully above the horizon.

The sun that was in the *wrong place*.

"So, where are we?" asked Merta. "You said the island can actually *move*?"

"Let me explain," said Alia. "When the Eight hunted for the Hamelyn Piper, Ural Casimir missed no opportunity to tell us about legendary Sorcerers. The Sorcerer he most admired was Lar-Sennen—the creator of the magical device that brought us here, and the various devices that Ural collected over the years."

Patch thought back to the Caves of Casimir and the cabinet that had contained Ural Casimir's most prized finds. Rundel and Erner had taken some of those devices with them to Tiviscan, hoping they would help them in their mission.

"The legends surrounding Lar-Sennen are many," said Alia. "But there was one so strange, so *exaggerated*, that not even Ural believed it. Lar-Sennen, the legend claimed, lived in a secret fortress. An island, called Massarken, protected with powerful magic that made it impossible to find or attack. Surrounded by an impenetrable barrier, great sea beasts guarded its coast. Devil-birds guarded the land."

"Devil-birds . . . ," said Merta. "I've not heard of them."

"I'm not surprised," said Alia. "They're a *myth*, even more ancient than the legends of Lar-Sennen. Vicious things! Razor-beaked with blades for claws, they have a special skill that makes them unique. When they hunt, they cannot be seen."

"Camouflage?" said Tobias.

"*Invisibility*," said Alia. "And Massarken has one more trick up its sleeve—the island can *sail* anywhere. At the center of the island, the legend said, was a wheelhouse that Lar-Sennen would steer his fortress by."

"You showed us a drawing of it!" said Patch, suddenly remembering. "An island, with a craggy hill at its heart. A small hut sat on the hill, a man holding a ship's wheel. And from the water came great tentacles . . ." He stared at Alia. They were *all* staring at her.

"We knew this was a Bestiary, a Sorcerer's *zoo*," she said. "But where would Lar-Sennen have kept his Bestiary? His most precious collection of magical animals? Where else but on his fortress island! On *Massarken!*"

They all turned to the sun, rising in the wrong place.

"A moving island," said Merta.

"Great tentacles from the sea," said Patch.

"Now I wish I'd paid closer attention to Ural's stories," said Tobias.

"The devil-birds!" said Barver. "Lethal, and *invisible*! That's what made you think of it . . ."

"Well, the tentacle got me thinking first," said Alia. "Then we tried our little experiment in the meadow. No creature could have moved fast enough to return to the trees without being seen—but what if they didn't flee at all? What if they were invisible, watching us the whole time?"

Patch shivered at the thought.

"But even last night, I didn't think that the legend—the full, ludicrous *moving-island* legend—could be true," said Alia. "Bits of it, perhaps, but not *that*. Then the mist rolled in, and the dawn light looked wrong, and I *knew*. In the night, the island had pulled up its anchor and sailed, and ended up pointing in a different direction."

"Wait!" said Tobias. "That must mean there's someone at the wheelhouse, steering!"

"You really *should* have paid more attention to Ural's

tales, Tobias," said Alia. "Because there's one last part to the legend of Massarken. When Lar-Sennen knew he was close to the end of his life, he retreated to his fortress island and was never seen again. But the island was a curious place. Some might have said that it was *alive*. And once Lar-Sennen was dead, the island was alone, fulfilling the last command that its creator had given it—to never be found! Alone, for centuries! And this is the final part of the legend: that Massarken, the island fortress of Lar-Sennen, couldn't withstand that long isolation, and fell prey to madness."

They all stared at her again.

"Madness?" said Tobias. "You think we're trapped on an island that has lost its *sanity*?"

"That's the legend," said Alia. "My point is that just because the island moved doesn't mean there's someone steering it. Before he retreated here, Lar-Sennen hadn't spent all his time in his fortress. That implies the island could manage well enough on its own. Hiding when it needed to. *Moving* when necessary. Barver, your father speaks of this place as if it's alive, yes? Looking after its prisoners..."

Barver nodded, but a moment later he gasped. "Not just looking after!" he cried. "Capturing new ones too—my dad and Alkeran."

"Yes," said Alia. "A Bestiary might have some animals

in enough numbers to breed, but others would have to be restocked from time to time..."

Restocked. Patch felt queasy at the thought. He wondered how many griffins had been held prisoner here in the long years the island had been alone. How many had lived out their whole lives, chained, never understanding where they were or why they'd been captured.

"You said Lar-Sennen was compassionate," said Patch. "That he was Ural's greatest hero. So how could he be so cruel, to imprison griffins in his Bestiary?"

"A good question," said Alia. "Indeed, my first thoughts about *whose* Bestiary we'd found ourselves in leaned toward a *dark* Sorcerer for exactly that reason. Ural may have had quite a rose-tinted view of things. Perhaps Lar-Sennen wasn't really much better than his great enemy, Quarastus." Alia pointed to the distant hill. "But if the legends are true, then there's a wheelhouse up there. If we reach it, we can steer to the coast near Tiviscan! And I promise you—if we can't tame this island, then so help me we'll *strand* it there!"

"I like the sound of that," said Tobias.

"But the devil-birds!" said Patch. "And even if we get past them, there'll be other creatures of the Bestiary to face!"

"Yes, yes," said Alia. "But we have an army of the best Pipers and soldiers you could ever want on your side. We'll get through those trees, devil-birds be damned! And the other creatures will hardly slow us down."

"What if the island doesn't like what we're doing?" said Barver.

"Then we'll be quick and catch it by surprise!" said Alia. "*We can do it!*" She noticed everyone looking at her with a combination of dismay and doubt. "Tobias! Back me up here."

"You want to catch the mad island by surprise," he said, raising an eyebrow. "I might phrase it differently when I tell the army."

"It'll work," said Alia. "Barver, your father must stay here until we can free him from his chain. Cramber and Wintel can't travel, of course. A small group of Pipers and soldiers will remain with them. Merta, I leave it up to you whether you want to come with us or stay."

"This expedition will be our last hope," said Merta. "Fail and we'll be trapped. So I'll come with you and offer any help I can. I know I'm leaving Cramber and Wintel in good hands."

"Good," said Alia. "Barver, your fire will prove invaluable. Patch, I'd appreciate it if you were to stay here and be safe, but I know you'll insist on coming whatever I say."

"Absolutely," said Patch. "Where Barver goes, I go."

Alia nodded. "I'll be positioned at the center of our forces. You must promise to stay beside me at all times."

"I will," said Patch.

"I'll hold back on sorcery unless absolutely necessary," said Alia. "That's what seemed to upset the island most. It's the power of the *Pipers* that'll get us through—their Songs will make a path, ripping the bone trees from their roots! Although whatever we do, we must make it past them before dark."

"Why before dark?" said Patch.

"The legends say that devil-birds can't sustain their invisibility for long in daylight, because it tires them too quickly," said Alia. "That will help us."

Patch raised an eyebrow. "What's the point of being invisible if you can only do it when it's dark?" he said.

"A very *human* way to think about things," said Merta. "There are many nocturnal prey animals, Patch, who can see perfectly well at night."

Tobias had been deep in thought, hand on his chin. "Triple rank, Short Fives, pulsed shielding, with archery and pike support," he said, almost to himself. "That should do it, I reckon. Leave the horses in camp, though—they'd be too easily panicked."

"Is that a *plan* you're forming there, Tobias?" said Alia.

"It is," said Tobias. He looked out to the sun, now well above the horizon. "We must begin preparations as soon as possible."

As the army gathered in the meadow, Barver went to see his father to explain what they'd learned and what was going to happen.

"How did he react?" Patch asked on his return.

"He was relieved to finally know the truth of this place," said Barver. "But he was also anxious about our plans to venture through the bone trees. Worried that the island might react somehow."

"What can it do?" said Patch. The sight of the army assembling in the meadow gave him a confidence he'd not felt since their arrival. "A tentacle can't reach us inland. As long as we can hold those devil-birds at bay, we'll make it!"

Tobias made the army practice the formations they would employ. Three lines of Pipers would take the front, using formidable Battle Songs to bring down the bone trees and clear their path. The noise alone would, they hoped, keep the devil-birds away. Two circles of Pipers would maintain Shielding Songs for added protection, with an outer circle of pike-armed soldiers and an inner circle of archers. "Our advance will be steady but remorseless!" cried Tobias as the army showed its mettle.

Alia stood with Patch, Barver, and Merta within the circle of archers.

"Impressive," said Merta, watching the preparation. And it *was* impressive—the front lines of Pipers moved with a fluidity that made the whole maneuver seem like a dance, one they'd been practicing all their lives.

All too soon, the rehearsal was over. Tobias came to the center to join Alia and the others. Ahead of them, they could see their target: the hill, where legends claimed a wheelhouse sat, ready to steer an island.

"To the bone trees!" ordered Tobias, and the army began to march.

9
The Black Knight Speaks
Wren

The Black Knight sat cross-legged, looking at Wren with a mixture of contempt and enjoyment. She knew he could see how scared she was, but it was difficult for her to hide it.

She looked—of *course* she did—at his replacement piece of armor, the silver sheen of polished steel covering his lower leg. She wondered how much the loss reduced the armor's capabilities; the fact that he'd whistled a Song to save her from the river suggested that it wasn't by much.

He saw her look. "The piece will be replaced," he said with a cold smile. "Soon."

Her glance moved up to the armor's chest piece and the deep indentation at its center—a hole made for the magical amulet that would *complete* the armor. A hole that was currently empty.

"Do you know what this armor can grant the wearer?" he asked.

"Immortality," said Wren, trying to sound dismissive, like it bored her. "But you need some old amulet. And you have no idea where it is."

The Hamelyn Piper narrowed his eyes. "*Some old amulet?*" he said, mocking her. "A jewel that's said to be more ancient even than *humans themselves*. Its name is *Vivificantem*, the Life-Giver. Yet without this armor, it would destroy anyone who tried to wield it."

Wren smiled. "You *definitely* have no idea where it is." She half expected him to hit her, but he just looked away.

"I know how to find it," he said. It sounded more like *hope* than certainty.

She looked at his face more closely now than she'd ever done before. He was younger than she'd thought, she realized, but there was a cruelty in his eyes that seemed older. His dark hair was cut so short it was almost stubble. She saw the wounds on his face—ragged scars down one side, his ear gone—and thought of Tobias, with his own scar running from jawbone to forehead.

"Your scar," she said. "I've seen its twin."

He nodded. "On Tobias Palafox, yes," he said. "The Eight tracked me down and almost caught me. We came close to killing each other there and then. I know he was the leader of that ramshackle fighting force you saved in Gossamer

Valley. The deserters who joined my army have told me all I need to know. *Almost* all."

"Like what?" said Wren, trying to sound as dismissive as she could.

"That they came from the Kintner Bastion," he said. "Joined by Alia Corrigan, also one of the Eight, who came with a group of griffins to aid with scouting. Last, but not least, was a dracogriff—the same dracogriff who I bent to my will with the Obsidiac Organ, only for the bungling creature to fly into the Organ and destroy it." He shook his head, looking almost *wistful*. "It would have given me great satisfaction to have killed them all in one strike."

The words *bungling creature* burned in Wren's ears, and she had to fight the urge to defend Barver.

He leaned toward her. "And now we come to *you*, girl."

Here it is, thought Wren—the Hamelyn Piper had finally remembered he'd seen her before, riding on Barver that day. Part of her *wanted* him to remember; a bigger part of her knew that it would only make her captivity harder, when he realized that the theft of his armor hadn't been the first time she'd helped thwart him.

But as it turned out, he hadn't remembered her at all. "Who *are* you, I wondered," he said. "You, who stole a piece of my armor? How could you carry out such an *expert* piece of trickery? And to wield sorcery the way you did? It didn't take me long to work it out. You're an *apprentice*. And your master? The Sorcerer who used the armor you flung down into the valley to work such a powerful spell and relocate the entire force? Well, Palafox was a simple Piper, all brute force and no elegance; Corrigan was capable of drab Shielding Songs, very effective but terribly unimaginative. And neither was gifted with even a drop of sorcery!"

Wren kept her face perfectly still, not wanting to give anything away.

"Which leaves one possibility," said the Hamelyn Piper. "With two members of the Eight present, I believe there was another. Ural Casimir himself!" He watched Wren eagerly. "Well? Am I right?"

Wren's thoughts whirled, and it took her a moment to know how to reply. They'd suspected the Hamelyn Piper was somehow connected to Ural Casimir's murder, yet he clearly had no idea Casimir was dead. It seemed to her that the more things the Hamelyn Piper was wrong about, the better. "How did you know?" she said at last.

"Casimir is the only person who was ever smart enough to stop me," he said. "I've spent years trying to find him, but he went into hiding and his identity was a mystery." There was an ornate belt around his waist; a spyglass and a small dagger hung from it, and there were several pouch-pockets. He reached into one and produced a small metal box an inch or so across. Wren was shocked to recognize it as the same kind of box that had poisoned Rundel. "I am a vengeful man," said the Hamelyn Piper. "I had sixty of these little things made by a Sorcerer in the far North. They should poison anyone who was within a hundred feet of me when I fought Tobias Palafox and got these scars. A difficult magic to create and *expensive*, but the only way I knew to target the Eight." He shook his head. "I was eager for revenge, but I had to be patient. At last, the opportunity came. There is an ancient book, one Casimir had always sought. When a rumor reached me that a copy had been found and sold, I sent someone to discover who'd bought it. But tragedy struck—the bookseller died before my associate could torture the information out of him. I sent my people to every customer the bookseller had ever had, yet the book was not found." He sighed. "Some deaths were involved—my people can be rather heavy-handed sometimes. I'd hoped Casimir was one of the fatalities. It seems my hopes were misplaced. I assume Casimir has the book, then?"

Wren said nothing. She thought at once of Rundel and Erner. When she escaped, she would be able to tell them she'd solved both the murder of Ural Casimir and Rundel's poisoning.

"But tell me . . . ," said the Hamelyn Piper. "The device that was used to escape me required a piece of my obsidiac armor to power it. Did Casimir build it himself, or was it one of the devices from his collection?"

This took Wren by surprise, and her eyes widened for an instant—long enough to give the answer away.

"Ah!" said the Hamelyn Piper. "One from his collection! An original Lar-Sennen, most likely! Astounding to think something so old can still work at all."

"It worked perfectly," said Wren, defiant. "My friends escaped!"

The Hamelyn Piper smiled. "And I suppose you'll never tell me where they went?"

"Never!" cried Wren.

His smile widened. "I could make you tell," he said. "It wouldn't be hard. A little pain and all your secrets would spill. But it doesn't matter where you *think* they ended up." A flash of confusion showed on Wren's face, and he relished it. "There's been no report of an army of Pipers suddenly appearing out of thin air, I can tell you that. And such news tends to travel fast. A thousand-year-old magical antique, powered by more obsidiac than Lar-Sennen could ever have had in mind when he built it? My dear girl, they could be on the farthest continent, lost in unexplored territories. They could be at the bottom of the ocean. They could be on the *moon*." He leaned forward. "When I captured you, I promised that you'd watch your friends die as punishment for what you did. I suspect I'll have to break that promise. Because wherever your friends are, I guarantee one thing—they're not my concern anymore. I doubt they're *anyone's* concern."

Wren glared at him, horrified at the thought.

"You think I'm a monster," he said.

She wiped tears from her eyes. "You enjoyed telling me that you think my friends are dead. And you thought nothing of killing dragon children just to create your stupid armor. Only a monster could come up with a plan like that!"

His mood seemed to suddenly change. Instead of his apparent delight in tormenting Wren, he looked weary. "So you know the dark secret of the obsidiac," he said. He looked at his own armor for a moment, then shook his head and stood. "I've wasted enough time here. Perhaps we'll talk again." He turned to leave but paused. "There are worse monsters than me in the world, child. That plan was not *my* idea."

Then the Black Knight strode off into the darkness.

10
Forward March
Patch & Barver

As the army marched toward the edge of the bone trees, Patch saw Tobias's gaze move between the tops of the trees and the meadow-grass in front of them.

He was judging the distance, Patch realized—because those trees would soon come crashing down. The nearer the Pipers were to the tree line, the more accurate their Battle Songs would be, but the greater the danger.

"Position!" Tobias cried, and the army halted as one. "Short Fives, by rank! Begin!"

The three leading ranks of Battle Pipers began to play, building up their Songs—the Short Fives, a short-range destructive blast.

The first rank started their Song and kept perfectly synchronized. The second rank began playing after fifteen seconds or so, the two Songs weaving together like the melody sung in a children's round. After the same gap had passed, the third rank joined in, and the resulting three Songs combined into a sound so beautiful that it was hard to believe the end result would be destructive.

And then: the notes of the first rank's Song rose in pitch, climbing the scales rapidly until the Song was almost a scream. The final, highest note was called the *release note*. The moment it sounded, the Song flew at the trees, hitting them low on their trunks, shattering wood. Patch was almost surprised to see that those creepy trees were made of wood after all, given how unpleasantly bone-like they were.

None yet fell, however. The next rank of Pipers strode forward, and the second Song was unleashed. Trunks splintered, and the bone trees began to topple.

Now the third and final rank stepped to the fore and let fly their Song; trees that had withstood the first two Songs gave way at last.

"Hold!" cried Tobias, and they waited for the crunch and crack of falling timber to stop. Now it was time to venture beyond the tree line. From that point on, death could come at them from all sides.

Patch scanned the gloom behind that first line of devastated trees, looking for any sign of the devil-birds. Barver, on Patch's left, was looking just as intently. "Anything?" Patch whispered to him.

"Nothing," said Barver. "Although if they're truly invisible, I'm not sure if that helps."

Alia stood to Patch's right. "In daylight they can't be *completely* invisible," she said. "They would look like a creature made of glass, according to the legends. And even that would be hard for them to keep up for long."

"Shield contingent ready!" called Tobias. "Pikes and archers ready!" The circle of Battle Pipers who had the task of creating Shielding Songs began to build their melodies. Behind them, the archers readied their bows; in front, the outermost circle of soldiers formed a dense ring of sharp pikes. "Short Fives, recommence!" called Tobias, and the leading ranks started their Songs once more.

Alia looked to Barver, and to Patch, and nodded. "Now it really begins," she said.

For an hour they moved forward into the trees. The front ranks settled into a rhythm—they would release their Songs in turn until four full cycles had completed. Once those twelve devastating blasts had hit the trees in front of them, a burst of Shielding Songs would be sent out into the forest ahead. All eyes would watch for any disturbance that could indicate the presence of devil-birds.

So far, there had been none.

Then the clearing would start. Soldiers moved as much of the debris to the sides as they could, as quickly as possible. Barver and Merta did the heavy lifting, dealing with the larger trunks. There was almost no vegetation on the floor of the bone-tree forest, which was a blessing.

Once the clearing was complete, the army would make its way forward again, the front ranks of Pipers repeating their performance for the next audience of trees.

It seemed so simple, and Patch was at the center of the army—the safest possible place. Yet at every moment he felt that disaster was seconds away, that the devil-birds would swarm through their defenses and kill every single one of them. Fear filled him from head to toe as they made their slow progress through the forest.

He looked back, seeing the corridor of destruction they'd left behind them and the relative safety of the meadow receding into the distance. The forest ahead was still thick, giving no hint of how much farther they would have to venture.

At last, though, things changed. After yet another toppling of the trees, the soldiers moved forward with Barver and Merta, ready to clear the way so the army could progress. A shout came up, and Barver hurried to where the call had come from. Patch strained to see as a soldier ran over to Barver, carrying rope. Then Barver came back to the center of the army to show Tobias and Alia.

The dracogriff threw a large bundle of knotted rope to the ground.

"There!" he said. "The first of them, caught in the blasts."

It took Patch a moment to understand what he was seeing. It wasn't just rope, of course—there was a shape among the knots, one that made little sense to Patch's eyes. *Like a creature made of glass*, Alia had said, but this sorry specimen was starting to become more visible even as he watched, small regions that showed dense blue feathers, the rest transparent and oddly shimmering. Its true size was hard to gauge, but it seemed *big*.

"Dead?" said Alia.

"I hope so," said Barver. "I tied it up all the same. It doesn't seem to be breathing."

"Possibly alone, but no guarantee of that," said Tobias, thoughtful. He called to his army: "Eyes on the shadows! Watch for movement!"

Alia kneeled by the devil-bird.

"Be careful," said Tobias. Some of the shimmering body darkened, and a clawed foot became visible, the lethal claws three inches long. Alia seemed to reconsider and stood back from it.

"When it's fully visible I want to examine it," she said. "It'll help to know exactly what these things are capable of. Barver, can you carry it as we move?"

"Of course," said Barver, without a flicker of concern.

Patch looked at the creature's body and wondered just how many there were out among the bone trees.

It wasn't long before they found out.

Five more rounds of destruction, clearing, and advance went without incident.

The captured devil-bird had become fully visible now, and Alia found it fascinating. She freed up one wing to allow it to be stretched to its full extent of six feet, the narrow feathers a deep blue.

Unlike any other bird Patch had seen, the devil-birds had an additional clawed hand halfway down the wing, the three claws even longer than those on its feet. He was relieved when Barver retied the wing firmly to the rest of the bundle.

The feathers had a curious stiffness to them and gave a sense that they too could cut through skin. The head was long and narrow, ending in a hideously elongated beak crammed with serrated teeth—another feature none of them had ever seen in a bird.

Every time Barver picked it up and moved it forward, he had an expression of real distaste.

Patch couldn't help staring at it, even though it made him feel ill to see the blade-like claws. "I wish you'd get rid of that," he told Alia.

Alia shook her head. "There are things to be learned from it," she said.

Another round of Short Fives was completed. Barver and Merta were called to the front to help clear the debris, Barver leaving the corpse of the devil-bird behind. The worst of it, for Patch, was watching his friend go to the very edge of safety, while he was surrounded by the protection of all the Pipers and soldiers. He stared at the shadows intently, every muscle in his body wound tight.

He had a sudden sensation of being watched and spun around, but there was only the corpse of the devil-bird, tightly bound in rope.

Then a call came out from the left flank: "Movement in the trees!" One of the pike soldiers stood, pointing into the forest beyond, but Patch could see nothing.

The defensive circle of Pipers maintained their Shielding Songs. Patch turned to look at Alia and Tobias. Their expressions were tense.

Another call came, this time from the right flank; then another call from the front. It was enough for Tobias: "Shields loose by pairs, all sides!" he ordered, and a set of Shielding Songs was released from half of the Shield Pipers. The Pipers immediately began building their Songs again, at which point the other half would release theirs. Shielding Songs were normally held in place, acting as a defensive barrier—this was a way to use them as an attack, to drive back an enemy, but it would be an exhausting race to build the Songs fast enough.

"They'll tire quickly at that pace," said Alia.

"We can't afford to be hemmed in," said Tobias. "We need to kill the creatures or scare them off. Just one of those things getting through would be a catastrophe."

There was a bright flash ahead—Barver was unleashing his fire.

"I'm going to the front," said Tobias. "We'll see if Short Fives can take down the devil-birds! Keep pressing with the Shields, Alia, for as long as they can manage!"

"I will," she said. Patch could see purple sparks circling her fingertips, and she noticed him looking. "There'll be no sorcery yet," she said. "That's what the island seems to take exception to, and I don't dare provoke it unless I have no choice."

"How many of them are there?" said Patch. Another blast of fire raged ahead of them.

"Hard to tell," said Alia, but now everywhere Patch looked he could see movement—fragments of body becoming visible, the creatures tiring quickly in the light and dropping their disguises, letting out a cry as they did—terrible screeches that echoed around Patch.

The high-pitched release note of Short Fives sounded from the front rank, and dozens of devil-birds were flung backward.

"Archers ready!" cried Alia. "Careful targeting!"

The arrows began to fly, passing unhindered out through the Shielding Songs, but it was disheartening to watch. Even the surest of shots seemed to be brushed aside by the devil-birds, while those few that stuck deep were snapped away by claw or beak, and not one of the creatures fell.

"Save your arrows!" cried Alia, and the archers ceased. "Pray that the Short Fives are having a better effect," she muttered, almost to herself.

Something drew Patch's eye—again, it was the rope-bound devil-bird, and Patch silently cursed the thing. And then he looked closer. For quite some time now, Patch thought, it had been fully visible—yet he must have been mistaken, for now part of its head was translucent. And had it always had its legs bent that way?

He was about to say something when its red eyes snapped open. Shock took the breath from him. The words Tobias had spoken echoed in his mind: *just one of those things getting through would be a catastrophe.*

"Alia!" he cried out, but as Alia turned to see, the devil-bird's razor claws sliced through the rope in one motion. It rose and bounded toward him. Patch tripped in his haste to back away, and in an instant he felt a searing pain in his ankle as an agonizing grip pulled him into the air.

11
Questions, Questions
Erner & Rundel

Three more hours of sleep were all that Rundel and Erner had, but Erner was grateful for it. After that, they went straight to the Council residences, which took up the central floor of the northern wing of the Castle.

First, they knocked on Lady Rumsey's door.

"Virtus Stone," she said as she opened it. "Time for my *grilling?*" She smiled as they entered, but she seemed nervous.

Erner looked around. It was the first time he'd ever seen a Council member's room, and it was extraordinary, far more luxurious than Rundel's quarters. It was clad in elegant carved wood; bright tapestries and paintings hung from the walls.

"Take a seat and we'll begin," said Lady Rumsey. They sat at a table in front of a blazing fireplace. Erner took out a small notebook.

"My apprentice will take notes," said Rundel. He put his hand in his pocket. Erner knew that was where the strange pyramid device was, primed and ready with obsidiac to see if the truth was told.

With each member of the Council, it would prove to be more or less the same—the extravagant quarters, polite-yet-wary greeting, and a little unease as the questions came. Lady Rumsey first, then Lord Cobb, Lord Pewter, and Lord Winkless. Erner took notes for all four.

Rundel would always begin in the same way: "As I informed the Council this morning, Ural Casimir was killed. Did you know of his death before I told you?"

Each Council member said they'd not known—which was as expected, as nobody knew Casimir's true identity. If the pyramid had indicated a lie, it would have been damning evidence of their involvement.

Rundel's next question: "Was the new quest to hunt the Hamelyn Piper—the *Great Pursuit*—the idea of Lord Drevis?"

A unanimous *yes*.

Then: "And when he decided to leave on an expedition himself, did he discuss it with the Council?"

Lady Rumsey had thought about it for a moment before frowning. "No," she said. "We only found out once he'd gone. He'd left us a letter explaining that he wanted to keep his destination secret, but that he would return within a month."

"Were Battle Pipers sent on the expeditions?" Rundel asked her. "Is there any word from Kintner Bastion?"

"We did receive something from the Bastion about a training exercise," said Lady Rumsey. "Half of their number, as I understand it! It could be Lord Drevis, I suppose, using a training exercise to keep their true purpose disguised?"

Hearing that, Erner smiled to himself. It sounded exactly how Tobias would have done things, so at least that part of the plan seemed to have gone well.

Eventually, the questions turned to Skamos, which the Council members each thought a strange topic to bring up as it had nothing to do with Ural Casimir. But for both Rundel and Erner, any information on what could have happened to Barver, Patch, Wren, and Alia was vital.

"The dragons used a new kind of weapon," Lord Cobb told them. "Great spheres that exploded with terrifying force. The city was leveled, once it had been evacuated. We've decided to play it down for as long as possible, to avoid panic. Especially now that the Dragon Triumvirate has . . ." He shook his head, but then seemed to change his mind. "No, it's time you knew, Rundel. There are reports that the Dragon Triumvirate is no longer in power—that military leaders have taken over the affairs of dragonkind, under the command of a general called Kasterkan."

Erner felt a sudden chill. The Dragon Territories had been ruled by three monarchs for thousands of years—the

Dragon Triumvirate. For that ancient system to have been overthrown was shocking.

Lord Cobb and Lady Rumsey both thought it made war between humans and dragons more likely.

Lord Winkless was dismissive. "The dragon military wants only to seal off its lands and have nothing more to do with humans," he said. "There's no expectation of war. As for their terrible new weapon, the repairs to the Battle Horns in the Keep have made them more powerful than ever before. I oversaw the work, and the weapons used in Skamos pose little threat to us."

Lord Pewter was more wary, however. "I fear the dragons may wish to settle old scores," he said. "And that makes them very dangerous . . ."

The questions continued. It was often the more innocent ones that were the most important, Erner noticed—while asking about the reassignment of Custodian Pipers to the Great Pursuit, for example, Rundel would throw in little questions about loyalty and trust that, on their own, might have caused offense. As it was, the Council members answered everything they were asked, without objection or anger.

Back in Rundel's quarters, Erner was keen to learn what his master thought. "Well?" he said. "Are they to be trusted?"

Rundel took the pyramid device from one pocket. From the other, he took the cylinder—the device that was supposed to detect magical persuasion—and the spare fragments of obsidiac. He set them all on the desk in front of him.

The cylinder had a metal ring around the center which—according to Alia—would turn in the presence of someone who was being magically controlled by another.

"This showed no signs of a problem, for any of the Council," said Rundel. "Which is good, although we can't really be certain that it works at all. We do know the pyramid is effective at spotting lies, though, after testing it with you. Each of the Council lied at times. Small things, nothing very significant." He tapped the device. "But *useful*. It guided my questions, and helped reveal truths I may not have wormed out of them otherwise."

"So can we trust the Council?" asked Erner. "Can we tell them of the Black Knight?"

Rundel seemed troubled. "Let's assume that the cylinder device works and none of them is under the magical control of someone else. Their answers to my questions gave me no reason to doubt their loyalty—to Tiviscan, at least." He looked at Erner. "Tell me what *you* think."

Erner was caught off guard by the request. "Me, Master?"

"Yes," said Rundel.

Erner took a slow breath and put his thoughts in order. "Well . . . ," he said. "Perhaps the wariness of Tobias and

Alia has left too great a mark on me. You say there were no lies, none that mattered anyway, but . . ."

"Go on," said Rundel.

"Something's not right," said Erner. He shook his head. "I don't know what. It's just instinct."

Rundel nodded slowly. "A Custodian should never ignore their instinct," he said. "And I feel the same way. We *should* trust them . . . and yet my instinct tells me to wait. Perhaps things will be clearer tomorrow."

There was a knock at the door. Rundel went to answer it, but suddenly turned his head to Erner. "Quickly, hide those!" he said, nodding to the two devices and the fragments of obsidiac on the desk. Erner scooped them into the pockets of his Custodian's robes.

Rundel opened the door.

Outside stood Lord Pewter, looking rather anxious. "I need to speak with you, Rundel," he said. "Alone."

Rundel nodded to Erner. "Give us privacy," he told him, and as Lord Pewter entered, Erner left and waited in the hallway.

"What is it?" asked Rundel.

Lord Pewter glanced around the room nervously. "I should have told you this at once," he said. "But . . . I feared being heard—even in my own quarters!"

Rundel frowned. "Surely your quarters are safe?"

Lord Pewter drew close, speaking in whispers. "Nothing here is *safe*, Rundel. Nobody can be trusted! Except you!"

The words took Rundel by surprise. "Surely the other members of the Council are—"

Lord Pewter interrupted: "No! You don't understand!"

"Then tell me," said Rundel.

Lord Pewter nodded, and Rundel could see his hands tremble. "It began the day Lord Drevis went on his expedition. I was approached by a young Custodian called Valdemar." Pewter looked genuinely frightened. "Her behavior was strange," he said. "She seemed almost in pain as she spoke, and her words filled me with dread."

"*Tell me*," said Rundel.

"She claimed she was under the control of the Hamelyn Piper," he said. "A puppet, her mind enslaved! That she'd helped with the construction of the terrible Pipe Organ. And that she was not the only one!"

Now Rundel understood the fear on Lord Pewter's face. "If she was under his control, how could she confess to you?"

"She'd found a way to block his influence," said Lord Pewter. "But at a terrible cost! Pain that was almost *unbearable*—as if her whole body was on fire. This was an act of such courage, Rundel! But what she told me next was even worse. Everything the Hamelyn Piper had done was with one purpose, to obtain obsidiac—to actually *create* it! That's how he got enough obsidiac for the Pipe Organ."

"Create obsidiac?" said Rundel. "How?" Of course, he already knew—Barver had revealed the terrible truth, that the obsidiac was formed from the bones of dragon children, buried for a decade—but he wasn't going to let Lord Pewter know that.

"The details are too horrible," said Pewter. "I'll explain in time, but for now the most important thing is this: the Hamelyn Piper was only the *apprentice*. There is another villain, Rundel—an even more terrible one, the master who guided the Hamelyn Piper's hand! Valdemar warned me that I could trust nobody, for she was not the only puppet in Tiviscan. And then she screamed out, the pain overwhelming her . . . She collapsed where she stood, Rundel! Dead!" He shook his head, tears pouring down his cheeks. "Since that day, I've lived in fear. But now that you've returned, you're the only one I know I can trust!"

Rundel felt a great apprehension build within him as he asked the most important question of all. "Do you know who it is, Lord? Who is this *master* you speak of?"

"To know that . . . ," said Lord Pewter, "I must tell you something else Valdemar revealed to me. The Hamelyn Piper *betrayed* his master. He stole the obsidiac to make the Pipe Organ, wanting all the power for himself. When his scheme failed, he fled and hid. So, if you want to know the identity of his master, you must ask yourself: Who has done most to find the Hamelyn Piper? Who was most driven to track him down?"

"No," said Rundel. There was only one answer, and he couldn't bring himself to say it.

"*Yes*," said Pewter. "The man who has launched the largest hunt in the history of Tiviscan, the Great Pursuit! *Lord Drevis himself!*"

"I don't . . . I *can't* believe it," said Rundel. "Lord Drevis is the best of us!"

"It's the truth," said Pewter. "Trust me."

"But how do you know you can trust *me*?" said Rundel.

Lord Pewter smiled for the first time since entering the room. "Rundel Stone, if *you* are not immune to magical mind control, then we're truly lost. No, I trust you. And I need your help. Lord Drevis thinks of us as fools—weak and unable to see what's really going on. My plan is to convince the Council members to make *me* Leader of the Pipers' Council, before Lord Drevis returns, and take action while we still can. Until now, I didn't have the courage, but if I have your support, they'll have to agree. Will you support me?"

Rundel shook his head. "I simply can't believe that Lord Drevis would betray us . . ."

"Neither could I, at first," said Pewter. "But if I can convince you, will you support my move to become Leader of the Council?"

"Show me evidence that will convince me," said Rundel. "And I'll support you."

"There is something I can show you," said Pewter. "Three miles west in the forest lie the ruins of an old outpost. There's a pine close by that grows tall among the oaks. Meet me there one hour after dawn. Come alone." He strode toward the door and opened it, looking back again at Rundel. "Be careful," he said. "And trust nobody!" He leaned out of the doorway, looking anxiously to the left and right before setting off.

Erner had been listening.

He knew his master would disapprove, but Erner had paused at the door even though it was wrong to eavesdrop when Rundel had insisted on privacy. He was almost caught in the act as the door opened, but somehow there'd been enough time to get out of sight in a small recess along the corridor. Once Lord Pewter was gone, Erner went back to Rundel's door and went inside.

Rundel was sitting at his desk. He caught the expression on Erner's face and frowned. "Whatever is the matter, lad?"

"Virtus," said Erner. He knew he had to confess to listening, and the shame burned deep within him, but he had no choice. Because as he'd listened, he'd realized a truth that Rundel *had* to be told. "There's something I must tell you!" he said. "Something *terrible* . . ."

12
Out of Time
Patch & Barver

Patch screamed as he was taken higher by the devil-bird. He was hanging upside down beneath it—his ankle in the vicious grip of the creature's claws, his flesh pierced.

Below him, Alia cried out his name, purple sparks pouring from her fingers; she'd clearly decided the time had come to let loose her sorcery. The circle of Battle Pipers maintaining their Shielding Songs had started to notice Patch's predicament—and the fact that the supposedly dead devil-bird was very much alive and *inside* their shields.

The creature seemed uncertain where to go, spiraling upward with a shrill *caw*. A rush of purple light came, Alia's blast striking its wing. It plunged back toward her, lashing out with its beak as it drew close. Alia moved out of the way just in time and the bird flew on, crashing into the circle of Pipers from the rear before flying away from the army, taking Patch into the forest—unhindered by the shields, which from inside didn't act as a barrier.

Around him, Patch saw the other devil-birds advancing on the ground and in the air. The disruption to the Pipers had left a small breach in the Shielding Songs, and he watched with dismay as some of the creatures made it through.

He hit a tree hard with his shoulder and almost blacked out. The bird was taking him farther into the forest, eager to keep its prey to itself, but its flight was uncertain. Another flash of purple struck it, and it lost height suddenly. Patch instinctively tensed, then hit the ground and rolled as the pressure on his ankle vanished. The sounds of the fighting seemed distant now—the Shielding Songs, the Short Fives, and the screeches of the devil-birds.

His abductor had landed thirty feet away. Its wing seemed injured, but rather than nursing the wound it kept flicking the wing out with an angry *caw*, expecting it to suddenly work. The little translucency it had regained before breaking free of the rope had gone, and it was fully visible.

At last it stopped, and its head turned slowly to where Patch lay. *There is a glint of something cruel in its eye*, Patch thought as it began to crawl toward him.

The devil-bird came slowly, its movements uneven. It was obviously hurt, but then again so was Patch. A fiery pain came from his ankle, and he didn't want to look at the damage the devil-bird had done there. All Patch could manage was a slow retreat, pushing back with his elbows.

The bird had closed the distance by half and was picking up speed when another loud *caw* sounded. A second devil-bird landed, this one with wings that were almost invisible, much of its torso and limbs glass-like. It saw the other bird and gave a short series of chirps that almost sounded like a laugh before turning its red eyes on Patch and hopping toward him. The first bird wasn't having any of it, though. Prompted to action, it rushed toward its foe, jabbing at it with its sharp beak. The newcomer was taken by surprise: the injured bird's beak struck home at the neck, plunging deep, felling its opponent in one blow. These creatures were vicious even with their own kind, Patch realized with horror. The victorious devil-bird stood over its dying victim, looking proud of itself for having seen off a competitor. It had just enough time to preen for a moment and take another step toward Patch before a burst of intense fire incinerated it.

"They're certainly not fireproof," said Barver.

"You were quiet," said Patch. "I had no idea you were there."

"I had to be stealthy," said Barver. "Those things are unpredictable when they're cornered." He jabbed a thumb toward the continuing battle, and Patch was aware again of the distant sounds of fighting. "It's madness back there."

"You should leave me and go back to help," said Patch. "They need you!"

Barver scowled. "Leave you?" he said. "No chance! Besides, I think our forces have the upper hand now that Alia has thrown caution to the wind." The purple flashes of Alia's sorcery had become almost continuous. "Can you stand?"

Patch shook his head and gestured to his ankle. "I haven't dared look yet, but I'll not be walking anytime soon."

Barver crouched beside him. He touched Patch's foot, and the pain made Patch yell out.

"Shh!" said Barver, looking around worriedly. "Try to stay quiet. You're bleeding badly. I have to stop the blood before we go anywhere."

At last Patch gathered the nerve and glanced down at his wound. His ankle was an absolute mess, so drenched in red it was hard to make out exactly what the damage was. The flow of blood visibly pulsed in time to his heartbeat. He suddenly felt horribly weak.

Barver reached into his harness packs and pulled out a long piece of cloth. "This will hurt," he said before gently pulling off Patch's boot. The pain was too much—Patch blacked out briefly. The next thing he knew, Barver had finished wrapping the cloth around the injury and was giving him an anxious look. "Your Pipe is in my packs," said Barver. "Would it help?"

Patch managed to shake his head. "Too weak to play."

"Let's get you back to Alia and Tobias," said Barver. "I'll carry you, okay?"

Patch nodded, but as Barver bent to pick him up, a curious noise joined the sounds of the battle.

"What—" said Barver, but the noise grew so rapidly in volume that speaking was pointless. It was like a *scream*, but coming from the ground itself—for ten seconds, twenty, getting continually louder. Patch covered his ears. Then, in an instant, it stopped. And more than that—the sounds of *battle* had stopped too. Barver looked at him, wide-eyed, then picked him up. With Patch in his arms, he stealthily made his way back toward the now-silent battlefield.

Everything was frozen.

There was an odd shimmer in the air that reminded Patch of the Leap Device that had brought them to the island and the mirror-like ripple that had marked its limits. The shimmer surrounded the fighting, and everything within was like a statue, unmoving. Many of the Pipers and soldiers had their hands over their ears, just like Patch had when the strange ground scream had become unbearable.

For those at the front lines of fighting, though, there'd been no option but to ignore the sound; soldiers with pikes and swords were locked in static combat with the birds, Pipers behind them frozen in position as they tried to finish their Songs.

"I think the island finally reacted to Alia's magic," said Barver.

"The *island* did this?" said Patch, aware of how weak his voice was. "What do we do now?"

Barver looked back in the direction the army had come—the long corridor of destruction that led to the meadow. "The priority has to be for someone to reach the wheelhouse," he said. "There are Healing Pipers with Wintel and Cramber. I'll take you there and then continue the journey to the wheelhouse by myself."

"You can't, not alone!" said Patch.

"I'll be quicker alone," said Barver. "The devil-birds are trapped here too, and who knows how long this magic will last? We can't wait around."

"Take a few of the Pipers and soldiers left at the camp with you," said Patch. "Promise me!"

Barver gave a grudging nod. "Very well," he said. "Although they'll just slow me down." His eyes widened, and he shushed Patch. A little distance away, a devil-bird was moving. Presumably, like them, it had been out of range of the time-freezing magic. They watched as it approached the shimmer, obviously curious. When it was very close, the shimmer seemed to spark outwards slightly, and the devil-bird was engulfed at once—frozen in time like the rest of the battle.

Barver instinctively took a large step back from the shimmer. "We'll give it a wide berth, I think," he said. He turned, aiming for the meadow, but then he stopped.

Patch saw it too.

That devil-bird hadn't just been a solitary straggler. Not at all. The birds were mostly translucent, but Patch saw the telltale shifting of light wherever he looked.

They didn't seem to have spotted Barver and Patch. Yet. Barver nodded in the opposite direction. "I think it's clear that way," he whispered. "We should find safety and get back to camp by a different route." He backed off, keeping to the shadows.

For a moment Patch thought they would get away with it. *Just a little farther*, he kept thinking, then Barver stopped in his tracks. Some of the birds were looking in their direction. Keeping absolutely still was the only chance they had.

One of the creatures let out a shriek and took to the air, moving toward them in a way Patch hadn't yet witnessed— it reached the trunk of a tree and clung on, then launched itself again, short flights from tree to tree that proved surprisingly speedy. Most of the forest was too dense for them to fly in, Patch realized. Perhaps this was the way they usually got around.

Suddenly more birds started to do the same, and the whole flock was moving in their direction.

Barver couldn't afford to be gentle anymore—he ran as fast as he could through the trees, Patch in agony as he was jostled.

"There!" cried Barver. "Ahead!"

Patch looked and saw what Barver had seen—something lighter up ahead, through the trees. As they drew nearer, Patch realized what it was—the bone-tree forest came to an end at last, and beyond was a meadow.

Surely we can't have come full circle, he thought, but no. The trees at the other side of this meadow were pines, not the sycamores of camp.

"We can make it!" said Barver. The devil-birds were closing on them. They leaped from trunk to trunk, not slowing at all, unrelenting.

Barver reached the edge of the bone trees and ran over the meadow-grass.

"Look!" said Patch.

"I see it!" cried Barver. A short way outside the line of pines ahead of them, boundary posts ran, the rope hanging between them. If they could make it that far, they'd be safe, as long as their assumption that the devil-birds couldn't pass the boundary was true.

It suddenly felt like a *very* big assumption.

The birds reached the edge of the bone trees and seemed hesitant. For a moment Patch dared hope that the bright sunlight and open space of the meadow was too much for them, but one by one they leaped into the sky, their fully visible wings outstretched, the light too bright for their camouflage.

They were coming fast, and Barver was only halfway across the meadow, stealing glances behind him as he went. "Shield your face!" said Barver. "I'm going to try and scare them off!"

As Barver turned his head back, Patch knew exactly what was coming. He buried his face in the feathers on Barver's chest and heard the roar of fire as the dracogriff let loose his flames.

"Let's see what they make of *that*!" cried Barver, and Patch looked. It had certainly had an effect—most of the birds were circling uneasily, wary of continuing their pursuit. Not all, though. Some were still coming at them.

"Not far!" cried Barver. He kept glancing back, and the boundary was tantalizingly close. "Another blast!" he said; Patch hid his face once more and Barver turned, but this time the roar of the fire was cut short. "I'm out!" said Barver. He'd been using his fire in the battle, and then to incinerate Patch's kidnapper, so his store had already been low. "Hold on tight!"

Barver cried out as he ran, a roar of voice instead of fire.

Behind them, the devil-birds pulled back as they approached the boundary, but there was still one coming at them, closer, closer . . .

With a final roar, Barver hurled himself over the boundary rope, rolling once with Patch in his arms, then coming to a halt. The sole remaining devil-bird, too stubborn to give up its chase, burst into flame as it crossed the boundary, screeching as it fell to earth. It tumbled through the undergrowth and came to a halt, twitching for a moment before growing still.

"That wasn't my doing," said Barver, confused for a moment.

"Now we know why they don't go past the boundaries," said Patch.

Barver started to laugh. The relief of escape was enough for Patch to ignore the pain in his ankle just for a moment, and he laughed too.

The devil-birds were making their way back across the meadow. At last they disappeared into the bone trees.

"Come on," said Barver. "Let's get you comfortable, then I'll tend to your wounds."

13
Hedgehog of Horror
Patch & Barver

Barver carried Patch in among the pine trees and set him down gently, sitting him up against a trunk. The ground was soft with pine needles.

"Can I have water?" said Patch, his throat suddenly dry. Barver took the water pouch from his harness and passed it to him. As Patch drank, he noticed smoke rising a little distance away, coming from the trail of burning left behind by the unfortunate devil-bird. Small flames still flickered in places.

"Let me extinguish that," said Barver. "I don't think the undergrowth is dry enough to catch, but better to be careful." He went over to the smoldering trail, kicking and stamping until the flames were out. Then he bent down and prodded at a dark mound. "Oh, *no*," he said. "Poor wee thing." He picked something up and returned, his hands cupped in front of him.

"What is it?" said Patch.

"Caught in the fire, bless it," said Barver, holding his hands out for Patch to see. There, rolled up tightly, was a hedgehog. It was trembling, and across its spines was a scorch mark. Barver took the water pouch from Patch and poured water over the animal's burns. Patch winced as he heard a definite *sizzle*. The hedgehog let out a pitiful squeak. "That's not good," said Barver. He set it down beside Patch and strode off, rummaging in the undergrowth and around the base of tree trunks. When he came back, he placed a squirming mound of earthworms, slugs, and snails in front of the curled-up hedgehog. "Maybe some food would help it?" he said. He poured more of the water onto the scorch mark; this time there was no sizzle, and the animal was silent, but it stayed tightly curled up. "Ah," said Barver, holding the water pouch upside down as the last drips fell from it. "We'll need more to clean your wounds, Patch. I'll see if I can find a stream nearby."

Patch nodded. Despite the pain in his ankle, he felt drowsy—probably from the loss of blood.

Barver stood, but seemed hesitant.

"What's wrong?" said Patch.

"I'm nervous," said Barver. He hit his chest a few times with his fist. "I won't have any fire to use for a while, and

I'm worried about what might be out there. You know, in this enclosure."

Patch suddenly felt a lot less drowsy. It hadn't occurred to him, but of *course* . . . The boundary had to mark an enclosure, and in that enclosure there would be another kind of terrifying magical monster.

And when Barver left, Patch would be *alone*. "Be quick . . . ," said Patch.

"I will," said Barver. "I'll not go too far from the boundary; that way I'll be unlikely to come across . . . whatever it is." He drew himself up, took a deep breath, and off he went.

As the sound of Barver's movement faded, Patch strained to listen for other sounds, any signs of *giants* stomping through the trees. *Snarling beasts could burst through the foliage at any moment*, he thought, and here he was, a sliver away from passing out.

From beside him came the nibbling of the hedgehog, which had finally uncurled and was tucking into its pile of slimy treats, a worm held between its tiny paws. "Look at you," said Patch. "Minding your own business, and we come barging in with a flaming devil-bird to ruin your day." The burn on the animal's side was nasty, Patch saw. A wound had opened up among the spines, red and raw. For such a little creature, it didn't bode well.

His thoughts turned to his own prognosis and he sat up higher, stifling a cry as pain shot through his leg. He looked at his ankle. The dressing Barver had put on it was soaked through with blood. It was no wonder he felt so weak. He sighed and looked back to the hedgehog. It was making quick work of the pile Barver had gathered for it and was now munching a plump slug.

"At least you have an appetite," he said. "That's a good sign." *And the little thing needs good signs,* he thought, *given how badly it's hurt.* Although . . . having a second look, the wound didn't seem nearly so bad. And it really *did* have an appetite—it finished that writhing slug in no time at all, picking up a snail now, seemingly *ravenous.*

Another surge of pain came from his ankle, and a brief cry escaped his lips. The hedgehog reacted in a curious way: it looked at Patch and then at his ankle, its little nose twitching furiously as it sniffed the air. And then it began to move toward Patch's leg.

Patch looked to the blood-soaked ankle and back to the ravenous hedgehog, and a terrible thought came to him.

It was so very, *very* hungry. And it could smell his *blood*.

A sudden terror gripped him, as he realized that this was no ordinary hedgehog. He'd been so worried about what hideous monsters were in the enclosure, that it hadn't occurred to him that *this* was the magical creature held prisoner here.

His mind raced, trying to recall any tales he'd heard of monstrous hedgehogs with a taste for human flesh, and even though no memories came he knew he must be right. "No . . . ," he said, feeling weaker by the second. "Please . . ."

He tried to cry out for Barver but managed only a pitiful call. The little animal kept moving toward his leg. *The scent of blood is too strong a draw for it*, thought Patch. *Its desire for human flesh must be sated!*

The hedgehog reached his knee and hauled itself up. Patch tried to move, but the pain was too great. He felt faint, his eyes closing no matter how desperately he fought to keep them open.

The hedgehog made its relentless way along Patch's leg toward his blood-soaked ankle. It raised its front paws and placed them on the dressing. Patch couldn't look—in his mind's eye he saw its jaws open wide, its horrible maw bearing down to rip and tear at its new meal . . .

But he felt *warmth* instead of agony.

He opened his eyes and was certain he was hallucinating, for the little hedgehog was giving off a golden glow from its spines, and as the glow intensified, his ankle grew numb. Soon the pain was gone completely, and the hedgehog became as bright as a blacksmith's furnace.

Then the light vanished. The hedgehog plopped off Patch's leg and returned to its pile of slimy treats, tucking in with renewed vigor. Patch noticed that there was no sign of its own wound now—no sign at all.

And what of my ankle? he thought. He sat forward and began to unwind the dressing.

"Don't do that!" came Barver's anxious voice as he emerged from the trees.

Patch looked up. "It's okay," he said. "The hedgehog is magical. It healed me!"

Barver's expression was one of absolute despair, which Patch could understand—his friend thought Patch was so weak from loss of blood that he'd lost all his senses.

"I mean it," said Patch, continuing to unwind the bandages. By the time Barver reached him, the ankle was revealed—pristine, undamaged.

Barver stared at it. Then he stared at the adorable hedgehog as it finished off its last worm and looked up at him with a delightful little squeak.

Barver gathered a generous pile of assorted creepy-crawlies and laid out a banquet for their new hero before lying down next to Patch.

"Perhaps our journey to the hilltop won't be as bad as we feared," said Barver. "It hadn't occurred to me that the residents of the Bestiary could be quite so *cute*."

Patch was lacing up his boot as best he could, given that the devil-bird had cut right through the leather in a few places. "I doubt the rest will be so friendly," he said. "We need to be ready before we move on to the next one. How's your flame store?"

"I drained the last drop," said Barver. "It'd be better if I was full before we continue, but that would take an hour or so."

"We could do with a rest anyway," said Patch. He nodded to the scorched trail the devil-bird had left. "Do you think all the animals burst into flames if they cross the boundaries?"

"Perhaps," said Barver. "Although I doubt they'd cross over by accident. All the other devil-birds turned back, remember. Only one of them was stubborn enough to keep going. They must be able to sense the danger."

At that, the little hedgehog began to take an interest in Barver. It clambered up onto his chest and gave his face a good look-over. "What's it doing?" said Barver uneasily.

Patch smiled. Barver's face had a few fresh cuts, inflicted by the devil-birds. "I think it may have found its next healing task," said Patch. "I'd just let it get on with it, if I were you."

And it certainly *did* get on with it. While Barver rested, the hedgehog crawled up and down him, and every now and again a burst of golden light accompanied another act of healing. It spent time on his wings too, ending with a particularly bright display around Barver's shoulder. Patch supplied it with regular refills of slugs and snails.

After it had finished with Barver and eaten its fill, the hedgehog tottered off into the nearby bushes, much to Barver's sorrow. "I liked having that little one around," he said. "All my usual aches and pains seem to have gone."

"Could you pass me my Pipe, please?" said Patch. "I want some practice before we go on." Barver rummaged in his packs and handed Patch his Pipe. "The Songs the Pipers played to get us through the bone trees would be handy in a tight spot. I want to try and reproduce them." He went to the edge of the meadow, staying well inside the enclosure boundary.

The Song they'd used to knock down the trees was called the Short Fives. While it had a lot of similarity to the various Push Songs he already knew, Songs of that kind of power weren't taught to the trainees at Tiviscan. Even so, Patch had a good ear for picking things up.

He made Barver stand well back, just in case, and began with one of the basic Push Songs. It was the same one he'd played when he first faced off against the Hamelyn Piper, quick to build and reliable. He was sure the Short Fives used almost the same melodic shifts, but there were a couple of additional layers he'd noticed as the Battle Pipers had cut their way through the bone trees earlier. One was a deep rhythmic pulse, and it was that pulse that seemed to make up the last part of the Song, getting more rapid and high-pitched until the final release note was played. The other was a fast and intricate melody that Patch reckoned he could just about remember.

He spent a few minutes trying each of the parts, seeing how they fit together. Barver watched in interested silence. After a while, Patch decided to try building the Song in full. Even though he felt that the intricate melody had escaped him, he hoped he'd caught enough of it to be worth a go.

He increased the speed of the rhythmic pulse until it had the same kind of frantic shriek he remembered from the Short Fives. He could feel the power of the Push being altered and strengthened by the modifying melodies.

It was time to see what happened. Louder and faster, faster and louder, until he released the Song and—*WOOOOMMMMMMPPPHH!*

He picked himself up off the ground, wiping away the mud that had splattered his face. His ears were still ringing as he turned to Barver, who was staring back in shock. Patch gave him a thumbs up and looked around. Surrounding him was a newly formed ditch, ten feet away and at least two feet deep. "I'll have to work out why I couldn't aim the Song," he said. "Overall, though, not bad! Not bad at all!" He put the Pipe to his lips, ready to have another go.

Barver, perhaps wisely, took a few steps farther back.

14

The Eternal King
Wren

The Hamelyn Piper's visit had left Wren deeply anxious. Once he'd gone, her mind whirred as she thought about his reasons for talking to her. Some of it had been to gloat; he'd seemed to actually *enjoy* suggesting that the army in Gossamer Valley, and her friends, might be dead. She had a strange sense, though, that he wanted to *confide* in her.

As for his bizarre suggestion that his evil plans had been someone else's idea . . . He was surely just toying with her.

Even though she was exhausted by her near-drowning in the river, she decided to practice her shape-shifting exercises, the blanket covering her in case she succeeded. She managed to produce a tail easily this time. Then, to her joy, she was able to shrink her leg a little, her foot halfway to becoming the paw of a rat.

Her hands seemed more resistant to change, though, and without transforming those she wouldn't be able to free herself from the manacles. They were designed to drain a Sorcerer of their magic, and she could feel that they were somehow blocking her efforts. She could only hope that they wouldn't make it impossible, and that she would find a way. When the morning sun woke her, she moved as close as she could to the still-warm embers of the fire. From her pocket she took out the piece of bread she'd kept aside from her meal the night before. She tore it into crumbs and scattered them, then waited until the crows in the trees around camp picked up enough courage to come and eat.

Her guards watched in amusement.

"You'll regret wasting it like that," said one. "What kind of idiot feeds the birds rather than themselves?"

She ignored them. Their amusement meant that they didn't chase the birds off, and she could watch the creatures carefully as they pecked at the crumbs. She imagined herself growing those feathers, her body shrinking and getting lighter . . .

The crumbs quickly vanished, and two birds picked a fight over the last morsels. The fight was brief, and Wren was delighted to see a crow's feather drift to the ground within her reach.

She took the precious feather in her hand, marveling

at the beauty of it before tucking it into a pocket for later study.

The guards added more wood to the embers of the fire, and it was soon blazing again. They also brought her water when she asked for it and gave her a meal of simple stew and bread. She kept some of the bread aside for the birds in the morning, of course, but the continuing good treatment puzzled her. When she had a brief coughing fit she noticed them watch her with wary eyes, and she remembered the Hamelyn Piper's words when he'd saved her from the river: *You don't escape me so easily.*

Clearly, dying from a chill wasn't going to be allowed either, and her guards were *very* aware of it. She coughed dramatically from time to time, to remind them.

As darkness fell, she settled down under her blanket to rest for a while, wondering how she was going to escape—especially if she couldn't transform her hands while they were clapped in the manacles. She tried to squeeze her hands free, but she reckoned she was a whole thumb too big.

She heard someone approach. With a sinking heart, she knew who it was before they spoke.

"Wake up, girl," said the Hamelyn Piper.

Wren pulled her blanket back and sat up. The Black Knight was gesturing to his leg and the replacement piece of obsidiac armor that was there, glinting in the light of the fire. "You see?" he said. "Complete once more." He sat, his legs crossed.

"I suppose we'll be off to battle soon, then," she said.

"We set out tomorrow," he replied. "We'll crush anyone who stands in our way."

"Our way to where?" said Wren.

The Hamelyn Piper smiled. "I will finish what I started, girl. I have a score to settle in Tiviscan, you can trust me on *that*."

"*Trust* you?" she said. "You killed dragon children. You killed human children. You sent your own twin brother to suffer in prison instead of you!"

The mention of his brother seemed to hit a nerve.

"He deserved to rot in those dungeons!" he said. "A spiteful, vindictive brother, he was. I was to go to Tiviscan to train. I had the gift of Piping, but he did not, and he hated me for that. When my father died, my brother made sure I was blamed for his death. My mother cast me out when I was no older than you! I lost no sleep when I condemned him to his fate."

Wren paused, unsure what to say for a moment. The Hamelyn Piper had definitely come to confide in her tonight, it seemed. "You studied in Tiviscan, then?" she asked.

"That was my plan," he said. "But instead, my destiny was greater. Soon after my mother disowned me, my *master* sought me out."

"Your master?" said Wren.

The Hamelyn Piper smiled. "The man whose idea all this was. I told you, there are worse monsters than me in the world. I had a more powerful gift for Piping than anyone he'd seen in years. He trained me in secret, and with one purpose—to bring about his great plan so that he could create this armor and live forever. *Rule* forever, an eternal king. With me by his side, or so he claimed."

"He was a Piper?" she said; in her mind she pictured an old hermit, selfish and cruel, finding this boy to mold into a weapon.

"He was a *liar*," said the Black Knight. "And I was fooled, for years. I finally discovered his great secret, though—who he really was. A dark Sorcerer, capable of magical disguises . . . I've never even seen his true face. He'd promised me we would rule together, but in truth he only needed me to do his dirty work and then take the blame. I knew that I had to betray him."

"And have the armor for yourself."

"Of course," he said. "He didn't realize what I'd done. All those years of waiting for the obsidiac to be ready, and he never suspected I'd already turned against him." He smiled, pleased by his own cleverness.

"Is that why we're going to Tiviscan?" said Wren. "To confront him?"

"Instinct tells me he's there," said the Hamelyn Piper.

"Wearing a different face, no doubt, but I have my suspicions about *whose*. I'll start at the top and work my way down if I have to. Tiviscan isn't impregnable."

"It was dragons who broke its defenses before," said Wren. "And you've wasted all your explosive spheres."

The man's smile was unnerving. "More are coming," he said. "The dragons will join me."

"Their hatred of *you* was the reason they attacked the last time!"

"Circumstances have changed," he said. "And now they're in my debt. I showed them how to *make* their spheres. They had a blend of substances that would explode with great force, but it was unstable and dangerous, liable to go off on its own. Some powdered obsidiac in the mixture was all it needed, something only I could provide."

"You're lying!" she said. "It's *blasphemy* for dragons to use obsidiac."

"Kasterkan is in charge now," said the Black Knight. "His actions at Skamos won him plenty of support, and his weapons give him the upper hand. The Triumvirate had no choice but to stand aside. Now *he* gets to say what counts as blasphemy." He tapped the leg of his armor. "The dragons are still ignorant of the true nature of obsidiac. Perhaps one day they'll learn its secret too and harvest their own dead for weapons. I wouldn't put it past them. For now, though, they must turn to me."

Wren frowned. "But the dragons have a legend—The

End of the Skies, when the earth gives up a vast store of obsidiac and *everything* is destroyed. Aren't they afraid the legend is coming true?"

"People interpret things in ways that suit them," said the Hamelyn Piper. "Kasterkan claims the old legend was about the end of the *Triumvirate* and thus predicted a new era for dragons. With him in command, of course."

"And you in command over the world of humans," she said with disgust.

"Be grateful, girl," said the Hamelyn Piper. "When I rule this world, it will be with a firm hand, not a cruel one. But if my master had ruled . . . the suffering would have been unspeakable."

Anger surged through Wren. "*Not* cruel?" she said. "The children of Hamelyn died with the Dispersal, a Song used for the execution of criminals!"

"The fastest way to end their lives," he insisted. "Painless!"

"Painless?" she said. "So the pain of their parents counts for nothing?"

The Black Knight shook his head. "On the contrary," he said. "The pain of their parents was *everything*! If I'd taken only the dragon children, the dragons would have wiped humans from the face of the world in their rage. There had to be pain for humankind, pain of the same degree. A parent's grief for a child."

"You could have stopped this whole thing before the children died at your hands!" she cried. "You didn't, because you wanted the armor for yourself. You wanted the *power* for yourself. But you *will* be stopped, I promise you!"

"Only one thing was capable of stopping me, and I dealt with that long ago," he said. "My triumph has been foreseen, girl. It is *inevitable*."

"Foreseen?" said Wren, dismissive. "How?"

"I dreamed of it all, and everything I dreamed has come true."

"A prophetic dream?" scoffed Wren. "Oh, please . . ."

He narrowed his eyes. "I dreamed of the armor exactly as you see it long before my master told me his plans. I saw myself with the amulet before I even knew it existed. So don't *sneer*. Such dreams have guided my decisions from the start. Even my choice of Hamelyn."

"You *chose* Hamelyn?" said Wren.

"Of course," he said with a smug smile. "Did you think the rats just *happened* to infest the town? I could have stolen the children from anywhere. All that mattered was that it made for a story that would be told in every corner of the world."

Wren felt shocked, but she had only one question now.

"Then why *did* you choose Hamelyn?"

The Black Knight looked at her for a few seconds, his smile fading, and Wren sensed that his need to confide had faded too—that he felt he'd said too much. He scowled. "I had my reasons," he said, standing. "I don't have to justify myself to *you*. The world will have me as its eternal king, and it will rejoice."

And as he walked away, he added: "Or *else*."

15
ISLAND OF MONSTERS
Patch & Barver

After three more attempts at recreating the Short Fives, Patch felt he had a decent grasp of things. His aim still wasn't great, but at least he'd managed to limit the destruction to *mainly in front*, rather than *all around*.

"Just give me plenty of warning," said Barver as they set off. "So I can take cover."

"You don't need to worry," said Patch. "I think I'm too slow to take *anything* by surprise. I'm nowhere near as fast as the Pipers of Kintner!"

Barver shook his head and smiled. "You mean you're not as fast as the greatest Battle Pipers in all the world? You really are hard on yourself sometimes."

They had decided to walk straight through the pines of the hedgehog enclosure, aiming toward the hilltop ahead.

Once or twice they caught glimpses of movement around them as more of the magical hedgehogs snuffled for slugs and bugs, but they knew there was nothing to fear.

Not *yet*.

When they reached the boundary markers rather than the meadows that had separated the enclosures thus far, the forest of pines continued. Beyond lay a second set of markers and rope-fence thirty feet away.

"We could follow along the boundary for a bit," said Barver. "Rather than enter that other enclosure."

Patch frowned. As appealing an idea as that was, it wouldn't take them any closer to the hilltop. "Time is precious," he said. "How are your flames?"

Barver patted his chest and smiled. "Not full, but I have plenty," he said. "Together with your Songs, I'm sure we can chase away any beasties we meet."

Patch nodded. "So it's decided, then," he said. He stepped nervously over the boundary fence. "After all, we've faced giant tentacles and vicious devil-birds. Perhaps the creatures are less nasty the closer you get to the hilltop?"

"Perhaps they are," said Barver, joining him. They both looked at the new enclosure ahead. The pines seemed no different than those they'd spent the last half hour walking through.

How bad could it be? thought Patch.

They were about to find out.

After fifteen minutes in the new enclosure the forest thickened, slowing their progress. They could still make out the hilltop through the trees, but only just.

At least we've not encountered anything dangerous, thought Patch. For all they knew, the residents of this enclosure were a kind of ladybug with the power of clairvoyance.

Barver was the problem for once. As the forest became more dense, he had to hack away at the lowest branches just to get through, and even then the sharp ends would scratch at his wings. Patch, meanwhile, was moving freely through the gaps. Stubborn as ever, Barver pressed on, but when one wing got caught he strained so hard that he ripped a small tear in it and cursed loudly. "It's no good," he said. "I can't get through this. We'll have to backtrack and find an easier route."

"Are you sure?" said Patch. "Maybe it doesn't stay this dense for long. I'll go a little ahead and see." He ventured off, the trees not slowing him at all.

"Unless it opens up right away, we need to backtrack!" insisted Barver.

From ahead, he heard Patch's voice. "I think it's thinning out!" called Patch. "I can see much more sky ahead, and . . ."

"You already sound too far away for my liking!" said Barver. "Forget it, Patch—we'll backtrack and find a quicker way." He waited for Patch's reply. None came. "Patch?" he said. "*Patch?*"

Patch hadn't replied because he was too busy *falling*. Branches whipped against his face as he plummeted down a near-vertical slope. About to scream for help, he hit an outcrop of rock and was too winded to make anything more than a whimper.

Down he tumbled as the slope became less steep. At last he came to a halt. He looked back up to where he'd come from—at least two hundred feet above. He called for Barver and heard nothing.

He could see now why he'd thought the trees thinned out ahead. It was a huge deep hollow he'd fallen into, murky and dim; the few pines growing here were sparse and sickly. He'd come to rest among fallen age-bleached branches that pressed uncomfortably into his back. He shook the dizziness from his head and stood, checking himself briefly for injury.

He felt a sudden *fear* wash over him. His hand went to his pocket for his Pipe, but it wasn't there. He thought he saw it within reach, but it was only once he grabbed it that he realized it *wasn't* his Pipe.

It was a *bone*.

He turned and saw that bleached branches covered the entire floor of the large clearing in the hollow. And they weren't bleached branches, not at all.

They were bones too.

Trembling, he held up the bone in his hand, the one he'd thought was his Pipe, and with a creeping dread he saw that it looked very much like an arm bone. A *human* arm bone.

He dropped it in shock. Looking up to where he'd fallen from, he tried to cry Barver's name, but what came from his throat was barely a croak, because he could sense something now.

Eyes, watching him.

There were so many dark places where *things* could hide. He looked around, turning quickly, overpowered by the feeling that something was *behind* him.

He stumbled into the middle of the clearing, tripping over the bones on the ground, and then the sensation of imminent horror grew too much for him. He fell to his knees and covered his head with his arms.

A terrible sound came, a screaming *roar* like nothing he'd ever heard before. Patch raised his head and saw it: emerging from the shadows was a vast and hideous creature, bulbous and slimy, oozing greenish fluid from folds in its skin, covered in warts and horns and spikes and scales. It lumbered across the ground, crushing the bones it trod on, drooling through a massive mouth with huge razor teeth so crooked it was almost as if they'd been thrown into the gums at random.

And so tall! It must have been three times the height of Barver. The monster came closer and closer, but then it stopped and sat down, facing Patch with a look that could only be hunger.

Patch stood and turned, ready to run, but his heart sank when he saw a second creature emerge to block his path. He turned again and cried out when he saw there was another creature—and another!

A ring of them, closing off all hope of escape.

The monsters roared and chomped their horrifying teeth. The smell of their breath was unspeakable.

Patch sank to his knees, fear leaking out of every pore. "No . . . ," he said, for there was one more horror approaching, making its way through the trees surrounding the clearing. Patch stared at it in disbelief. *Hundreds* of feet high, this new horror sent up white clouds of bone dust with each crushing step.

There could be no doubt—this was the end! The new creature looked like a gigantic demon, its slavering mouth baring a malevolent grin, every inch of its body covered in spikes and barbs.

The massive demon leaned down from its great height, closer and closer. *Don't look*, Patch told himself. *Just close your eyes.*

"It's okay!" boomed the demon, in a voice that was exactly like Barver's. "Everything's fine!"

Patch wouldn't be so easily fooled and closed his eyes even tighter. Yet there was no sudden attack, no unbearable pain. Nothing happened. At last he opened his eyes and saw the demonic face, leering at him only a few feet away. "What new torment is this, you devil!" cried Patch. "Just kill me and get it over with!"

"Oh, sorry," said the creature. "Give me a second, it'll stop soon." It reached out a vast, horrific claw. Patch yelped and closed his eyes again.

A strangled squawk came from somewhere to Patch's left.

"All done," said the voice of Barver. "You're safe now."

Patch's mind was filled with the vision of the demon's face, surely still within arm's reach, but after a few moments he nervously opened his eyes.

He swore loudly.

The hollow was no longer littered with bones—only the occasional fallen branch. Barver stood above him, exactly where he'd seen the demon. He was holding what looked like a cockerel, perhaps twice the usual size, hanging upside down by its feet.

Not *quite* a cockerel, he could see now—more color in the feathers, and with long, thick eyelashes surrounding eyes that seemed to be permanently wide open, as if comically surprised.

Barver playfully waggled the cockerel-like thing. It squawked, then hung limp.

"It's a cockatrice," said Barver. "Very dangerous."

"A what?" said Patch. He looked around to see what else was in the hollow, but there was nothing—no sign of the monsters that had formed the ring around him. "But . . . they had me surrounded!"

"There was just this," said Barver. He waggled the creature again. "A cockatrice hunts with fear. Your mind changes what you see into images of impossible terrors! Monsters so large, so hideous, so completely undefeatable that their prey will simply give up, paralyzed with dread. The extremes of terror eventually stop the heart from beating. And there you go—dinner! Sorry I took so long to reach you. It wasn't easy to find a way through."

Patch glared at the cockatrice. He stood up and brushed himself off, offended that something that looked so harmless had tried to kill him.

"Hard to believe, isn't it?" said Barver. "After all, anyone who escaped their attacks would report seeing huge, horrifying beasts. And those who didn't escape would be found partially eaten, clearly having died from fright. That's how legends are born."

The cockatrice stared back at Patch with its wide-open eyes and let out a low, wary cluck. It flapped its wings in annoyance, but Barver's grip was firm.

"We're lucky it wasn't a basilisk," said Barver. "A very different prospect, basilisks. A cockatrice is just very sneaky, and their fear trickery doesn't affect me."

"How come?" said Patch.

Barver smiled. "Birds, dragons, and griffins are immune to its powers." He waggled it again, to its irritation.

Patch scowled at the creature. "So what will we do with it?" The cockatrice looked at him with those odd, staring eyes. "Are they *edible*?" he said.

16
THE WHEELHOUSE
Patch & Barver

In the end, they didn't eat the cockatrice.

Barver had been certain (well, *almost* certain) that it was safe to consume, but Patch's anger faded. The creature had behaved according to its nature, and killing it seemed rather spiteful. So instead, Barver let the cockatrice go. It gave an angry cluck then flapped and hopped away until it was safely in the shadows.

"You're sure they don't pose a threat?" asked Patch as they made their way through the hollow. "There are bound to be more of them."

"With me here, they're no threat at all," said Barver.

Patch had managed to find his Pipe, which had been clearly in view once the cockatrice's visions weren't swamping his senses. As they walked, he practiced the finger movements for his Battle Song. All of his fear seemed to have been used up, leaving him feeling curiously brave, and he was eager to press onward to the hilltop by the most direct route they could find.

At the far side of the hollow, the slope was steep but manageable. As they climbed, the pines became more plentiful, but never quite as dense as before. Barver had little trouble, and soon enough they were back on flat ground and the hilltop was visible once again.

They passed through five more enclosures before they reached the base of the hill.

In the first was a great boar, taller than Patch. The moment it saw them, it charged, and its feet left a trail of sparks. It gouged at the earth as it came, and lightning flashed between its tusks.

A wall of Barver's fire greeted it. The beast thought better of its attack and halted. It snorted and sparked as it watched them go by.

In the second enclosure, they saw nothing. Yet they did *hear* things—whispers, wordless and urgent, reaching their ears as if from mere inches away. They were very glad to arrive at the other side.

In the third, they saw a huge elk, its antlers perhaps twenty feet across. It was a glorious sight at first, as it stood completely still looking off to one side. Then it turned its head toward them and they saw that its eyes glowed orange and it had great fang-like teeth. Patch shivered and began to prepare his Song while Barver readied his flame, but neither was needed. The creature did not move from that spot.

In the fourth enclosure, it was the breaking of branches that alerted them. Here, the pines gave way to enormous birch trees, and standing up beside one was a massive bear—or so they thought. Patch had never seen anything quite like it, and neither had Barver. It was the height of a large dragon, and from each of its front feet emerged long claws, terrifying things that would have given Patch nightmares for weeks if the creature hadn't seemed so slow-moving. It used its claws to draw the higher branches of the tree down to its mouth, its long tongue stripping away the leaves. It seemed oblivious to their presence. They watched it for a time and soon realized that, for all its size, it was a peaceful animal.

"I wonder what magical purpose it serves," said Barver as they moved on. They heard more branches snap elsewhere but saw no more of the docile beasts.

The fifth enclosure, the last before they reached the base of the hill, was covered in grass as tall as Patch. Some distance away they caught sight of what they assumed was the resident type of animal, and they were wary. It seemed to be a kind of deer, but given their experience with the orange-eyed elk they knew not to take things at face value.

They crouched down, the grass barely enough for Barver to hide in.

A moment later the deer turned to run, and a large cat-like predator leaped from its hiding place. The deer was brought down, the hunter and kill both concealed in the long grass.

The deer was clearly not the magical resident here after all.

"Deer for prey?" whispered Barver, an edge of complaint in his voice. "That seems unfair. My dad would have *much* preferred deer to the endless diet of rabbit and pigeon!"

"But what *is* it?" said Patch.

"Some kind of lion, perhaps," suggested Barver. "Let's keep going while it's busy with its food."

They'd barely taken three steps when the animal rose from the grass. It did look somewhat like a lion, but its head was bizarre—it resembled an old haggard man, with unruly tufts of white hair sprouting from the scalp and chin.

"Oh, no!" whispered Barver. "A manticore! Stay absolutely still!"

Patch did as Barver told him—he knew about manticores. In *The Adventures of the Eight*, the chapter called "The Terror of Imminus Rock" had gone into plenty of detail about the creatures. At the end of their tails were poisoned spines that they could shoot at a great distance.

The oddly human-like heads weren't even the strangest thing, though. That honor belonged to the *sounds* they made, which were also unnervingly human. Instead of roaring, for example, the creatures seemed to actually *say* the word "roar."

Patch thought hard about the stories he'd read. The only harmless manticores were *sleeping* ones, so if they stayed unnoticed for long enough, the manticore would likely eat its prey and fall asleep. That was how the Eight had managed it, according to *The Adventures*.

"Roar!" said the manticore.

It was looking in their direction, but after a moment it sniffed the air before dropping low into the grass again. They could hear the sounds of flesh being torn from the deer carcass.

"I think it's caught our scent but doesn't know where we are," said Barver. "We should try and sneak away if we can." Very slowly, and keeping as low as possible, Barver and Patch backed away.

"Grrr!" said the creature. "Snarl!"

Barver gestured for Patch to stop, and they waited. The manticore was up again, and through the grass they could just make out its rather creepy face. It was scowling as it looked around.

"It's too risky," whispered Barver. "We'd best stay still for now."

"Can you use your flame to scare it off?" said Patch.

"It's beyond my range," said Barver. "I'd just provoke it into firing its poisoned spines. What about your Battle

Song? Get it anywhere near the animal, and it'd be knocked out for certain!"

"I don't think that's a good idea," said Patch. "It takes me too long, and I can't do it quietly. It would hear. We should wait for it to sleep."

Barver frowned. "But we might be here for hours, and the hill is so close now! Besides, there could be other manticores nearby..."

"All right," whispered Patch. "I'll build it up as quietly as I can. But it'll get much louder near the end."

"I'll keep my eye on the manticore and warn you when it notices anything amiss," said Barver.

Patch nodded and started to build the Song. It wasn't easy to keep it quiet, but he tried his best.

"Oh, I think it's already noticed," whispered Barver.

Patch tried not to think about it and focused on the task in hand.

"It's heading this way," said Barver, anxiously. "Anytime now would be good."

"Roar!" said the manticore.

"Anytime now...," said Barver. "It's halfway here, it might launch its spines at any moment!"

"Grrr," said the manticore, which didn't help.

Patch started on the final sequence, the Song growing louder with every second. However strong it ended up being, however accurate the shot, it would have to be enough.

He saw Barver's eyes widen suddenly. "Too late!" cried the dracogriff.

Patch stood.

He had a fraction of a second to see the manticore staring right at him from thirty feet away with its disturbingly human face. The creature's tail rose, like a scorpion's readying to sting.

Patch released the Song, and the ground near the creature exploded into the air. The manticore was outraged. "Ow, ow, ow!" it said, pawing at its face. "Grrr! Roar! Snarl!"

Patch and Barver were already running.

By the time the manticore had blinked the dirt out of its eyes, they were long gone.

They sprinted through the long grass and reached the boundary without encountering anything else. Over the boundary they went and kept running until they were well out of range of any manticore's spines.

The long grass became shorter as they went up the slope of the hill. They felt rather exposed, but at least there was nowhere for anything to hide and jump out on them.

As they neared the top, Patch noticed how clearly they could see the land around them. There was none of the strange haze that had always been there when they were looking at the hill from a distance, which made sense—if the island could truly be sailed through the oceans, there would need to be a clear view from the wheelhouse.

They reached the summit. Patch had expected something grand and impressive, but instead there was just a small stone building. "The wheelhouse, I presume," he said.

They drew closer. The building was circular, ten feet high and perhaps thirty feet wide. Windows ran all around it, but they couldn't see anything through the dark glass. At the far side of the building was a door made of weathered wood.

"I'm not going to fit through that," said Barver.

"It's okay," said Patch. He pushed at the door and it opened.

Inside was a single room. It was gloomy, as very little light came in through the windows, and it took a moment for Patch's eyes to get used to the dark. Then he gulped—in the center of the room was a large ship's wheel, and at the wheel was a figure, hands stretched out to either side and gripping the handles.

There was no movement.

"Lar-Sennen, do you think?" whispered Barver.

"Um, hello there?" called Patch. When no reply came he took a deep breath and stepped inside, approaching the wheel.

The figure was a corpse, wizened and long dead. It had a lengthy beard and wore simple clothes—not the luxurious robes that Patch had imagined a great Sorcerer would have chosen. The corpse's head was tipped forward, leaning on another of the wheel's handles. Patch could see no obvious sign of injury.

"Well?" asked Barver, sticking his head as far as he could through the doorway.

"Dead," said Patch. He walked back to Barver, glad to be away from the corpse.

"Is it him, though?" said Barver.

"Maybe," said Patch. "Although it doesn't look like it's been here for a thousand years. A few decades, perhaps, but it's not *ancient*. And it's certainly not going to be answering any questions."

"I wouldn't be so sure of that," said a dry and dusty voice from behind him.

Barver's eyes widened in horror. He fell to the ground in a dead faint—blocking the doorway.

Very slowly, Patch turned around to see what had spoken.

17
Quarastus
Erner & Rundel

R undel Stone paused to take a breath, leaning on his cane. Around him, the forest was unnervingly silent, the morning sun bright through the overhead leaves.

Up ahead he could see the old outpost ruins that Lord Pewter had described. There were a dozen or more of these old buildings dotted around the vicinity of Tiviscan. Most were now like this one, lost and all but forgotten in deep forest—crumbling wrecks of what they once were.

It had taken him over an hour to get there after leaving before dawn. He'd brought a waterskin with him and took a well-earned drink. As he replaced the stopper, Lord Pewter emerged from the forest ahead.

"This way, Rundel," said Pewter, looking around anxiously as Rundel reached him. "You're sure you weren't followed?"

"I'm sure," said Rundel.

"And what of your apprentice?" said Pewter, leading the way toward the ruins. "Did you tell him where you were going?"

"I gave him errands to run that will take up his morning," said Rundel. "We'll be selecting Custodians to help in our investigation later, so there's much to arrange."

"Ah, yes," said Lord Pewter. "The investigation into the murder of Ural Casimir. Such strange timing . . ."

"Strange?" said Rundel.

"There was a Sorcerer that Casimir was a great fan of. You know the one I mean?"

"Lar-Sennen," said Rundel. "Yes, he mentioned him."

"Well, Lar-Sennen is involved in the plans of Lord Drevis," said Pewter. "Before she died, the Custodian Valdemar told me that the Obsidiac Pipe Organ came from a book that Lar-Sennen wrote. A book that contained *many* uses for obsidiac . . . uses even more terrifying than the Pipe Organ!" Lord Pewter stopped in his tracks and watched Rundel's face intently. "Do you know of such a book?"

"No," said Rundel. Pewter watched him for a few seconds before seeming satisfied, continuing toward the ruins. "Why?" said Rundel. "Do you think Lord Drevis has it?"

"The Hamelyn Piper does, certainly," said Lord Pewter.

"So you think Drevis was like Casimir, obsessed with Lar-Sennen?"

Lord Pewter scowled. "Lar-Sennen was a romantic," he said. "A starry-eyed idealist! Casimir was the same. No, the driving force behind the actions of the Hamelyn Piper is much darker, believe me. Did Casimir ever tell you much about Lar-Sennen?"

"Of course," said Rundel. "The Eight traveled together for many months. Ural would talk of Lar-Sennen endlessly until one of us told him to stop." He smiled. "Usually Tobias."

"Then you know of Lar-Sennen's greatest enemy, the Sorcerer Quarastus?"

"Yes," said Rundel. "Like Lar-Sennen, Quarastus died a thousand years ago. *Thankfully*, given the things Ural told us about him."

"Well," said Pewter. "Just as Lar-Sennen still has fans like Casimir, Quarastus still has *his*. Many dark Sorcerers hold him as their idol."

"You're suggesting Lord Drevis idolizes an evil Sorcerer?" Rundel shook his head. "This is too much to take in. I've known Lord Drevis for decades. He's one of the most honorable people I've ever met. Yet you tell me he's some kind of evil mastermind, following the path of a long-dead dark Sorcerer. I don't see that it's possible."

"That's why you're here," said Pewter. They had reached the outermost wall, or what was left of it. Steps led down into a dark passage belowground. "This way."

Rundel followed. The passage was dim, occasional holes in its roof letting in enough light to see by. Rundel eyed those holes warily, wondering just how safe it was to be inside such a decrepit structure. "Why here?" he said.

"You'll see soon enough," said Lord Pewter. "I've often come here to be alone and think. Council business can be wearing."

"You still think my support would be enough for them to make you leader?" said Rundel.

"Your opinion would swing things one way or another. You may be unaware of this, Rundel, but the other Council members hold you in as much awe as they hold Lord Drevis himself. The moment you arrived yesterday, I knew it—with you here, I can't become leader if you don't support me." They arrived at a large wooden door that seemed surprisingly solid. "This is the base of the old observation tower," said Pewter. "In a moment, all your questions shall be answered." Lying against the wall was a short gnarly stick, which Pewter lifted. "Would you hold this for a moment as I unlock the door?" he said, offering it to Rundel.

Rundel took it with his right hand, and an odd smile crossed the Council member's face.

Pewter turned to the door and unlocked it, pushing it inwards. The door seemed almost new, certainly not the half-rotted remnant Rundel would have expected in such a place.

Within was a large circular room. The stone walls were damp, thick tree roots breaking through the slabs in places. He could see one larger opening in the ceiling, a square three feet across. It had presumably once allowed access to the floor above, but not anymore—the hole was sealed with haphazard pieces of stone, suggesting that the upper floor was little more than rubble.

Stepping through the doorway, Lord Pewter turned. "Aren't you coming?"

As Rundel readied to follow, he realized that something was wrong. *Dreadfully* wrong.

He couldn't move. Not his legs, not his arms, not even his head. Only his eyes responded to his body's command, and he looked down now to see the curious gnarled stick that Pewter had passed to him. As he watched, the stick lengthened and sprouted new growth, fresh twigs spreading and thickening, engulfing his right hand before seeking out his left and engulfing that too, knocking his cane from his grasp.

Lord Pewter adopted an expression of mock-sorrow. "I'm almost disappointed in you," he said. "Luring you here was so much easier than I expected." He paused, taking a long deep breath. "*In*," he commanded, stepping back from the door.

Rundel wondered if Lord Pewter didn't realize he couldn't move his legs, but then he felt the wood around his hands shift, and he knew that the command hadn't been directed at *him*. Shoots sprouted from it, growing at an astonishing rate toward the doorway, seizing the frame and flexing, *pulling* him across the threshold and into the room, his legs dragging uselessly behind him. Hardly even knowing which way was up, he felt his robes tear against stone and branch as the wrenching wood ignored the pains it caused him, his joints twisting almost to the breaking point, his face hitting the wall hard, tooth mashing against lip, hot blood flowing into his mouth.

Laughter echoed around the darkness.

And then all was still again. He was vertical, his back pressing against stone. His legs felt encased, as did his arms, locked to his sides. The floor was littered with debris: chunks of stone, dead leaves, and mossy growths.

In front of him stood Lord Pewter, grinning. "I've always wanted to see you like this, Rundel," he said. "*Powerless.* You have an irritating self-righteousness that provokes such *loathing* in me. Watching you suffer is a joy!"

Rundel realized he could move again, those few parts of him that weren't restricted. He spat the blood from his mouth. "Why are you doing this?" he said. He could feel pains all over his body, and his right eye was starting to swell shut.

Lord Pewter smiled. "A lie is told best when much of it is true," he said. "For example, Custodian Valdemar *was* a victim of magical mind control, although it was *mine*, not the Hamelyn Piper's. She was almost managing to break free of it and confronted me. So I pushed her off a cliff." He shrugged. "What else was I supposed to do?"

"And Lord Drevis?" said Rundel.

Pewter grinned once more. With a flourish he moved to one side and held his arms toward the far wall. There, barely discernible in the gloom, another figure was held captive by the same kind of unnatural twisting wood that held Rundel. Pewter walked over and clicked his fingers. A small ball of light appeared and floated slowly upward.

Rundel gasped. The figure was wearing the lush robes of a Council member, the head lolled forward so the face wasn't visible, but Rundel knew at once who it was—Lord Drevis! Rundel looked for signs of life, but the figure didn't even seem to be breathing. "Is he dead?" he asked.

"Dead?" said Pewter. "No! Where would be the fun in that? Torturing him is one of my guilty pleasures. That's what I was doing before you arrived. He'll regain consciousness in a day or so." He strode back to Rundel. "You really didn't tell your apprentice where you were going? How trusting of you!"

"Leave Erner alone," said Rundel.

Pewter's grin widened. "Leave him alone? So quaint! I have my people in the Castle, Rundel. Those under my power will do whatever I need them to do. Or perhaps I'll take *his* mind too!" He looked at Rundel, clearly relishing the anguish he was causing. "Although taking a mind is harder than you think. With the Pipe Organ only a simple form of it was possible, a kind of *puppetry*. Easy for anyone to spot, really—just an empty husk carrying out orders. To truly *take* a mind is time-consuming. Things would be so much easier if I had the Council in my sway already. When I brought Drevis here, I thought I could break him eventually, but I soon grew bored of the idea."

"Why are you doing this?" said Rundel.

"The Hamelyn Piper has something that belongs to me," said Pewter. "I can afford no more complications. No risks."

"So *you* were the Hamelyn Piper's master . . . ," said Rundel.

"Exactly," said Pewter. "I discovered him when he was a boy—such potential as a Piper! I excel at magical disguise. I appeared to him in a different form and earned his trust. He never knew my true identity, yet I became like a father to him. I taught him what he needed to learn! But most important of all, he was ruthless even then. There are those who think a child is a blank sheet of paper onto which any future can be written. They're wrong. Take the Brightwater boy you condemned to a lifetime in the dungeons of Tiviscan—he has the same spark of ability that I saw in the Hamelyn Piper, but *tainted* with a sense of justice that would make him useless to me. The Hamelyn Piper had no such problem." Pewter shook his head and laughed. "I saw the darkness in his heart, and it made him perfect for my purpose."

"But he was smarter than you realized," said Rundel, satisfied to see Pewter wince at the thought. "He turned against you."

"He did," said Pewter. "He decided to take the obsidiac for himself. Perhaps he thought I would kill him once his task was complete. That was my intent, yes, although before I had the chance the Eight caught him and brought him back to Tiviscan. I was happy enough, though. His battles with the Eight had left him insensible and unable to reveal the truth. They threw him in the dungeons to rot. Or so I thought."

"It wasn't him," said Rundel. "It was his brother."

"Yes," said Pewter. "A twin I didn't even know he had, taking the blame in his stead, robbed of all memory. As a result, I knew nothing of his betrayal until he revealed his Pipe Organ and tried to make puppets of us all. My revenge will be glorious when the Great Pursuit finally snares him!"

"The Great Pursuit was your idea?" said Rundel.

"Oh, Drevis *started* it," sneered Pewter. "But he lacked the willingness to do what needed to be done and commit the Custodians *completely*, as if no other task mattered."

"So he had to disappear," said Rundel.

"Of course! I issued a flurry of orders in his name, while

everyone thought Drevis had set off on the Great Pursuit himself. When I convince the others to make me leader of the Council, I can use every last Custodian and Battle Piper to help my quest."

"You defile the honor of Pipers," spat Rundel. "You, a follower of Quarastus..."

Pewter smiled. "Oh, please, Rundel. You still don't see it, even when it's right in front of you!"

Rundel looked back at him, confused.

"As I told you," said Pewter. "Magical disguise is one of my greatest skills." Before Rundel's eyes he became taller, his hair darkening, his thin face fleshing out. "You've known me as Lord Pewter for so many years, yet here and now you see me for the first time. I'm no *follower* of Quarastus, Rundel. I *am* Quarastus." He began to laugh, the sound echoing around the stone walls. Gradually his appearance became that of Lord Pewter once more.

"My plans have been a thousand years in the making," he said. "And nobody is going to—"

Suddenly he stopped talking. He reached out to Rundel's chest and took hold of a small black pendant that sat there, tied around Rundel's neck. "Is that—" His eyes widened. "It can't be!"

Rundel felt no despair that the pendant had been noticed. Things had proven to be far worse than he feared, yes, but he didn't regret coming here, and to what—he had to assume—was his death. With his cut lip still bleeding, more blood had pooled in his mouth. He spat it out as hard as he could, making Pewter step back.

Rundel smiled, ignoring the pain. "It seems your secret is out," he said.

In a small stable far from Tiviscan Castle, Erner was watching. He wore a pendant—the twin of the one around Rundel Stone's neck.

Just as Rundel had brought the device to detect lies, and the device to detect magical persuasion, he'd brought another of the obsidiac-powered creations from the Caves of Casimir.

Alia had described it as a device to see from far distances, and her translation of the instructions had been vague, but as soon as Rundel had obtained the obsidiac fragments, the purpose and usage of the pendants had become very clear.

The green stone that made up each pendant *absorbed* obsidiac and darkened, turning black. Thereafter, whoever wore the pendants could see and hear what was happening to the other.

Pewter's visit to Rundel's room had changed everything. As Erner had listened outside the door, hearing Pewter speak of Lord Drevis and asking Rundel to come alone to a mysterious rendezvous, Erner had had the pyramid in his pocket and had felt it tremble and shake whenever Lord Pewter spoke.

It had been lies. All of it.

So Rundel had hatched a plan, and nothing Erner said could change his mind.

Erner would use the pendant and witness everything that happened. He'd watched with growing horror as Pewter revealed his treachery and took Rundel prisoner; as he saw Lord Drevis hanging lifeless from the wall; as Pewter *transformed* and announced his true nature.

And then the moment had come when Pewter saw what was around Rundel Stone's neck, snapping the cord from Rundel and holding up the pendant, glaring at it—glaring at *him* now, for the pendant's vision went both ways.

Lord Pewter—Quarastus—reached out to the pendant, his eyes burning with rage. Erner cried out in fear, getting to his feet and throwing the pendant to the ground.

His fear turned to terror as a hand came *through* the pendant, growing vast and seeking him out. Erner ran forward, a rock in his hands, and destroyed the pendant with one sweeping blow. At once, the huge hand vanished.

He was torn now. Rundel had sent him this far away in case all of the Council was involved, making Tiviscan too dangerous. He wanted to go back and do everything he could to help free his master, but Rundel had given him a mission—to find Alia and Tobias. As a dutiful apprentice, he had no choice.

He wore simple clothing, his Custodian Robes packed away. Traveling incognito was necessary, especially now that Lord Pewter knew he'd been watching. He led his horse out of the stable. The morning sun was bright, but the world seemed even darker now than it had before dawn.

18

Lar-Sennen
Patch & Barver

"Welcome to Massarken," said the dry, dusty voice in the wheelhouse. "You have no need to fear me!"

"I'll fear you all I like, thanks very much!" said Patch, his voice trembling. "You're a talking corpse!" He gave Barver's head a nudge with his foot, hoping his unconscious friend would wake.

"Ignore my body," said the voice. "It is only the dried remnants of what I once was."

Patch realized that the corpse holding the wheel hadn't moved at all. Instead, in the shadows behind it, another shape had appeared. As he looked, the shape seemed to brighten, a gentle light coming from it, and there it was— the glowing figure of a man, with the same long beard and simple clothes that the corpse had.

A *ghost*.

The ghost smiled at Patch. "Is that better?" it said.

"Who are you?" said Patch.

"Lar-Sennen," said the figure. "As you guessed."

"Lar-Sennen died a thousand years ago," said Patch. "Surely a body becomes nothing but dust and bones after a thousand years?"

The figure stepped around the wheel, looking sadly at the dead body holding it. "I certainly am a bit shriveled," said Lar-Sennen's ghost. "But I died only sixty years ago. I had lived an unnaturally long life by then. In the end, death catches up to us all. It's good at that. All the practice, I suppose."

The ghost came across the room toward Patch, but instead of feeling his terror growing, Patch was surprised to find his fears subsiding. He felt no malice from this specter.

The ghost looked at Barver. "Your friend is regaining consciousness," he said.

Barver was making anxious grumbling sounds, his eyes still closed. Patch kneeled down and placed his hand on his friend's snout. "Be calm, Barver," he said. "There's nothing to fear."

"He is of a nervous temperament, then?" said Lar-Sennen.

Patch scowled. "I've never met anyone braver! Spooky things are his sole weakness."

"*Spooky things*," repeated Lar-Sennen, seeming to find the words amusing. "I can understand that."

Barver cracked open one eye and peered warily at Lar-Sennen. "I'd hoped I'd dreamed you up, ghost," he said. "But apparently not." He pulled back from the doorway and sat up on the grass outside, his arms folded, looking decidedly cross.

"I, Lar-Sennen, Greatest Sorcerer of All Time, welcome you to Massarken," said the ghost. "And congratulate you on succeeding in your quest!"

Barver frowned. "What's he talking about?"

"I have no idea," said Patch.

"You have found me!" insisted the ghost. "You are Seekers of Lar-Sennen, are you not? I lived in hiding for a thousand years, waiting for a worthy candidate to come. Even in death, I have waited!" He bowed his head, sorrowful. "It was a long time."

"I'm sorry," said Patch. "We're not Seekers, whatever they are. We came to your island by mistake."

"By *mistake*?" said Lar-Sennen.

Barver scowled. "Don't you know?" he said. "I thought you must know everything that went on here!"

The ghost gestured to the dark windows. "These are the eyes of the island," he said. "When I lived, from here I could see everything that went on—even far out to sea! But for these past sixty years, the eyes of Massarken have lit up only when the island chooses. I have no power over it anymore." He looked at his translucent hands. "Not in this state. The island no longer obeys me, because it can no longer *hear* me. Massarken is my greatest creation. I granted it life, of a kind; I gave it wisdom, to a degree. The ability to see *ghosts*, however . . . that never occurred to me. And so when death finally claimed me and I returned in the form that stands before you now—unable even to leave the wheelhouse—I discovered to my frustration that the island had no idea I was here."

"What, then, of the griffins you took captive?" said Barver, clenching his fists. "Cruelly chained!"

"If I could have freed them, I would," said Lar-Sennen. "I swear it! Yet the blame is mine, yes. As I came closer to death, the magic I had used for centuries to extend my life was no longer enough. I ordered the island to seek griffins for my Bestiary—to trap intelligent beings for my own benefit. It is my greatest shame. It was said that the ancient magic of *pairing*—possible only between griffins and humans—could extend life even further. I had always vowed never to consider such cruelty, but in my desperation I made a terrible mistake and broke my vow. I died before I could take it back, yet the island carried out my command."

"How *many*?" shouted Barver. "How many griffins has the island imprisoned?"

"Only two," said Lar-Sennen. "The opportunity to catch them rarely comes up. One escaped. The island grew ill some years ago and was wracked with tremors. The illness was brief, but thankfully the poor soul got away while the island was distracted."

Barver glared at the ghost, but his anger subsided at last. "Do you even know how we came here?" he said.

"I know some of it," said Lar-Sennen. "There was a considerable surge in magical energy that even a ghost can sense. The eyes of the island showed some of what has occurred since. I saw your army of Pipers as it cut through the forest. I saw the devil-birds attack. I saw you healed!"

"The hedgehog!" said Patch. "Certainly my favorite of your animals."

"A *helsterhog*," corrected the ghost. "They *are* wonderful, I agree." He leaned closer to Patch, squinting. "Are you sure you're not a Seeker?"

"I don't know what you mean by *Seeker*," said Patch.

"Those who would prove their worth!" said the ghost. "Those who would take over Massarken so they may use my work for the good of the world! Those who bore my mark!"

"What mark?" said Patch.

The ghost spread his arms. "Look beneath you and you shall see!"

Patch looked down. There was a symbol inlaid in metal, covering the whole of the stone floor—a circle with a set of lines inscribed. It was a symbol he'd seen before. "The mysterious woman," he said.

Barver nodded. "The one who kidnapped Alkeran."

Patch looked at the marking on the floor again. When he'd first seen it, he'd thought that it resembled a bird's foot. Wren had thought it was like the root of a plant. But now he saw it for what it was: the combination of two letters, an *L* and an *S*, within a circle.

Lar-Sennen.

He turned to the ghost. "I saw a woman with that tattooed on her wrist," he said. "Would that be one of your Seekers?"

"Yes!" said the ghost with a smile. "Was she worthy? Driven by a deep sense of justice and hope?"

Barver shook his head. "Actually she was a bit of a wrong'un, as far as we can tell. She was definitely trying to *seek* this place, but she wasn't averse to using murder and kidnapping to do it."

The ghost's smile vanished, and he seemed rather dejected.

"We've got nothing to do with your Seekers," said Patch. "And we're certainly not here to take over Massarken. We really did come to your island by mistake."

"Not *quite* by mistake," said Barver. "We used one of your obsidiac devices to escape certain death, and we ended up here because you imprisoned my father—the griffin still held captive!"

Lar-Sennen opened and closed his mouth, but before he could reply, a thought struck Patch so hard it almost winded him.

"It's *all* because of you . . . ," Patch said. "Your book. *Thoughts of the Unlimited Dark*. You invented the Obsidiac Organ. You designed the Black Knight's armor. *It's all your fault*."

The ghost gaped in silence for a few seconds before managing to speak. "What?"

"He has no idea," said Barver. "None at all. He's been haunting this little wheelhouse for sixty years and hasn't the first *notion* of what trouble he's caused." He nudged Patch. "Tell him. All of it."

"Where to start?" said Patch. But it took him only a few seconds to realize how he should begin. It was obvious, really. "Ten years ago," he said, "the town of Hamelyn had a problem with rats . . ."

The ghost was crouching at the far side of the wheelhouse, wailing in sorrow.

"He's not taking it well," observed Barver.

"No," said Patch, but it was understandable. Lar-Sennen had listened to his story, enrapt. This was to be expected, given that the ghost had spent the last sixty years without even his island for company. But when he'd learned that his design for the Obsidiac Organ had actually been *made*, and worse—that his obsidiac armor was a reality, he'd been horrified.

At last Lar-Sennen came back to the doorway, still wailing.

"It wasn't possible!" the ghost cried. "It's not my fault!"

"I beg to differ," said Barver. "You wrote that book! You created those designs!"

Lar-Sennen nodded. "I created them to destroy my greatest foe."

"Your greatest foe?" said Patch.

"*Quarastus*," said Lar-Sennen. "An evil Sorcerer, rich and powerful, but he always wanted more. The only thing he feared was death. I already knew there were ways to extend life beyond a natural span—ways I vowed to keep secret. But if someone like Quarastus discovered the same methods, I dreaded the consequences. Quarastus would never stop gathering more power, more wealth, until he ruled the world with a brutal hand. It would mean *centuries* of terror! So I decided to *trick* him. I designed the armor and made sure he knew of it—why settle for mere centuries of life when you could have immortality? I knew he couldn't resist. It became his obsession, yet it would always be beyond his reach. He died penniless, all his money spent hunting for an amount of pure obsidiac that simply did not exist. His life was wasted on a fool's quest."

"A quest someone else has managed to complete," said Patch. "Because there *is* a way to create obsidiac, and somebody found it."

Lar-Sennen shook his head. "How could I have known?"

"But if it was all supposed to be a trick," said Barver, "why did you make the designs work?"

"Quarastus understood the principles behind the magic involved," said the ghost. "He didn't have the genius to invent the armor himself, but he could certainly tell if it was useless."

Barver and Patch shared a look.

"Well," said Patch. "Your genius could be the downfall of us all. The Hamelyn Piper has built that armor, and if he gets the amulet he'll be unstoppable. We need to warn the world and make sure that doesn't happen!" He pointed to the wheel. "Tell me how to steer your island!"

19
THE WITCH
Wren

In the morning, Wren watched the birds again. During the night, her practice had gone well. She was getting better at changing her feet—huge rat paws filling her shoes—and with her head hidden under her blanket she managed to change her ears and her nose, whiskers and all. She imagined the kind of shock her guards would have had if they saw her this way, and the thought made her smile.

It was all *rat*, though. Her attempts at a beak and a feather-covered head came to nothing. Her hands had been disappointing too. She could feel how the manacles suppressed her ability to change them, which would stop her escape attempt before it even began.

The guards were still the same ones she'd had since almost drowning, and she'd noticed how they'd taken turns to watch her during the night as three of the four slept on the little crates they used as seats—sitting upright to make it look like they were on duty, but slouched enough for her to tell they were asleep. From time to time, the guard watching her had dozed off too—only briefly, yes, but it would have been a perfect time to try and get away.

If only she could get out of the manacles.

She'd been hoping for some breakfast, but it wasn't to be; the order came through that the army would soon move on. The speed at which mercenaries could switch from calm inactivity to furious action was impressive, and they were marching within the hour.

To her left as she walked, in a valley below, was the river that had nearly killed her. After a few hours, that river was in a deep canyon, the army marching beside it along cliffs overlooking raging water.

The sky ahead looked angry. One of Wren's guards noted it. "Storm," they said with a wary shake of the head. "A bad one. We'll be stopping soon to prepare, mark my words!"

The guard was right. The order came back from the Black Knight to make ready to sit out the storm. The army itself was strung along the simple roadway at the top of the cliffs on a plateau that merged with forest. The clifftop road was too exposed, and so the soldiers erected their tents within the tree line to give some added shelter. Wren's hope of being inside one of those tents was quickly dashed as the guards drove the usual stake deep into exposed ground, fastening her manacles to it before taking up position surrounding her. Each had an oilskin wrapped around them, ready for the inevitable rain.

"Here," said a guard, handing her an oilskin. "Don't want you to *drown* again, do we?"

Wren's chain reached as far as a foot-wide rock on the ground, and she sat on that and hoped the storm wouldn't be as bad as the guards seemed to think.

By the time night came, though, it proved to be even worse.

The rain fell heavily for an hour as the winds gathered themselves and howled. At the base of the small rock Wren sat on, water pooled around her boots. She covered her head and as much of the rest of herself as she could, holding the oilskin tightly in her manacled hands. What few gaps there were let in flashes of lightning and damp blasts of cold air, and if she moved in just the right way she could see the guards sitting in the downpour, three of them hunched in that manner that made it clear they were trying to sleep. The fourth, however, was wide awake and looking right at her. She turned to face away from him.

The winds dropped and she tried tucking the oilskin under her arms to free up her hands. It billowed a little at times, but never enough to whip it away and give the elements free reign to soak her. Now that her hands weren't occupied, she wanted to try squeezing out of the manacles, just in case it was possible after all.

She pulled her right hand until the pain nearly made her cry out. The rain was helping, though, wetting her skin. She had a moment where she thought it was actually going to be enough. She gave an almighty tug and felt the bones in her hand grind together...

But the manacles wouldn't move any farther.

Her hand was in agony, and she knew that if it started to swell, there'd be no chance of getting it out—but now she found it wouldn't slide back either, no matter how hard she pushed.

She cursed her own thumb as the pain made her more and more cross. If only that thumb would—

It shrank.

Her hand slipped through the manacles, and she stared at it: a human-sized rat's paw. She let out a brief laugh and made her hand human again, then tried changing her left. This time it seemed easy, and she was entirely free from the manacles for the first time.

The sense she had then was astonishing. She could feel the *sorcery* flowing back into her and knew instinctively that if she wanted to become a rat again, she could do it in an instant. Now wasn't the time—but soon, if the guard watching her would only doze off. She flexed her hands, both human again, and grinned.

She would allow herself one little indulgence, though, before slipping back inside the manacles. With her hands free, she concentrated, wanting to change them *both* to oversized rat paws at the same time.

But the moment they changed, she felt the *need* intensify, the overwhelming craving to transform. It spread through her body, taking all the effort she could muster to suppress it, but the manacles slipped from her knees and fell to the ground, splashing into the water with a clunk of metal and rattle of chain that was unexpectedly loud.

Quickly she leaned down to grab them again. Her hands were still paws, she realized, and as she tried to focus and change them back, she sensed movement.

From right in front of her.

"And what do you think you're up to, girl?" came a voice. The guard. The oilskin was pulled away, and the guard stared at her, then staggered backward, falling to the wet ground.

Wren stood up, suddenly aware that she'd not quite stopped the change from spreading after all. Her nose was longer, she realized, as were her teeth. A flash of lightning showed her hand-paws with a terrible clarity, and she remembered wondering how funny it would be if the guards could see her in her half-rat state.

It wasn't funny, not at all.

The guard stared at her in utter horror. Wren's mind was spinning in panic. The situation had completely changed—if she wanted to escape, it was now or never.

Yet her panic froze Wren to the spot. As another lightning strike lit everything around her, the guard finally found his voice.

He pointed at her and cried out in one long fear-filled scream: "*Witch!*"

Wren looked to the other guards as they pulled back their oilskins to see her standing there, but the guard's yell had broken through her paralysis, and she ran. It was only as another flash of lightning lit the scene in front of her that she realized she'd gone the wrong way—toward the clifftop, rather than into the forest where she might have changed fully to rat and hidden.

She ran through the stinging rain, snatching glances behind her. When lightning came she could see exactly what was chasing her—the four guards were close, a scattering of other mercenaries coming behind them. She saw the cliff edge ahead and she knew what she would have to do.

She stumbled, barely managing to stay on her feet. With another glance behind, she saw how close things would be. Her pursuers were matching her pace, and there were more of them now. If any one of them slipped or fell, it would make no difference. If *she* fell, it would all be over.

Her lungs were burning with the effort of it and she could feel her strength fading, her legs crying out for her to stop, but she couldn't stop now.

Feathers, she thought. *Beak. Feet. Wings*.

As a rat, falling from the cliff into the gorge below would be a terrible risk. Falling as a human would be fatal, of course, but even as a rat the risk of injury was huge—hitting sharp rocks, or getting caught in the torrent of the river.

It would be easy to fully become a rat if she had no option, but she needed to become a *crow*.

Feathers. Beak. Feet. Wings. She pictured the birds she'd been studying, focusing in readiness for the moment her fall began. She ignored the angry shouts from behind her—so *close*.

In her last look back she could see the guards stopping, hands to their sides. Their chase was over, they thought. Where could she go? Wherever the girl ran now, they would catch her. As long as she didn't do anything stupid . . .

Feathers. Beak. Feet. Wings.

The lightning came again. The cliff edge was twenty feet away, the canyon ahead revealed in the harsh light. *A five-hundred-foot drop*, she thought. The water beneath was fast-flowing, unforgiving.

From behind came a shout of dismay as she leaped and closed her eyes.

Feathers. Beak. Feet. Wings.

She fell through the air, plummeting, yet she managed to concentrate enough that the changes began. The rush of air slowed her, her body shrinking now.

Feathers. Beak. Feet. Wings.

She stretched, twisted, and felt exhilaration flow through her as the rush of air changed, and she knew she was going *forward* as well as down. She opened her eyes, looking left and right, seeing the black feathers running along the sleek wings that bore her up.

But she saw at once that it wasn't *quite* what she'd been hoping for.

The wind buffeted her, and she turned herself to face back down the canyon with the wind coming from behind and buoying her up. She would need time to get used to flying, especially given how things had turned out.

Feathers and wings, yes—she'd managed that much.

And the rest? Paws and a furry body with a long, thin tail . . . It wasn't perfect, but it would have to do.

As the storm raged on, the little winged rat flew off into the dark night.

20
Guardian of Massarken
Patch & Barver

"If you wish to control the island," the ghost of Lar-Sennen said to Patch, "you must become the *Guardian of Massarken!*"

"That sounds ominous," said Patch. "Does it involve some kind of challenge?"

"Maybe a series of elaborate tests, and if you fail, you die?" suggested Barver.

Patch scowled at him. "Not helpful," he said, then turned back to Lar-Sennen. "But does it?"

"No," said the ghost. "You just have to put on a magical bracelet." He pointed to the corpse clinging to the ship's wheel, and Patch saw a glint of metal around the body's left wrist. "That one."

"Really?" said Patch. "That's all?"

Lar-Sennen smiled. "The test, dear boy, was making it here alive. Now take the bracelet."

Patch went to the body, reluctant to touch it. Its fingers were still clasped around the wheel handles.

"Go on," said Barver from the doorway. "I would help if I could fit inside."

"I know," said Patch, bracing himself. He pried the dead fingers away one by one. They still had a fierce grip, and as he straightened each of them the horrible sound came of tendons snapping. He winced every time. Once the final finger was released, the corpse fell to the side. It hit the floor with a bony clunk rather than crumbling to dust as Patch had expected.

Lar-Sennen's ghost looked at his own corpse, his spectral expression hard to read. To Patch, it seemed like disappointment as much as anything. "Perhaps a funeral pyre would be nice," said the ghost. "When we have the time. For now, put the remains over by the wall. Around the neck is a chain, at the end of which is a small bottle. Be sure to take that as well as the bracelet and place the chain around your own neck. We'll need it later."

Patch took a deep breath and reached to the neck of the body, finding the chain, freeing it from the dusty clothes, and pulling it over the corpse's thin hair. Suppressing his distaste, he put the chain over his own head before dragging the body to the wall. Only then did he remove the bracelet.

He stood and slowly slid it over his left hand.

He noticed Lar-Sennen *wince* slightly. "Why did you do that?" he asked.

"Do what?" said the ghost.

"You winced!" said Patch. "I saw it!"

The ghost looked slightly embarrassed. "If you'd had evil in your heart, you would have exploded." He smiled. "But you didn't explode!"

Barver shrugged. "Fair enough," he said.

The bracelet began to glow with a warm white light. "Ah, good," said Lar-Sennen, ignoring Patch's scowl.

"It's working. It will also glow anytime you ask it to, which is handy when light is scarce. Now repeat what I say: *Massarken, hear my command! Show me the devil-birds as they fight!*"

The instant the words left Patch's mouth, the dark windows around the wheelhouse grew light. Yet instead of the hilltop and its surroundings, Patch could see the frozen battlefield where the devil-birds were still caught in the midst of combat with the soldiers and Pipers of Kintner.

Lar-Sennen gave him a broad smile. "The island hears you," he said.

"Those devil-birds are horrible creatures," said Barver.

"Horrible in many ways, true, yet they have many magical uses," said the ghost. "They also prowl the island and the regions between enclosures. A useful deterrent!"

"I think most people would have opted for guard dogs," said Barver. "Easier to train, for a start."

"I am not *most people*," said Lar-Sennen. "Against your army, the devil-birds met their match. If the battle had continued, both sides would have been slaughtered! Massarken has the ability to halt time in small regions of the island. Even when I was alive, I wasn't always here—I was a very busy Sorcerer! If one of the creatures in my Bestiary grew ill or was injured, Massarken could stop time around it, protecting the animal until my return. Here, it's done it on a much larger scale."

Patch walked to the windows and looked out on the frozen battle. He saw Alia and Tobias, back-to-back, surrounded by devil-birds; and there was Merta, kicking out at one of the creatures as she plucked another from the air.

"Ask it to show us my father, Patch," called Barver.

"Massarken, hear my command!" said Patch. "Show me Gaverry Tenso, the captured griffin!"

The view of the devil-birds and the Pipers faded, and now they could see Barver's father sitting by the entrance to his cave. They could *hear* him too—hear him *sing*. It was a soothing song in a language Patch didn't recognize, but when he looked back at Barver he saw tears in his friend's eyes.

"An old griffin lullaby," said Barver, nodding. "I can remember him singing it to me when I was very young."

His father stopped singing and looked up to the sky. "Come back to me safe, son," he said.

"I'm here!" said Barver. "Dad! I'm here!"

"He cannot hear us," said Lar-Sennen.

"Surely you can release him from his collar and the chains that have bound him all these years?" said Barver.

Lar-Sennen shook his head. "It would be possible, but better to wait, I think."

"Why?" glowered Barver.

"Your father would need fair warning," said the ghost. "Otherwise the appearance of the Iron Crabs might cause him some distress."

Patch met Barver's eye. "The *Iron Crabs*?" he said.

"Yes," said the ghost. "Curious specimens, kept in an enclosure halfway around the island. It was they who forged the chain and collar, and they who would remove them. It would be wise for your father to know they're coming. They certainly give *me* the heebie-jeebies."

Barver, Patch noted, gave a slight shudder. "Very well," said the dracogriff. "As long as we can release him soon. In the meantime, we should check on Wintel and Cramber. If their recovery is faltering, they may need our help first."

"Massarken, hear my command!" said Patch. He was getting used to this. "Show me the injured griffins."

Again the scene in the windows faded, replaced by the small group of Pipers and soldiers who'd stayed behind in the camp and the two sleeping griffins. All seemed well—the breathing of the griffins was regular and strong, and the Pipers were smiling and cooking rabbits on a small fire. There was no urgency there.

"Good," said Barver. "Then our first action should be to rescue the army from their time trap and the devil-birds. But how can the army be freed without also freeing the birds and creating carnage?"

Lar-Sennen nodded. "Not a problem," he said. "Lead on, Patch!" He gestured toward the door.

"I thought you said you couldn't leave the wheelhouse?" said Patch.

"The bottle you wear around your neck is what allowed me to come back in this form," said the ghost. "But my movement is limited to twenty feet away from it at most." Patch pulled the tiny bottle from under his tunic and looked at it. "A Soul Bottle, it's called," said Lar-Sennen. "Without one of those, the chances of coming back as a ghost are practically nil. Please be careful with it. And do *not* drop it in the sea!"

"I wasn't going to," said Patch, although he could understand why the ghost was anxious to make sure that didn't happen.

They took a path along boundary fences at first, but eventually Lar-Sennen led them into an enclosure. Patch and Barver were reluctant; Lar-Sennen smiled. "You are quite safe," he said. "This is where the helsterhogs live. There are injuries to be dealt with, so we should take some with us." He frowned. "Although they can be difficult to find at this time of day."

They looked in the undergrowth for a while without luck, but then Patch had an idea. He pulled his Pipe from his pocket.

Lar-Sennen was delighted. "A Piper's Song!" he cried. "What will you play?"

"The Dream," said Patch. "Their greatest desires will lure them out. I'll weave their favorite slimy treats into the music, and hopefully they'll come from hiding. Although, Barver, I must warn you—I don't know how to play just for helsterhogs, or even hedgehogs for that matter, so it will be quite broad in its effects."

Barver frowned. "Meaning what exactly?"

"Well, you might find that slugs and worms suddenly sound delicious," said Patch. "Hopefully it won't feel too strange."

"They're not my first choice of snack," he said. "But I don't actually mind the occasional worm. I'll gather some while you play. It would seem rude to summon the little creatures without gifts to offer!"

Patch began. He built the basic melody for the Dream and then added counterpoints that he hoped would bring a sense of "delicious sliminess" to the desires that the Song invoked. He had only played for a few minutes when small twitching noses began to emerge from the bushes nearby, and three of the adorable animals were soon at his feet.

"Well done!" said Barver, offering the helsterhogs some worms before slurping one of them himself.

"These three should do nicely," said Lar-Sennen. "A little helsterhog goes a long way."

Barver took two of them, both easily fitting on one palm. He was immediately besotted. Patch took the third, and Barver gave him a handful of worms.

"Thanks . . . ," said Patch, grimacing.

Soon they stood at the enclosure boundary by the meadow, looking over at the creepy bone trees.

"Wait," said Patch. "There were other devil-birds that chased us, not just those that were frozen."

The ghost nodded. "A good point. Repeat these words: Massarken, hear my command! The devil-birds must return to their nests until nightfall!"

Patch repeated the words. They listened carefully for any hint of rustling in the bone trees, but only heard the helsterhogs chewing their worms.

"Not a thing," said Barver. "Hopefully they're long gone."

And off to the bone trees they went.

The battle between the devil-birds and the Pipers lay frozen before them—deadly foes locked in an unending fight for life. "Will you explain *now*, ghost?" said Barver. Since leaving the enclosure of the helsterhogs, he and Patch had asked repeatedly how they were going to end the time-freezing spell without just making the battle continue to rage. Lar-Sennen had never given a direct answer, and had merely claimed that "All would be well" and "You will see."

"Patch, will you please step toward the edge of the spell's effect?" said the ghost.

The Piper Army was surrounded by devil-birds, and so wherever Patch went it was devil-birds that were closest to him. He held his nerve and moved right up to the curious shimmer in the air. "Now what?" said Patch.

"Reach out," said Lar-Sennen. "Push your hand through the spell!"

Warily, Patch did as instructed. The shimmer surrounded his hand, accompanied by a sparkling ripple that flowed across his skin.

"You see?" said the ghost. "As Guardian, you are unaffected by the time spell."

Barver looked puzzled. "But how does that help us? Everyone else is still trapped."

"Patch must venture inside and carry each person out," said the ghost. "We'll be able to take the most injured first and treat them one at a time."

Patch's eyes widened. There were well over two hundred

people within the spell. It was going to be a long day. "Everyone?" he said. "Just by myself?"

Lar-Sennen gave a sympathetic nod. "The protection is specific to the one who commands Massarken," he said. "That is *you* and no other."

"Can't I just give the bracelet to somebody else?" he said. He tried to slide the bracelet off his wrist, but it seemed to have shrunk.

Lar-Sennen looked horrified. "No!" he said. "You are *Guardian*."

"What, for the rest of my life?" said Patch.

"Should you decide to give up the honor, there is a ritual that can be performed," said the ghost. "By the light of a full moon."

Patch frowned. He looked back to the battle and all the people he was going to have to move. His eyes widened again as he noticed Merta. "And what about the griffin?" he cried. "I can't lift her!"

"Well, you *could* carry the devil-birds out of the spell too," said the ghost. "As Guardian of Massarken they shouldn't attack you. Although they do tend to get a bit feisty, so I can't guarantee they wouldn't lash out."

Patch looked at the lethal claws of the nearest devil-birds. "I'll pass on that idea," he said.

"I have it!" said the ghost. "Move all the birds away from the griffin so they can't harm her when the spell is lifted, but keep them inside the spell so they remain frozen for now. Then when you order the spell removed, the devil-birds will return to their nests as Massarken commands, leaving the griffin unharmed."

"Move all the devil-birds . . . ," said Patch, suddenly feeling very *very* tired indeed. It really *was* going to be a long day.

21

Rescue of the Pipers
Patch & Barver

Patch made his way farther into the frozen-time spell until he reached the nearest injured Piper. She was on the ground, using a knife to fend off a vicious devil-bird on top of her. Its claws had raked through the Piper's clothing, leaving a deep gouge in her flesh that would need the attention of the helsterhogs. Patch lifted the stiff-limbed creature away, then began to drag the woman to safety.

Everything he touched felt as hard as stone.

At the edge of the spell, the shimmering followed the pair for some way, finally vanishing suddenly like a popped bubble. The Piper struggled and lashed out with the knife in her hand, her eyes wide with fear; Patch barely managed to step back out of harm's way. When she saw that she was no longer in danger, she collapsed, shivering with the pain of her wounds.

"Oh, yes, you need to be careful of that," said Lar-Sennen, a little late.

From then on, Patch was careful to remove the weapons of those he rescued and to always take a few quick steps away before the spell's effect vanished. Everyone he pulled from the fight was right in the middle of a life-or-death struggle, and who could have blamed them if they'd accidentally injured their rescuer?

He spent the next few hours untangling the frozen battle while the helsterhogs tended to the injuries under Barver's watchful eye. The devil-birds were carefully brought to one densely packed region within the spell, as far from Merta as Patch could manage.

He decided to leave Alia and Tobias until last. Their safety was the most important of all to him, and whenever he felt his energy flag, the sight of them both let him summon the strength to venture back inside.

The helsterhogs usually made quick work of healing the injured, but some of the Pipers and soldiers were beyond even their miracles. Each death hit everyone hard—the helsterhogs included. When a patient died in spite of their efforts, the helsterhogs curled up into balls and trembled.

Some of the uninjured Pipers helped by playing Healing

Songs; others played Songs to buoy Patch up, even though his legs were ready to give way.

And then at last he was done, and he brought first Tobias and then Alia from the clutches of the spell. Tobias was bleeding profusely from an injury to his side, requiring the immediate aid of the helsterhogs.

Alia, though, was unharmed. Flabbergasted when the spell's effect was broken, she stared at Patch and Barver; she stared at the gathered forces of the army, who were cheering her name and Patch's too. She turned and stared at the devil-birds, still trapped in time and crowded together—and at Merta, standing as if locked in a terrible fight even though the devil-birds she'd been battling against were gone.

Alia glared at Patch. "What on *earth* have you been up to now?" she said sternly. Then she noticed Lar-Sennen's ghost standing beside him. Her eyes widened. "And you are . . . ?" she said.

"Lar-Sennen, ma'am," said the ghost.

Alia, for once, was lost for words.

The moment came for Patch to order Massarken to end the time spell and free Merta. Before he did, the army readied itself in case the still-frozen devil-birds caused any trouble. Lar-Sennen thought it a possibility, as they could easily be disoriented once the spell ended, just as many of the soldiers and Pipers had been.

Ranks of Pipers lined up and prepared Shielding Songs, and then Patch gave Massarken the command. The shimmering air shrank back from the edges of the battlefield. The first devil-bird to be freed shook its head and shrieked before taking wing and disappearing into the bone trees; the others followed suit. The entire army sighed with relief when the last of them was gone.

Then Merta too was freed of the spell. She spent a few seconds flailing at the empty air around her before she saw the army safe and sound and realized that the devil-birds were nowhere to be seen.

And at that, Patch's exhausting work was complete. He lay down on the dry earth beneath him, every muscle in his body aching, and fell into the deepest sleep he'd ever known.

When he woke, he was still aching all over.

"It lives!" said a voice from beside him: Barver. "We thought you might never wake."

Patch sat up. He was back at camp, and everyone seemed to be taking a well-earned rest. He was surprised that it was still daylight. "What do you mean?" he said. "I can't have slept for more than a couple of hours."

Barver laughed. "You slept right through!" he said. "It's morning!"

Patch rubbed the sleep from his eyes. "Did I miss anything?"

At that, Wintel hurtled past a few feet from the ground, chased by a fully recovered Cramber—both griffins keeping their flight low enough that the island's magic didn't make them unconscious.

"You missed a few things," said Barver. "As you can see, the helsterhogs worked their usual wonders."

"Lar-Sennen should breed the cute little things by the thousands," said Patch. "Every town infirmary should have them."

Barver gave a sad shake of his head. "I already suggested it," he said. "The helsterhogs are the last of their kind, and they can't survive away from Massarken's protective magic for long. The same is true for many of the creatures here."

Patch noticed something at the center of camp—a row of bodies, reverently laid out. Those who'd been beyond the reach of the helsterhogs. Before he'd slept, there had been ten deaths he'd known of. Another five Pipers and soldiers had injuries so severe that the helsterhogs could only do so much, and their survival would be touch and go.

Now he counted thirteen bodies. Patch felt it as a physical blow. "Three more dead," he said. "I'd hoped . . ." But he could say no more.

"All was done that could have been done," said Barver. "The Healing Pipers think the rest of the injured will survive." He placed his hand on Patch's back as they both looked toward the dead in silence for a time. "You carried a great burden yesterday," said Barver at last. "You should be proud."

Patch put his hand to his chest and couldn't feel the Soul Bottle. At the same moment, he realized he'd seen nothing of the dead Sorcerer since he'd woken. "Where's Lar-Sennen?" he said.

"Alia took the Soul Bottle," said Barver. "At the ghost's request. While you slept he was keen to learn all he could about the events that led to us coming here. They're over there." He pointed to the edge of camp, where a group huddled around a large fire. Merta was there with Alia and Tobias and the glowing figure of Lar-Sennen.

"Your father is still chained?" said Patch.

"He is," said Barver. "You're the only one who can command Massarken to send the Iron Crabs. I suggested waking you earlier, but Dad insisted we wait until daylight so you got the sleep you needed. Although I reckon he didn't like the idea of the crabs coming while it was dark . . ."

"Then we should waste no more time," said Patch. "Your father's next meal will be eaten out here with the rest of us—*free*."

The Iron Crabs were a sight to behold.

Barver's father was visibly nervous as he waited outside his cave. After Patch gave Massarken the command, it took an hour before the crabs arrived, walking sideways between the sycamores. Many of the army had gathered to witness it. Most of the crabs were three feet or so across from leg tip to leg tip. Their shells were craggy, like rock. Their claws were enormous and gleamed like steel. Some crabs were smaller, some larger, and the largest of all was huge—eight feet at least, its claws easily five feet long.

The parade of crabs circled Barver's anxious father and made a start on the chain, their claws turning red with intense heat that allowed them to pinch through the metal as if it was soft clay. The collar remained, and Patch was suddenly worried that the largest crab would have that task. Such a vast claw coming close to your neck would not be a pleasant experience at all.

Instead, the removal of the collar was the role of the smallest of the crabs, each only a few inches across. They had been riding on the shell of the largest, and Patch hadn't even noticed them until they began to move onto the ground. They swarmed up the griffin's arms, covering the collar, and when they swarmed away again nothing remained of it.

The Iron Crabs marched off the same way they'd come, leaving Barver and his father to embrace.

"Free!" cried Barver, but his father was overcome and could say nothing. Barver took his father's hand and led him back to camp, to cheers and applause from the army and the other griffins.

A feast of rabbit and pigeon had been cooked as an act of both celebration and remembrance, but once tribute had been paid to the fallen, Patch insisted that he return to the wheelhouse and begin the journey to Tiviscan.

"You must eat first," said Alia.

"We can take food with us," said Patch. "It's time to go." Barver, of course, joined him, as did Alia and Tobias. Alia gave Patch the Soul Bottle, and Lar-Sennen guided them. They brought the hardworking helsterhogs, and when they reached their enclosure Barver took a moment to gather them some extra worms as thanks for their efforts.

Plus a handful for himself.

At the wheelhouse, Patch grasped the wheel. Alia and Tobias stood at either side while Barver watched from the doorway.

"How do I do this?" Patch asked the ghost. He could barely believe it, but he was about to take control of an entire *island*.

"Command Massarken to show you the way to Tiviscan," said Lar-Sennen. "A light will appear in the window to indicate your course. Steer with the wheel. It's quite thrilling."

Patch nodded. "Massarken, I command you!" he said. "Show me the way to Tiviscan!"

A light appeared to his far left, and he turned the wheel until it would turn no more. But nothing happened.

"Ah, yes," said Lar-Sennen. "Give the order for the speed. Full ahead!"

"Here we go, then," said Patch. "Massarken, I command you! Full ahead!"

They felt the slightest of vibrations under their feet, a gentle rumble; the light in the window of the wheelhouse began to move, and the position of the sun changed as they turned.

"Captain Patch Brightwater," said Barver in the voice of a gleeful pirate. "Of the good ship Massarken! Where be we headed, Cap'n?"

Patch turned and grinned at his friend. "To Tiviscan, me hearties!" he cried. "To Tiviscan!"

22
The Fugitives
Erner

For four days, Erner traveled.

Rundel had given him one goal: to find Alia and Tobias and tell them what had happened. The big question was *how* to find them. They knew what their plan had been—that Tobias would bring Pipers and soldiers from the Kintner Bastion while Alia tried to recruit dragons in Skamos to act as scouts. Then they would gather in Gossamer Valley near the Ortings and begin their hunt for the Black Knight.

But had *any* of that plan been successful?

The Ortings lay far to the east, so that's where Erner headed. At brief tavern stops he listened for news. None was encouraging.

Everything he heard about the events at Skamos made it sound even worse than he'd thought—rumors abounded that there had been terrible casualties. Even if those rumors were false, there seemed little chance that Alia's mission had succeeded—and every possibility that Barver, Patch, and Wren had been hurt.

Or worse.

There were also rumblings of news from the Ortings, albeit vague: strange tales of the sounds of battle heard from a distance, yet when they were investigated, only the scattered remains of tents were found.

Erner wondered what it could mean. It seemed a real possibility that Tobias had confronted the Black Knight and triumphed. Indeed, if Barver had been with them, word of their success might even have reached Tiviscan by now.

But on the afternoon of the fourth day, he encountered westbound riders and carts on the road who warned of the approach of an army. At first Erner was hopeful that this was Tobias leading his forces to Tiviscan. As the travelers told him more, though, his hopes faded. While none had seen the army for themselves, they'd heard terrible things and were eager to avoid being caught in its path. Soon enough he heard news that chilled him to the bone—some mentioned a knight dressed in black armor and put the size of the army in the thousands.

Suddenly the rumors of a brief battle in the Ortings took on a very different meaning. Instead of victory against a small band led by the Black Knight, if Tobias had come up against such a large army . . .

Erner didn't want to think about it. Whatever the truth, however terrible it was, he needed to see the approaching army for himself.

As afternoon turned to evening, the road grew ever thicker with refugees with tales of whole villages destroyed and brutal treatment of anyone who crossed the army's path. Some even told of hideous monsters. Again, none seemed to have witnessed any of this firsthand, but their fear was real enough.

Erner caught the attention of one man driving a cart filled with anxious people, a woman and two children sitting next to him. "Where are you headed?" he asked the man. "For the safety of Tiviscan?"

"No!" said the man. "We've heard that's where the army is headed! In a few miles the road splits, and we're turning north to Geshenfell, a day's journey away. So should you! Get out of their way and let the Pipers deal with it!"

Children wailed and horses whinnied as the overcrowding on the road worsened, a sense of panic starting to spread. Soon it became impossible for Erner to ride against the oncoming flow. The panic of the road had seeped into his horse too, so he turned to the roadside, dismounting to guide it through the trees until the noise fell enough to let him think. He sat on sparse grass, breathing slowly.

He looked at his horse, which had calmed enough to start grazing the meager pasture. "What now?" he asked the animal. "Do I pick my way through the forest? Do I wait and see if the road clears? Is it madness to continue east at all?" The horse didn't look up, and kept grazing. "No answer, eh?" said Erner, despairing. There was a flutter nearby as an unusually large crow flew down from a branch. "And you, bird . . . ," he said. "Do you have an answer?"

"As a matter of fact," said the crow, "I do."

Erner stared at the crow, unable to speak.

"Hold on a second," the crow told him. It hopped away, disappearing behind a thicket of bushes. A moment later Wren appeared and gave a little bow. "Ta daaa!" she said.

"Wren!" he cried, leaping up to embrace her. "I heard terrible news of Skamos and feared that . . ." He frowned. "Wait. You . . . you can turn into a crow? A *talking* one?"

Wren grinned. "Took me a few tries, but yes. I started off as a winged rat, but I got there in the end. I'm still a bit big for a crow, I think. The other crows get a bit skittish. Reckon I'll get that right soon enough! The talking is a bonus."

Erner suddenly noticed that one of her arms was still a wing, and he pointed at it, slightly horrified.

"Oops," said Wren. She shook it a few times, and when she was done, the arm was entirely human.

"I'm lucky you saw me," said Erner.

"Lucky?" said Wren. "I could hardly miss you! The only person heading east against the current. Couldn't you take a hint?"

"I needed to see the army for myself," he said. "So that I can report what I . . ." He froze as the fact of Wren—here, now, standing right in front of him—really sunk home. "Tell me!" he cried. "Tell me everything that's happened!"

So Wren told him of Skamos and the griffins and the battle of Gossamer Valley. Erner was gobsmacked as she explained how she'd stolen a piece of armor from the Black Knight—the Hamelyn Piper himself! When she described those terrible explosive spheres hurtling through the air toward the small army of Pipers and soldiers, Erner's heart was in his throat.

"But they got away," she said. "Just before the spheres blew up, everyone had gone."

"Where to?" said Erner.

"The same place Alia went when she tested the device in the Caves of Casimir," said Wren. "A beach in the Eastern Sea. That was the plan, at least . . ." She fell silent for a moment. "I'd hoped Barver would have got word out by now. There really hasn't been any news from them?"

"No," said Erner. "But you mentioned Barver was injured in the battle, and the griffins. Perhaps none of them were able to fly."

Wren nodded her head. "That must be it," she said, but Erner saw the sheen of tears in her eyes and could understand how worried she must be for their friends. And—although he didn't say as much—he thought how worried Patch and Barver and the others must be too, knowing that Wren had been left in the clutches of the Black Knight.

"And you escaped from the Hamelyn Piper!" he said.

Wren waved it away as if it was nothing. "A bit of practice with shape-shifting, that was all. I couldn't even manage a crow at first—just a winged rat, whatever you'd call *that*. It was enough, and that's what matters. I started to fly toward Tiviscan, hoping I'd be able to find you and Rundel and let you know what had happened, but I flew over a village and couldn't help imagining that army of mercenaries laying waste to everything. I stopped and became human and tried to convince the villagers to run. At first nobody believed me. So . . ." She looked down sheepishly for a moment. "Well, I told them of hideous feathered monsters who went ahead of the army and would, um, eat them all up, and when they still didn't believe I shouted out, 'Oh, no, I hear them coming!' and pretended to run away. Then I began changing to crow but sort of *stopped* halfway and jumped out of the shadows making scary noises." She seemed slightly embarrassed by the whole thing. "They believed it *then*, let me tell you! I made myself scarce and watched from the air. They were gone within ten minutes. I mean, maybe it was unfair of me, but . . ."

Erner wanted to tell her that she'd done the right thing, but there was only one thought on his mind. "You . . . *stopped halfway*? Between human and crow?"

Wren winced. "I know. It's more horrible than it sounds."

It already *sounds rather horrible*, Erner thought. He changed the subject. "How long have you been warning people?"

"Two days now," she said. "Every time I think I'm done I fly back to make sure the army is still following the same road. But they don't always go the way I expect, and then I've got entirely different villages to warn. The army is *huge*, Erner, and the Hamelyn Piper claimed there would be dragons joining them."

"Dragons?" said Erner, his blood running cold. "Can that even be possible?"

"I haven't seen any yet," said Wren. "But I don't think it was an idle boast."

"Is the army definitely headed for Tiviscan?" said Erner.

"Afraid so," said Wren. "The Hamelyn Piper said there's someone there he has a score to settle with."

Erner nodded. "*That* I already knew," he said. "You've told me your side of things. Now it's my turn."

Erner told her of the events at Tiviscan, ending with the revelation of Quarastus and the terrible fate of Lord Drevis and Rundel Stone.

"What are we to *do*?" said Wren.

"You must leave me and fly ahead to Tiviscan," said Erner. "Perhaps Barver has returned with news after all!"

"I still feel I should be warning everyone I can," said Wren. "And what could I do against an evil Sorcerer?"

"You told me how you showed your sorcery skills in the sewers of Skamos," he said. "Perhaps you could stand up to Quarastus better than you think."

Wren shook her head. "I'm a novice," she said. "We need an expert."

"Then we *must* find Alia somehow," said Erner. "She knows more about sorcery than anyone."

The idea struck them both at exactly the same time: Alia wasn't the only powerful Sorcerer they knew.

Underath.

"How far away is his castle, do you think?" said Wren.

"Not that far," said Erner, his Custodian training coming in useful. "It's near Axlebury . . . I'd say eighty miles or so, roughly northeast." He checked the sky for a moment, then pointed. "That way. But are your navigation skills up to the task of finding it?"

"I think so," she said. "Besides, I can always change back to human and ask for directions."

"Will Underath agree to help?" said Erner. "That's the question. You know him best, surely?"

"I suppose I do," said Wren. "He did seem a changed man when we reunited him with the griffin Alkeran. A kinder man, certainly, and less selfish after he'd had a taste of life without magic. By now I fear he's well fed and as selfish as ever. He might not want to help *anyone*. I'll do my best, though! What about you?"

"Someone on the road said they were heading to Geshenfell, to the north," said Erner. "Geshenfell has a Custodian outpost. They can send a rider to warn Tiviscan of the army's approach. Find me there when you return."

"Will you tell them about Lord Pewter's treachery?" said Wren.

"I wish I could," he said. "But nobody would believe it. And I think Rundel's only chance is if we have surprise on our side." He looked suddenly forlorn. "Yet if he dies, it'll be my fault."

"Don't lose heart, Erner!" said Wren. "I'll convince Underath to help. Trust me!"

Erner nodded, trying to suppress his worry. Wren was one of the most capable people he'd ever met, and if she felt confident, then so should he.

Wren hid in the thicket of bushes where she'd changed from crow to human. After a moment, she reappeared as a crow, flying up to the treetops and away. Then the crow turned and came back, landing in front of Erner.

"Which way was it again?" cawed Wren.

Erner pointed. Wren took to the skies, and Erner found himself worrying once more.

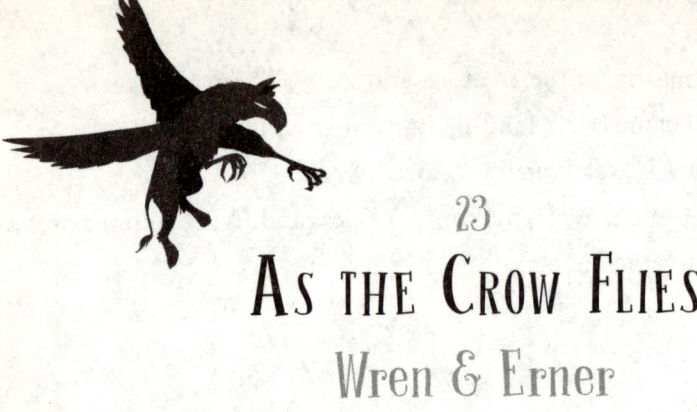

23
As the Crow Flies
Wren & Erner

Wren wasn't used to the wind yet, not by a long shot. As a crow, even the slightest breeze had a huge effect on her. She observed the other birds and saw that they simply accepted it, riding the currents of air without fighting them the way she did.

It had been worse as a winged rat, of course. As she flew toward Underath's castle, she thought back to that first flight she'd had, escaping the Hamelyn Piper's army, plunging down into the canyon as the storm had raged around her. She'd put enough distance between herself and the Black Knight's army to ease her doubts, finding a snug cave to sleep in and wait out the storm, but she'd known that she needed to master the shape of a bird if she was going to get much farther.

When morning had come, she'd practiced shape-shifting until she managed to become mostly crow, albeit with the tail of a rat and a pair of teeth poking out from the end of her beak. She'd flown to a high branch to get her bearings, and another crow had landed next to her. As soon as it caught sight of the *almost-crow* it had given a timid shriek and flown off, hitting the trunk of a tree and plummeting to the ground before picking itself up and flying away.

"Sorry!" Wren had called out—pure instinct taking over. It had taken her a moment to realize that she'd actually managed to *speak*. She tried a few words and phrases, delighted and relieved. After all, as a rat she could use her paws to speak in Merisax signs, but as a crow her wings wouldn't be up to the task. She wondered if she'd somehow *tweaked* the crow a little to allow the words to come, and she experimented by becoming a rat and seeing if the same thing happened, but it didn't. Perhaps the rat shape was simply too fixed, or else the form of a crow didn't need that much of a change to allow speech.

Now, on her way to Underath's castle, she felt as comfortable in her crow form as she did as a rat. The teeth were long gone, thankfully, as was the rat's tail.

Any fears of being unable to find her destination proved unfounded. She recognized Fendscouth Tor from quite a distance, the great hill on which Underath's castle sat.

There was something different about it, but it was only when she got closer that she could see what had changed—surrounding the castle was richly colored meadowland, where before there'd only been sparse grass. A wide range of tall flowers grew there now. She hoped it was a sign of Underath's mood, rather than just some extravagant display of his regained powers.

Landing outside the meadow's extent, she transformed back to human. She'd told Erner she would convince Underath, and as she'd flown she'd come up with a plan.

She expected the Sorcerer to be reluctant to help—after all, she was going to ask him to take sides against a powerful and evil Sorcerer, and Underath had a strong sense of self-preservation. *He will*, Wren thought, *come up with an excuse that will keep him away from any danger without revealing that he is scared*.

The most likely excuse would be Alkeran, she reckoned—the griffin who was Underath's greatest friend, whose life they had saved only weeks before. Alkeran was everything to Underath; she'd not appreciated how much the griffin meant to him until she'd seen how devastated the Sorcerer was when he was gone, or how overjoyed he was to have Alkeran back.

"Poor Alkeran needs his rest!" he would say. "I don't want him put at risk!"

That was why Wren didn't intend to waste time trying

to convince Underath to help—because if she convinced *Alkeran*, Underath would have no choice.

Erner sat outside the Custodian outpost and tried to sleep. Once Wren had gone, he'd taken his horse back to the crowded road, turning northward to Geshenfell and riding as hard as he could to get ahead of the refugees. Before he reached the outpost, he put his Custodian robes back on—lives were at stake, and he needed to be taken seriously. He told the Custodians stationed there about the influx of refugees that were coming their way and the reason they were fleeing. One Custodian took the outpost's fastest horse and rode for Tiviscan, while the rest set about preparing to rally the townsfolk to help the frightened travelers who would soon arrive.

Erner handed his horse to the outpost's stable hand. "She did a fine job," he said, patting her. "She deserves the best straw and some rest!"

"Do you need a fresh mount?" the stable hand asked him.

Erner looked up to the sky. "I've made other arrangements," he said, keeping his fingers crossed for Wren. Changing out of his robes again, he sat by the outpost wall and closed his eyes. The first trickle of refugees had begun to arrive by then, and the town already had an air of focused activity.

Sleep eluded him for a time. Every muscle in his body cried out for rest, but whenever he grew drowsy the same nightmare image would flash before him—of a great arm emerging from the pendant, groping around to grab him before he managed to bring down the rock and end it.

Sleep finally took him. The next thing he knew, someone was gently kicking his leg. He opened his eyes and looked up to see the figure of Wren Cobble above him.

"Well?" he said, and the smile on Wren's face was answer enough.

"We're camped out of town to the west," she said.

The camp was deep in the forest.

"I insisted on telling Underath and Alkeran together, but really it was Alkeran I focused on," Wren explained as they approached. "The moment I mentioned Quarastus, Underath stared at me and kept staring. When I was finished, Alkeran asked me to leave them to talk. Half an hour later, he told me they would come, once Underath had gathered some supplies. Even so, the Sorcerer still hasn't said a word."

They emerged into a small clearing, at the center of which was a fire. Underath was sitting near it, staring into the flames. He didn't even glance at them. He was wearing simple clothes, albeit of fine quality. There was nothing to mark him as a Sorcerer, which Erner found encouraging. If Underath's ego had grown back, then surely his pride would have seen him clad in something over the top and entirely impractical.

Alkeran was curled up near the heat. When he heard Wren and Erner approach, he came over to meet them. Around his neck and chest was a harness and pack, a smaller version of the kind Barver always wore. Erner presumed it contained the supplies that Wren had mentioned.

"Has he spoken yet?" asked Wren.

"Not yet," said Alkeran. "Give him time. It's been quite a shock for him."

"How so?" asked Erner.

"When I first met Underath, his life was on a dark path," said the griffin. "He belonged to a group who revered evil Sorcerers of the past. When I learned of this, I was appalled, but Underath refused to listen. The group visited the castle only once after Underath found me and never again." He sighed deeply and shook his head. "They had wanted to kill me, it turned out. Underath ejected them from his home. I was proud of him."

Wren's eyes widened. "Proud?" she said. "It's not exactly the highest of moral standards, is it? 'Don't let people murder your friend.'"

"Every single one of those Sorcerers would have done it in an instant," said Alkeran. "But for Underath, that was the turning point—the moment he understood that he was different from them. It's not easy to discard the things you once thought essential, and he struggled with it for some time. But he succeeded. And now your news brings it back. You see, of all the dark Sorcerers they revered, there was one they considered highest of all . . ."

"Quarastus," said Erner.

"Yes," said another voice, and they turned to see Underath standing by the fire, facing them. "They wanted to kill Alkeran to learn what magic griffins held. Certainly, a *pairing* is one of the most mysterious and powerful of magics, as Alkeran and I know firsthand. Two beings, able to *share* their life essence—something only *ever* achieved between human and griffin. It kept me alive after my heart had been ripped from my chest! It kept Alkeran alive even as he was submerged in the sea for untold hours! I feel sick when I think back to that day in my castle, when those I thought were my friends suggested slitting Alkeran's throat." He clenched his fists, and a flickering of green sparks danced around his knuckles. "This wasn't long after I'd first met Alkeran and nursed him back to health. We'd yet to form our deep friendship, let alone perform the ritual that paired us. When the suggestion to kill him was made, to my shame I said nothing at first. Only when

I saw one of the Sorcerers bring out a knife did I react and send them away!"

"But you will help us, won't you?" said Erner. "Help us face Quarastus."

"I'll help rescue Lord Drevis and Rundel Stone," said Underath. "I promise no more than that." He sat cross-legged near the fire. "We should rest for a few hours," he said. "We'll leave soon after midnight so we can use darkness to cover our arrival in the forests of Tiviscan. There we will see how we might free the two prisoners." He suddenly clapped his hands together. A green flash lit up his face, and his head sagged. They heard a steady snoring.

"Now *that's* a useful trick," said Wren.

"He will wake in two hours exactly," said Alkeran. "And he'll be fully rested. I got him to try it out on me once, but the results weren't ideal."

"You didn't fall asleep immediately?" said Wren.

"I didn't fall asleep for three whole *days*," said Alkeran with a grimace. "I suggest we try and rest the old-fashioned way."

24
THE PRISON
Wren & Erner

As planned, they left just after midnight—Underath, Erner, and Wren all taking position on Alkeran's feathered back. Erner guided them to the west of Tiviscan, making sure to stay a good distance away from the Castle to avoid any risk of being sighted. They landed in a region of rocky moorland within the forest and waited until dawn broke.

Then it was Wren's turn to fly, her crow form making her an ideal spy to check whether the coast was clear. Off she flew, quickly spotting the tall pine which, according to Erner, marked the location of the ruined outpost.

It was even more of a ruin than she'd expected—above the first two floors, it was little more than a pile of rubble, and most of it had been swallowed by the forest. Trampled grass led to one wall, where ragged steps headed down. That, she presumed, was the way Lord Pewter had entered, but she didn't plan to use it. Erner had seen everything that Rundel had seen when he was taken prisoner and had mentioned small holes in the roof of Lord Pewter's improvised "dungeon." That seemed like the better option, with less chance of being spotted if Lord Pewter happened to be there.

The heap of fallen blocks that covered the tower had plenty of crow-sized gaps between them for Wren to carefully pick her way through. Down she went, and she eventually found a hole that led to the wide circular room below. She wriggled her top half into the hole and saw a figure directly below her, held captive against the wall by thick twisting wood as Erner had described. The figure's head rose slightly with each breath.

It was Rundel.

She could see the doorway but wanted to catch sight of Lord Drevis on the other side of the room before she returned to the others. If she could just push through the hole a little farther . . .

The sound of something rattling made her freeze—a key being inserted into a lock. She kept as still as possible in the gloom to avoid being noticed.

The door swung open and in came Lord Pewter, closing the door behind him.

"Good morning, gentlemen," he said. "In terrible pain, I hope?"

"Why . . . have you . . . come?" said Rundel, his voice robbed of all strength. Wren could *hear* just how much he must be suffering.

"You're hurting my feelings, Rundel," said Pewter. "I came to check on my favorite prisoners! Oh, yes—and to gloat. The Council took a vote last night. Finally they've seen sense and made me Leader of the Pipers' Council!"

So they betrayed us after all, thought Wren. *Even if they don't know it.*

"Now every single Custodian will devote themselves to hunting the Hamelyn Piper," continued Pewter. "The sooner I bring that traitor to heel, the better." He took an apple from a pocket and bit into it messily, allowing the juice to dribble down his chin. "Oh, how thoughtless of me! I'm sure you must be dreadfully thirsty and so *very* hungry." He grinned and discarded the apple on the ground.

"Drevis has . . . said nothing since yesterday," Rundel said, clearly struggling to speak at all. "You've given us . . . no water in . . . three days. He'll die!"

"You'll *both* die," said Pewter. "But not until I let you. I hold all the power here, Rundel Stone. But all the power in Tiviscan is *nothing* compared to what I'll have soon. More power than you can even imagine!" Suddenly he grew taller, and wider, his face distorting. He became a nightmare creature the size of a bear, black-furred with great fangs and red eyes. The creature leaned toward Rundel and gave a long, menacing growl before shrinking back to the grinning form of Lord Pewter. "I *do* enjoy our talks," he said, then opened the door and left. The sound of the key in the lock echoed around the chamber.

Wren carefully worked her way back up through the remains of the tower. She hopped to the top of the ruins, making sure she could see the steps she'd noted earlier. Eventually, Lord Pewter emerged from the shadows. He was moving slowly and seemed breathless. Suddenly he staggered to the side, barely managing to stay upright, and Wren saw him transform again. This time, instead of becoming a fearsome monster, Pewter seemed to shrivel away. His face grew pitifully gaunt, the whites of his eyes became a sickly yellow, and his clothes looked like they were wrapped around sticks rather than a body.

Gradually, the change reversed. After a minute or so, Pewter seemed to catch his breath again. He gathered himself then continued on his way, picking up his pace as he headed in the direction of Tiviscan.

Wren flew back and told the others what had happened. Then, back in human form, she led them to the outpost.

"There!" said Erner, pointing to the steps he'd seen Lord Pewter and Rundel go down. "The entrance is that way."

Alkeran hid himself behind the ruins and kept watch as the others went down the steps.

"I'll try and sense any traps he may have left," said Underath. "And see what magical protection has been put in place to guard his prisoners."

"He boasted that Rundel's cries for help couldn't be heard," said Erner.

"That kind of containment is simple enough," said Underath. "Easy to feel when we reach the walls themselves." A long curving passageway brought them before the wooden door. Underath held out his hands and waved in the air near the door and the wall, never quite touching either stone or wood. "There are formidable protections here," he said. "As you mentioned, Erner—no sounds or magic can escape the walls. There are alarms set too. Any use of magic nearby would alert him at once. The most significant spells are cast around the doorway. The wood and frame are strengthened, and the lock is well protected. Even if we *could* smash it down, he would know about it at once."

"I saw the room clearly through the pendant," said Erner. "I remember seeing a hatchway in the ceiling, blocked up with debris. What if we *moved* that debris? Would that trigger Pewter's alarms?"

"It shouldn't," said Underath.

Wren frowned. "*Move* the debris?" she said. "Have you any idea how heavy that must be?"

The other two watched her for a few seconds until the penny dropped.

Piece by piece, Alkeran moved the fallen masonry from the top of the ruins. At last he'd cleared enough to reveal the square hatchway. Underath, Erner, and Wren were lifted up, and they crouched by the hatch.

"Here," called Alkeran, producing a length of rope from his harness pack. He threw one end to Underath. "Lower yourself down gently."

Underath descended.

Wren and Erner looked through the hatchway and saw Lord Drevis and Rundel—both worryingly still, their heads lolled forward.

Underath did a slow shuffling sweep of the room. "You can come down now," he whispered. "As silently as you can, please."

Wren used the rope next, then Erner, who went at once to Rundel. His master's breathing was slow and unsteady; Erner reached out to the thick twisting branches that held Rundel to the wall, eager to wrench them clear and free his friend.

"Wait!" said Underath. "We must be careful. There may

still be magic left in the arboreal spells. They could regrow faster than we can tear at them—hunting for a prisoner to seize."

"What can we do?" asked Wren.

"Sorcery can't be used," said Underath. "Piping either. Pewter would know of it at once." He pulled a thin silver-bladed dagger from a sheath at his waist. "This is a Torpal Knife. It can cut the branches easily and shouldn't give us away, but we must be quick."

They freed Rundel first. Underath's knife sliced effortlessly through the vegetation holding him, and Rundel slumped down, Erner and Wren only just managing to keep hold of him. Though barely conscious, the Virtus Piper opened his eyes briefly and mumbled Erner's name. They guided him to the rope, tying a loop under his shoulders and easing him through the hatch as Alkeran gently pulled him up.

Lord Drevis was more of a challenge, his body utterly limp. Bleeding sores festered where the rough wood had chafed his flesh. Wren and Erner shared a desperate look, knowing the man had been trapped here for weeks. The fact that he was *alive* seemed astonishing.

They half-dragged, half-carried him, and soon he too was being raised out of the prison. It was a long few seconds, then, as they waited for Alkeran to throw the rope down again. Wren and Erner could see how Underath looked warily at the cut ends of the ensnaring branches. There was movement there, small and inconsequential at first, the tiniest of twigs growing, then larger ones.

The rope finally appeared. "Quickly!" instructed Underath. "You two go first!"

As Wren reached the hatch and climbed the rope, she heard the sound of creaking wood and swishing leaves from below. She looked back to see Underath wielding his Torpal Knife, slashing furiously as twisting branches reached out to seize him.

"Hurry!" called Erner. Wren pulled herself through the hatch and helped Erner up. Smaller branches and leaves shot forward, grasping for Erner's legs as he came. They both fell back from the hole, breathless. They could no longer see anything through it but foliage.

"Underath!" cried Alkeran urgently. For a moment there was no reply, only a terrible creaking and rustling. Alkeran was distraught.

Then the Sorcerer's voice came from below. "Pull!" he shouted, and Alkeran pulled the rope hard. Underath shot through the leaves, his knife flashing through the air. Beneath him, the probing branches seemed unwilling to come beyond the hatchway, and retreated.

Underath spat out a leaf and grinned. "It would have been much easier if I could have used magic," he said. "But nowhere *near* as exhilarating!"

They made sure to get some distance from the ruins, finding a stream before Alkeran set down the two patients in his care—and a sorry sight they were.

Rundel opened his eyes. "Water...," he begged. Underath pulled out a small silver cup from under his belt, passing it to Erner.

Erner filled it from the stream, then helped Rundel to sit up so he could drink. Underath turned to Lord Drevis, who was in a dire state, his lips cracked and encrusted with blood, his face thin and filthy, covered in weeping sores. His eyelids flickered briefly, but beyond that it was hard to tell he was even alive.

"Can you help him?" asked Rundel, desperate.

Underath stroked his chin. "There should be just enough for you both," he muttered, then went to Alkeran's harness pack. He rummaged around and brought out a small box. Inside, packed in wads of cotton, was a bottle that held a golden liquid, which seemed to produce its own light.

Wren was captivated. "What is it?"

"The strongest healing potion there is," said Underath. "After my brush with death I decided to make some, but the ingredients are exceedingly rare. *Exceedingly*..." He drifted to silence.

Alkeran coughed and gave him a hard stare. "Not reconsidering, I hope?" said the griffin.

"No," said Underath, heaving a sigh. He took the bottle from its protective box. "It won't fix everything, but it'll get them on their feet. And then you can thank me for a *very* successful rescue."

Wren shared a worried look with Erner. "Will you leave us, Underath?" she asked. "Or will you stay and fight?"

Underath raised an eyebrow. "I only promised to help rescue these two prisoners," he said. "Pitting myself against the most evil Sorcerer in history is a different matter entirely."

Wren noticed Alkeran frowning at his friend.

"But if he's so powerful, what can *we* hope to do?" said Erner in despair.

At that, Underath surprised them all by *smiling*. "Plenty," he said. "I believe his power is more limited than you think. When I had my shoe-heart, all of my magic was needed just to keep me alive. I believe Quarastus has the same problem. You told me, Wren, that he seemed to grow ancient before your eyes?"

"Yes," said Wren. "Just after showing off, turning himself into some kind of monster."

Underath nodded. "He's managed to extend his life for a thousand years, but the cost is great. What we think of as his *normal* appearance is a disguise, you see. One he must sustain constantly to go undiscovered! Making himself look monstrous should have taken very little of his power—yet he hardly had any magic left. He used too much, and his disguise slipped. He revealed his true form—clinging to life by his fingernails! He must spend almost every ounce of magic he has simply keeping death at bay. Maintaining his life, and his disguise, leaves him with little to spare."

"What about when he captured me?" said Rundel. "That was powerful magic!"

"Erner told me he had a stick of some form, which transformed?" said Underath.

Rundel and Erner both nodded.

"An old technique," said Underath. "You use an object to store a spell or magical energy. We call those *braids*. He can build up the magic in the object gradually, over days or weeks, until he's created what he needs."

Rundel frowned. "Then surely he has more of them," he said.

"I'm certain he does," said Underath. "But don't you see? However many he has, once it's gone he'll be defenseless!" He gave them all a knowing smile. "And why would I run from such a fight?"

It took a moment for his words to sink in, but then Alkeran smiled, and so did Wren and Erner.

Even Rundel, cracked lips and all, broke into a smile— but this was a smile that spoke of vengeance. "So let's get on with it," he said. "Give me and Lord Drevis your potion!"

"I will," said Underath. He measured half the bottle's contents into the silver cup, then paused. "Rundel Stone, I must warn you. This will hurt. Your colleague Lord Drevis is unconscious, and that's a mercy. This will be the most excruciating pain you have ever experienced. There's a risk that the shock will kill you."

Rundel gave an impatient grunt. He took the cup and sniffed the contents, wincing at the odor. "I have a traitor to arrest," he said, and drank the potion down.

25
THE UNMASKING
Wren, Erner & Rundel

The chamber of the Pipers' Council was two-thirds of the way up the towering Castle Keep. It was a huge room; around the sides were rows of stepped seating, which allowed for an audience whenever the Court of the Council was in session. At the far end of the chamber, the judges' bench was set up high, overlooking everything else. Currently the chamber was almost empty, and the central floor seemed vast. All it contained now was a single table with four chairs where four robed figures sat: Lord Cobb, Lady Rumsey, Lord Winkless, and—of course—Lord Pewter.

Quarastus.

Wren watched them as they talked. She was perched on the outside ledge of a small window near the top of the chamber. Of course, she was *very* high up the side of the

Keep itself, but heights meant little to her in crow form. She'd chosen this particular window out of the many that circled the chamber wall because one of the small rectangular panes was broken, with only a little jagged glass remaining. She could hear everything that went on inside and make sure there were no surprises that might affect the plan Rundel had hatched.

A pigeon flapped down awkwardly on the ledge beside her, making a terrible racket. She looked at it pointedly. "Find another ledge, buster," she told it. The pigeon froze, made a curiously high-pitched *coo*, then took to the air. It did not look back.

Below her, the members of the Council argued. Word from the Custodian outpost in Geshenfell had arrived, letting them know of the approaching army and who was leading it. The news had come as a shock for them all, but particularly for Lord Pewter. Wren thought of the triumph in his voice when he'd told Rundel that he'd been made Leader of the Council. Right now he looked like he was drinking vinegar.

"And to think," said Lord Winkless, "we believed catching the Hamelyn Piper would be so much easier if he came here to try and steal the remains of his Pipe Organ." He gave a humorless laugh. "Be careful what you wish for . . ."

"It *would* have been easier," said Lord Cobb. "We just didn't expect him to show up with a vast army!"

"We came close to sending all the Custodians in the Castle off on the *Great Pursuit*!" said Lady Rumsey. "It would have left the Castle almost unprotected!"

"Your first decision as Leader of the Council could have been a *disaster*, Lord Pewter," said Lord Cobb. "Had word of this army arrived in a day or two, after you'd sent the Custodians away, I dread to think how bad things might have been."

"Be calm," said Lord Pewter. "The Custodians are still here, and the Battle Horns are ready to protect us." He gestured above their heads; when she'd flown to the Keep, Wren had taken a quick look at the great Battle Horns that protruded from the roof—seven of them in all, their heads like the ends of trumpets, the largest at least six feet across.

"I've said it before and I'll say it again," said Lord Cobb. "We should have used the obsidiac to build the strongest possible Battle Horns!"

"Let's not argue about that again," said Lord Winkless. "Such Pipes would have had unpredictable capabilities and may have proved useless for defense. The risk was far too great."

All four looked to the great doors at the far side of the chamber. "Well, let's get this over with," said Lord Cobb.

"Public meetings . . . A waste of time, in my opinion. Time that would be better spent planning."

"We must calm the fears of all Tiviscan!" said Lady Rumsey. She stood and went to the near wall, reaching for a rope that was tied to a bell above the judges' bench. She rang it three times and sat down again as the grand doors opened. People began to stream inside—Custodian Pipers, Castle Guards, and townsfolk, filling the floor space once the seating was gone.

This was the second time Wren had flown to the Castle to snoop. The first had been soon after Rundel and Drevis had taken Underath's fearsome potion, and she'd been glad to go as soon as Erner suggested it. At the time, Rundel was in dreadful agony—although at least he'd stopped screaming, which he'd started doing within seconds of drinking the strange golden liquid.

Lord Drevis, though unconscious, had begun to flail on the ground as if in a hideous nightmare, so Wren took to the air, grateful to have a mission to carry out.

There were plenty of crows around Tiviscan Castle, so her spying was easy enough. Indeed, she'd actually been *watching* Lord Pewter when he'd first heard the news of the Hamelyn Piper's army. It had clearly shaken him that the Hamelyn Piper hadn't been hiding in fear all this time, desperate to avoid discovery—something the Great Pursuit relied on. Instead, he'd been gathering a vast army, preparing to march on Tiviscan.

An emergency meeting was announced—to be held within the hour—which all Castle residents could attend as well as the townsfolk. Wren had quickly taken the news back to the others. She was glad to find Rundel and Lord Drevis utterly transformed from their wretched states. Underath had magically cleaned their clothes, and they'd even managed to bathe in the stream once the Sorcerer had warmed it up for them.

Lord Drevis was still clearly marked by his ordeal, his lips scabbed, several sores on his face not quite healed. Rundel, however, was very much his old self. Even his limp seemed to have gone, and Wren wondered if Underath's cure had managed to chase away the last of the poison that had almost killed him.

Once Wren told them everything she'd heard, Rundel quickly came up with a plan, sending her back to observe. And now, as she perched on the ledge of the Keep, the emergency meeting commenced.

Lady Rumsey used a gavel until the hubbub in the chamber subsided. "Settle down, please," she called. "You're all aware by now of the reports we've received of an approaching army supposedly led by the Hamelyn Piper himself." She needed the gavel once more as anxious murmurs rippled around the chamber. "This meeting has been called to reassure you all that we're doing everything that can be done and to answer any questions you may have."

One of the Castle Guard came forward. "If the reports are true, the army is huge," said the soldier. "We could be overwhelmed. And there are rumors of dragons joining them!"

At the mention of dragons there was an uproar. Lady Rumsey hit the gavel on the table so hard that Wren was amazed nothing broke.

"I'll put that to Lord Cobb!" said Lady Rumsey.

Lord Cobb stood. "The rumors of dragons are just scaremongering," he said. "Think about it—when the dragons besieged Tiviscan, it was to seek the Hamelyn Piper's death! They wouldn't become allies with a man they *hate*."

It is a reasonable argument, thought Wren, *even if it is completely wrong*.

More murmurs rippled around the chamber.

"Any more questions?" asked Lady Rumsey.

A Custodian Piper stepped forward. "Is there word of the return of any expeditions? We could better protect the Castle if more Custodians were here."

Pewter stood. "Yes, thankfully," he said. "We've already received word that some will be returning soon." Wren hadn't heard the Council mention this before, and she noticed the other Council members share an uneasy look. It was clearly a lie. "Any more questions?" said Pewter, in a way that strongly hinted he wanted none.

"I have a question," came a voice. Wren felt herself tense. It was Rundel Stone.

The moment Rundel pulled back the hood of his robe, Pewter gasped. The crowd near Rundel moved aside, giving him room.

"My question is this," said Rundel. "Is a man who imprisons and tortures his enemies worthy of leading the Pipers' Council? Is a man who lies to those around him—while plotting the betrayal of us all—a man of honor?" He raised a hand and pointed at his target. "Lord Pewter! I am here to arrest you for *treason*."

All eyes turned to Pewter, who put on a decent show of bewilderment. "This is madness!" he said. "Virtus Stone has become deranged. He talks nonsense!"

At that, another hooded figure stepped forward to stand beside Rundel. He pulled back his hood: Lord Drevis. This time *everyone* gasped.

"You imprisoned Lord Drevis," said Rundel. "And you claimed he had ventured secretly with one of the expeditions. Do you deny it?"

"Of course I deny it!" said Pewter. "I'm innocent!"

"Then you imprisoned *me*, fearing I would get in the way of your plans," said Rundel. "*Do you deny it?*"

Pewter looked to his fellow Council members. "My friends, I . . ."

But Rundel wasn't going to give him time to speak. "The man we know as Lord Pewter is, in truth, a Sorcerer, ancient beyond imagining, evil beyond comprehension. He has committed treason and must be seized at once!"

Wren could see the hint of a smile on Pewter's face. "This is clearly ridiculous," he said. "It's sad to see great men reduced to such a preposterous accusation."

The rest of the Council looked to each other, uncertain. Lady Rumsey banged her gavel. "We must . . . We must consider what evidence you have, Virtus Stone."

Rundel shook his head. "There's no time for that," he said. "Underath! Make him reveal himself!"

A third figure stepped out. As part of the crowd, Underath had been inconspicuous. The moment he strode forward, he did it with a confidence and poise that made absolute silence fall in the chamber. And in that silence, he raised his hands and sent a sudden blast of green sparks directly at Pewter.

Pewter barely flinched as he was hit by the blast, but Wren could see the anger on his face. Then he feigned agony, falling back to his seat, calling out in a pitiful voice: "A Sorcerer? Protect me!"

Lady Rumsey stood and shouted: "Outrage! Sorcery in the Council chamber is forbidden!" She took her Pipe from her belt and began to play, and when Underath released a second surge of sparks, it burst harmlessly a few feet from Pewter against an invisible barrier. Wren was impressed by the speed with which Lady Rumsey had put up the shield.

"Custodians!" called Lady Rumsey. "The Song of the Sorcerer's Bind!"

Pewter stayed in his seat, but the other Council members rose, and from the crowd Custodians moved to join them, all drawing their Pipes and following Lady Rumsey's lead. The Song grew quickly, and within seconds Wren could *feel* it: the same kind of sensation she'd had when the Hamelyn Piper had put those red manacles around her wrists, draining the sorcery from her. That must be the purpose of this Song, she realized—to drain a Sorcerer's power and leave them weak. She could see Underath stagger back, held up by Rundel.

For a terrible moment she wondered if it would affect her ability to shape-shift, and she couldn't help but glance back over the ledge she was on and the vast drop to the bottom of the Keep that waited for her if she was forced back into human form. Thankfully, whatever magic allowed her to change shape seemed to be unaffected.

The same could not be said for Pewter, however. Shielding Songs were one thing, but he must have expected the Custodians to seize Underath, not do *this*. His face grew more and more gaunt, his ancient self becoming visible, and he seemed to be in terrible pain. "Stop!" he cried, struggling back to his feet. He reached into a pocket and his face quickly returned to normal. Wren suspected he'd used one of the things Underath had mentioned—a braid to replenish his powers.

"Stop it *now*!" he screamed. The sound was unnaturally amplified. A blast of pure force rippled through the air, exploding outwards from where Pewter stood, knocking the other members of the Council and the nearest Custodians to the floor. Throughout the chamber, people were hit by the shock wave.

Silence fell, and Wren saw a smile grow on Pewter's face. Everyone was staring at him now. He gave a simple gesture with one hand, and suddenly the three Custodians nearest him stood, dragging the other Council members to their feet. Each Custodian was blank-faced, and Wren felt a sudden chill of fear as she saw them cast aside their Pipes and pull long-bladed knives from their robes—knives they held to the throats of the Council.

"Bravo, Rundel," said Pewter, mock-clapping. "I look forward to finding out how you escaped, but you succeeded! I am *revealed*." There was movement here and there—other Custodians bringing Pipes to lips, Underath raising a hand ready to attack. But Pewter saw it all, and the knives pressed harder against the throats of the Council. "Ah, ah, ah! One move against me and the Council will die!"

The would-be attackers stopped at once.

"What was it you called me, Rundel?" said Pewter. "Oh, yes, *ancient beyond imagining, evil beyond comprehension.* I'll take it as a compliment."

"A confession if ever I heard one," said Rundel, defiant. It was stalemate, Wren could see—the knives to the throats of the Council stopped any thought of action. Somebody had to do *something*, though . . . so why not her? She forced herself through the hole in the window and plummeted down, flying at Pewter from the side. She cawed a moment before she reached him, flapping and pecking. He turned in surprise, arms raised to protect himself. "Give yourself up, Quarastus!" she cawed at him. His eyes widened, hearing her speak, and for a moment he froze; then he swiped at her and connected hard, sending her into the wall behind him.

But the distraction had been long enough! Underath raised his hand once more, and the blank-faced Custodians dropped their knives as if they were too hot to hold. The Council members took matters into their own hands—or *knee* in the case of Lady Rumsey, who brought hers up into the groin of her captor. From around them, other Custodians came to their aid.

Wren limped back into the air and perched by the judges'

bench above them. Pewter surveyed the scene with a scowl before reaching to his pocket once more.

"Look out!" cawed Wren, launching herself toward Pewter, but just before she reached him he seemed to burst into flame, then vanished. The last thing she saw was his scowl turn into a triumphant sneer as he made his escape.

The three Custodians who'd held knives to the Council's throat were secured, their wrists tied, but Wren saw the confusion on their faces—Pewter's puppets didn't seem to know what they'd done. She saw Erner standing next to Rundel and flew over to his shoulder.

"Are you okay?" Erner asked her. She nodded.

Lady Rumsey, Lord Cobb, and Lord Winkless strode over to them.

"Clear the chamber!" called Lady Rumsey. She studied the curious band of heroes in front of her as Custodians guided people outside. "Can someone explain what the *devil* is going on here?"

But then there was a call from the doorway, and against the flow of people came a young woman in a Castle Guard uniform, waving a wax-sealed letter in the air.

Lord Winkless sighed. "What is it *now*?"

"A message for the Council!" called the young woman, and when she reached them she handed it to Lady Rumsey.

"Well?" said Lord Cobb impatiently. "What does it say?"

Lady Rumsey opened the seal and looked at the message. "This is from the Castle Guard station near the coast," she said. "There's been a sighting . . . Something approaches from the sea."

Rundel shook his head, frowning. "Does the Hamelyn Piper send an invasion fleet as well as his army?"

"No," said Lady Rumsey.

"A returning expedition, then?" said Lord Cobb, suddenly hopeful. "Reinforcements, just in the nick of time!"

"That's not what the message says either," said Lady Rumsey. "It says that it looks like . . ." She shook her head. "It says that it looks like an *island*."

26
Massarken Arrives

"Land ahoy!" shouted Barver.

Dead ahead was a tall rock known as The Spindle, which sat a quarter of a mile out to sea. Behind it was a pebble beach that rose up into forest. Ten miles farther inland, Patch knew, lay Tiviscan Castle. He looked to Lar-Sennen glowing feebly near the window.

"Almost there!" he told the ghost with a grin.

It was certainly a relief. In the last two days, the only time Patch had left the wheelhouse for long was when they'd built a funeral pyre for Lar-Sennen's remains—a very curious funeral, given that the corpse's ghost was in attendance.

Lar-Sennen smiled back. "Command Massarken to make landfall," he said. "It'll get as close to shore as it can safely go."

Patch gave the command to the island, feeling nervous. "Is there anything I should know about how to guide it in?"

"Your command was all that was needed," said Lar-Sennen. "It can handle things from here. You should make preparations to venture ashore!"

Barver's father insisted on seeing his cave for the last time. "Strange of me, I know," he said to Barver and Patch. "A prison, yes, but also a home."

He went inside, and Barver was reluctant to follow. Patch knew why: Barver still hadn't told his dad about his mother's death, and it couldn't wait any longer. The dracogriff steeled himself and joined his father in the cave.

Patch was left alone, without even Lar-Sennen's ghost for company, because Alia had the Soul Bottle. It had crossed Patch's mind that Alia might well be the perfect Guardian for the island, although he'd not yet mentioned this to her or to Lar-Sennen.

After a while Barver came out of the cave, looking heartbroken. "He wants a little time to himself," he said.

"You told him," said Patch.

Barver nodded. "He said that somehow he'd already known. He gave me this." He held up his hand, and in his palm was one of the intricate carvings that had adorned the cave. This one was only five inches across, and it seemed almost impossible to believe that the griffin had used just his claws to carve it. "He said he was going to leave all his other carvings behind," said Barver. "This was the only one that was really important to him, and he wanted me to have it."

It depicted three figures standing in a circle, holding hands. Three griffins, Patch thought at first, one much smaller than the other two. Then he realized that one of the larger figures was carved with scales, not feathers, and had a snout rather than a beak, and he understood. A dragon, a griffin, and their child.

Patch looked at Barver and saw a great tear fall from his friend's eye.

The soldiers and Pipers of Kintner insisted on packing up their meager camp rather than abandoning it. It had served them well, those few bits and pieces that had happened to be packed in saddles when the Leap Device had brought them here.

Once Patch had ordered the devil-birds to their nests once more, Lar-Sennen guided them a little way across the island to where the land sloped down and led to a rocky cove. The cove was large enough for the whole of their convoy to assemble: two hundred and sixty humans, thirty-nine horses, four griffins, one dracogriff, and a ghost. They watched as the island drew ever nearer to the bright shores ahead.

"When we are close enough to shore, a causeway will form," Lar-Sennen told Patch. "This is the only path through the barrier that protects the island! You'll be able to tell the moment you pass through." He turned to Gaverry. "Then you can fly properly at last."

Gaverry stretched out his wings with care for those nearby. "Not a moment too soon!" he said. Merta, Wintel, and Cramber cheered.

Barver gave his father a stern look. "You're not to overdo things!" he said. "It's been far too many years, and you'll need to start slowly."

Gaverry grinned and slapped Barver on the back. "Remember I'm *your* father," he said. "Not the other way around!"

Soon Massarken slowed to a halt, even though the beach ahead of them was still some distance away.

"What now?" said Patch.

"Ask the island to open the way," said Lar-Sennen.

"Okay," said Patch. "Here goes. Massarken, I command you! Open the way!"

The ground shuddered, and a curious sound echoed around them—somewhere between whale song and the roar of a great lion. Suddenly the sea ahead erupted in turmoil, the waters frothing. A vast tentacle, even bigger than the one they'd seen before, began to rise. It was curled tightly at first, its skin encrusted in rock. Slowly it unfurled, laying out a path a hundred feet wide, its narrow tip burying itself in the pebble beach ahead.

The tentacle was still, and the churning waters settled. "Your causeway awaits!" announced Lar-Sennen. He gestured to the Soul Bottle hanging around Alia's neck, then nodded to a large boulder in the center of the cove. "Leave the bottle there. Like so many of the creatures on this island, I cannot survive away from Massarken's protective magic."

Alia nodded and took the chain from her neck, setting the bottle on the top of the boulder. "Will it be safe?" she said.

"It will," said the ghost. He turned to Patch. "You'll find it there when you return."

"Return?" said Patch.

"Absolutely!" said Lar-Sennen. "As the Guardian of Massarken, you have responsibilities now. For the sixty years since my death, the island has been without guidance. So come back once your difficulties have been dealt with and we can plan for the future! We shall fulfill my dream of finding new homes for those animals that can be set free and improving the lives of those who must stay under Massarken's protection!"

"But I'm not sure I *want* to be the Guardian," said Patch. "I planned to train as a Healing Piper."

Lar-Sennen frowned. "The decision will be yours alone," he said. "But I like you, lad, and would be sad if you declined. All I would ask is this: find someone you trust to take your place as Guardian. You owe Massarken that at least."

Patch noticed Alia suddenly perk up, intrigued.

"But choose wisely," said the ghost. "The creatures of this island depend on you! And remember, if the person you choose has evil in their heart . . ."

"They'll explode when they put on the bracelet, I know," said Patch.

Alia's eyes widened briefly.

"Promise me you'll return before you decide," said Lar-Sennen. "Perhaps I can convince you to stay."

"I promise," said Patch. He had a sudden urge to give the ghost a hug, but knowing that was impossible he simply smiled. "I'll return as soon as the *difficulties* are resolved."

"And good luck to you!" said the ghost. "Once you've gone the island will seek deeper waters and hide once again, but the Guardian can always find it!"

Walking on the tentacle was like walking on solid rock. Halfway to the beach Patch sensed he was approaching the island's invisible barrier and signaled for everyone to stop. It felt like approaching a stone wall and expecting the wall to let you pass through it.

Closing his eyes he took another few steps, feeling the barrier around him, then behind. He was suddenly elated—being on the outside of that barrier had seemed impossible only days before. He continued along the tentacle, but as Barver came through the barrier behind him Patch heard a gasp.

"What is it?" asked Patch.

"Is that *Alkeran*?" said Barver, pointing to the sky ahead. Patch could see the griffin now, swooping down and landing on the rocks. From his back, two figures dismounted.

"*I don't believe it*," said Barver, but as Patch was about to ask *what* it was he didn't believe, Barver took to the air, grabbing Patch around the waist without explanation or apology.

"Hey!" cried Patch, cross and uncomfortable, flying backward. "What are you *doing*?" He saw the other griffins spread their wings and fly the moment they were free of the island. Barver's dad veered left and right worryingly, his expression one of grim determination and vague alarm.

Barver landed on the beach, setting Patch down. Turning, Patch was to about to give his friend a piece of his mind when he froze and found he couldn't speak. There was the griffin Alkeran; beside him stood Underath.

And beside Underath, her face both astonished and overjoyed, was Wren.

She said nothing and just ran up to them; the three hugged each other long and hard. For Patch, time seemed to stop and the rest of the world disappeared. He was crying, even though he felt happier than he could ever remember feeling.

At last Wren stepped back, and the three regarded each other with tears and wide smiles.

Patch looked at Wren, her very presence leaving him absolutely baffled. There was only one question on his mind: "*How?*" he said.

Wren shrugged. "I was about to ask both of *you* the same thing," she replied.

The tearful reunions weren't limited to Patch, Wren, and Barver. Alia almost squeezed the life out of Wren when she finally got her chance.

Alkeran and Gaverry also had their moment. This was the first time they'd seen each other since that fateful day so many years before, when they'd both been pilots for a fishing fleet just before the island captured them.

Even the worrying news Wren gave them from Tiviscan and beyond couldn't quite bring the celebratory mood crashing down. Alkeran and Gaverry took to the skies again, laughing, while Barver watched nervously. "He's just not ready to exert himself like that," he said.

Patch kept finding himself in sudden tears every time he looked at Wren. Here was one of his two best friends, someone he was convinced had died to save them all, yet she was alive and well.

"So much mucus!" said Barver, staring at Patch's dripping nose.

Patch took a great wet *sniff* then wiped the rest away with his sleeve, and the three of them burst into laughter.

"Oh, I have a new thing!" said Wren eagerly. "Barver, could you just hold up your wing?"

Barver did, and Wren stood behind it. A moment later a crow flew out and hopped around on the rocks.

"Ta daaa!" said the crow, before flying back behind Barver's wing and becoming human-Wren again.

Barver and Patch were impressed. "Can you do sharks yet?" asked Barver.

"I can do crows and rats," said Wren. "And crow-rats. But give me time . . ."

27
Tiviscan Prepares

Once all of their number had crossed to the beach, the great tentacle withdrew from the pebbles, rolling itself back up before submerging. Massarken began to move away, shrouding itself in mist as it went to hide far out to sea.

Tiviscan was ten miles inland. Alkeran and Underath flew back to the Castle with the news that reinforcements were here; Barver and the other griffins chose to accompany the soldiers and Pipers on their march, spending much of the journey airborne to make the most of their freedom. None relished it more than Gaverry, of course. Patch and Wren watched father and son fly together, and it warmed their hearts.

At last the Castle was in sight, and they came to the rising road that linked the lower forest routes to the higher plains. Patch thought back to when he'd come along this road in the custody of Rundel Stone and Erner, when Wren was still a rat and they'd not even met Barver.

"How is Erner doing?" he asked.

"He's well," said Wren. "He and Rundel are using one of the devices from the Caves of Casimir to work out if anyone else is a victim of magical persuasion. When news of your mysterious island first reached Tiviscan, we'd already caught three Custodians who were under the control of Quarastus, and they have the whole Castle to get through. The town too, since the citizens will be coming inside the walls before the Hamelyn Piper gets here. By the time me and Underath left to check out the island, they'd only just got started."

Patch had had a cold lump of fear in his belly ever since Wren had told them all of Lord Pewter's true nature. "*Quarastus*," he said. "I always *liked* Lord Pewter, Wren. He seemed kind, yet all along he was evil. And now I can't help thinking he's watching everything we do."

"He probably is," said Wren. "Waiting until the dust settles before he makes his next move. But we have the more immediate concern of the Hamelyn Piper and his army..."

As they reached Tiviscan, the people of the town cheered them as if they'd already been saved from the Black Knight.

The air of celebration made Patch feel uneasy. There were thousands of mercenaries headed their way, probably armed with the same weaponry that had devastated an entire city. What difference could the addition of a few dozen Battle Pipers and a couple of hundred soldiers make?

Passing through the town square, Patch took a moment at the central statue. The hand pump and trough at the statue's base were a welcome sight after a long hike. He pumped the handle until fresh cold water poured out of the iron spout, then put his hand into the flow to drink.

"Oh, good idea!" said Barver, plunging his face into the trough and drinking noisily.

Patch kept pumping the handle for his friend and looked up at the statue of Erbo Monash—the man who first formed the Pipers' Council. Under the plinth was carved a motto: *Evil cannot triumph against the music of hope.*

It is a pleasant enough sentiment, he thought, but he wasn't sure that it was true.

Underath and Alkeran stood just outside the Castle Gate and nodded to Patch and Barver as they drew level.

"I thought you'd have gone home by now," said Barver.

"We both owe you our lives," said Alkeran. "We're not going to abandon you when you need us most." The griffin looked pointedly at Underath. "Isn't that right?"

"I won't lie to you," said the Sorcerer. "It's never been my nature to do things for a greater good. But facing Quarastus is the closest I've come, and I think I've developed a *taste* for it. Besides, Alkeran would never forgive me if I didn't stay."

Through the gates, the Castle Guards lined the way, saluting the new arrivals. By the Castle Keep stood the members of the Council, Rundel Stone beside them. Alia and Tobias were overjoyed to be reunited with Lord Drevis, and even Rundel Stone broke from his usual stern expression and managed a smile.

The largest smile of all, though, was on Erner's face as he hurried over to greet them.

"Patch!" he said. "When Underath and Alkeran brought the news that you were coming, I went to get you this." He held out a folded brown coat. "I promised you I'd look after it."

It was the deerskin coat Patch's grandfather had made for him, which Erner had taken for safekeeping before his trial. "Thank you, Erner," he said, almost overcome.

After taking out his Pipe, he removed the coat he'd had since escaping Tiviscan—found in the forest soon after he and Wren had met Barver—and put it safely in one of Barver's harness packs. It had served him well, and he certainly wasn't going to discard it, but it couldn't compete with his grandfather's expert crafting.

He took the deerskin coat from Erner and put it on, tucking his Pipe inside. Plunging his hands into the pockets, he thought of home.

Lord Drevis convened an urgent meeting of the Pipers' Council, instructing Alia and Tobias to join them along with anyone they thought could provide important insights. Barver, Patch, and Wren came—the heroes who had once actually faced the Hamelyn Piper and triumphed. Underath and Alkeran were there too, while Merta represented the other griffins.

They gathered in the East Hall.

"Virtus Stone and his apprentice will not join us," said Lord Drevis. "They've been working to unmask any more of Lord Pewter's agents and have a magical device that makes it possible."

"Have any more been found?" asked Alia.

"None yet," said Drevis. "With luck, there were only the three who held knives to the Council's throats. Lord Pewter may be . . ." He shook his head. "We must call him by his real name. *Quarastus* may be gone for now, but we can be certain he'll return. At least we can make sure he has no more agents in Tiviscan. In the meantime, there's a more immediate crisis, and we have plans to draw up. A scouting party has confirmed that the Hamelyn Piper's forces are approaching from the southeast. Wren's warning of an alliance with the dragons has proved true. At least a hundred now accompany them, under the command of General Kasterkan—who also led the attack on Skamos."

Lady Rumsey scowled. "That's the thing I understand least of all," she said. "Why would dragons make an ally of their sworn enemy? Surely they know that the Black Knight is the Hamelyn Piper?"

"The dragons helped him in Gossamer Valley too," said Alia. "Bringing him the same weapons they used in Skamos."

"The Hamelyn Piper told me the design requires powdered obsidiac, which he supplies," said Wren. "He showed General Kasterkan how to make them. They had some kind of deal."

"That explains some of it," said Lord Winkless. "The dragon military, led by Kasterkan, has claimed power over the Dragon Triumvirate, forcing its members into hiding. How it happened, we don't know, but *he* now controls the dragons. Whatever deal they made, it clearly includes helping the Hamelyn Piper's forces now."

"You know more about Kasterkan than any of us, Barver," said Alia. "What do you think?"

Barver frowned. "In spite of all that's ever happened between the Dragon Triumvirate and the Pipers, there was respect between them—enough to maintain peace between humans and dragons for centuries," he said. "Kasterkan knows that the Pipers might help the Triumvirate overthrow him."

Tobias grunted and gave a sour smile. "And so he wants Tiviscan defeated," he said. "Whatever it takes." He looked to Lord Drevis. "How much time do we have to prepare?"

"We expect the army to reach Tiviscan by morning," said Lord Drevis.

Alia and Tobias looked horrified. "Our position is much worse than I feared," said Alia. "The fate of Skamos could be the fate of Tiviscan . . ."

But there was no such horror on the face of Lord Drevis or any of the Council members.

"There's no reason to despair," said Drevis. "The Castle is well provisioned for a siege. The people of Tiviscan will take refuge within its walls, down in the underground stores."

Alia frowned. "But *Skamos*," she said. "We can be sure the dragons have brought more of their terrible weapons."

"The great Battle Horns in the Keep will protect us," said Lord Drevis.

"I'm certain that the Hamelyn Piper knows *exactly* what the Battle Horns are capable of," said Alia. "Don't you think he'll have taken that into account? He knows the limits of our defenses."

"And those Horns didn't help much when the dragons last besieged Tiviscan!" snapped Tobias. "All it took was one sneak attack and the Castle was defenseless."

"We'll not be taken by surprise again," said Lord Drevis. "The Pipers of the Keep will begin playing Shielding Songs at nightfall and will not stop until the siege is ended. And as for the Hamelyn Piper knowing the limits of our defenses . . ." He smiled. "That is where his downfall lies. Lord Winkless, if you would explain?"

Lord Winkless nodded. "The Battle Horns have been repaired since the Castle was last attacked," he said. "News pamphlets across the world have reported an official announcement from the Pipers' Council stating that the Horns are as good as new. But we lied." He smiled, with a glint in his eye. "They are *not* as good as new. They are *better*."

"In what way?" asked Alia.

"I carefully studied the remains of the Pipes of the Obsidiac Organ, and—"

Alia gasped. "You used the *obsidiac*?" she said, glaring at him.

"No!" said Lord Winkless. "But the design of the Pipe Organ revealed other ways to increase the power of the Battle Horns. Their range is far greater and their capabilities well beyond what the Hamelyn Piper would expect. More than powerful enough to protect us from those explosives."

"And now we have the best Battle Pipers and soldiers that Kintner Bastion could provide," said Lord Drevis. "When the Black Knight comes, the one thing he'll not expect is a direct attack on his troops, but that's what we'll give him! The combined force of our own army and the Battle Horns will be devastating! The mercenaries and dragons will abandon the fight when they see they can't win."

Alia looked to all of the veterans of Skamos and Gossamer Valley. "Those of us who have actually witnessed that weapon being used may not share your confidence, Lord Drevis. Because if you're wrong, we shall be *annihilated*."

28
A Lullaby

"I feel useless down here," moaned Patch.

After the meeting, Alia and Tobias had been very clear about what they expected of Patch and Wren—they would join the civilians of Tiviscan, taking shelter in the safety of the Castle's underground storage vaults.

There were ten large vaulted chambers, and in each chamber at least a hundred people claimed a little space and tried to find some form of comfort and perhaps even sleep. But sleep was not an easy thing to find in the circumstances. Barver and the griffins were all above ground. The corridors within the stores were too narrow for them, and Patch doubted that Merta and Gaverry could even have made it through the entrance.

"Oh, stop complaining," said Wren. "The Hamelyn

Piper won't *arrive* until morning. It's not like we're missing anything. And there's not the *slightest* chance of me staying down here tomorrow."

Patch frowned at her. "We gave Alia a solemn promise that we would," he said. "And I may not like it, but she has a point. Whatever battle rages tomorrow, we've already done our bit. It's down to the soldiers and Pipers now. Alia just wants us out of harm's way."

"She feels guilty about what happened in Gossamer Valley, that's all," said Wren. "You heard how confident Lord Drevis was. The Hamelyn Piper is about to be defeated once and for all, and I intend to enjoy every minute."

"Alia didn't share his confidence," said Patch.

"Sometimes she just worries too much," said Wren. "And so do you."

Soon after midnight, deep tones began to echo around the chamber.

"The Battle Horns!" said Patch. He listened carefully as the tones shifted. The Songs of the vast Battle Horns differed significantly from those played on an ordinary Pipe, and down here only the lowest notes reached them clearly. Even so, Patch recognized the rhythms that underpinned the defensive Songs he knew, which the music of the Battle Horns was based on.

Hushed whispers echoed around the chamber too, accompanied by the gentle sobs of children, terrified by what was going on. Patch saw a few young trainee Pipers huddled in the far corner, their expressions anxious. They gripped their Pipes, he saw, and it made him take his own Pipe from his coat. Holding it was a comfort.

He wished he could be as sure of victory as Wren seemed. Tobias had certainly grown more confident as the plans had been drawn up, convinced that the power of the great Battle Horns would take the Hamelyn Piper by surprise.

But Patch still found it hard to imagine *anything* protecting them from those exploding spheres.

"Surely you have something for that?" said Wren, rousing him from his thoughts.

"What?" he said, then looked to where she was pointing: two crying toddlers in the arms of their parents. The parents looked distressed, unable to soothe their children. Patch nodded, glad that Wren had drawn him out of himself. "Indeed I do," he said, and stood, walking to the corner where the five trainee Pipers sat. He kneeled beside them, his voice low. "Which of the Songs of Peace do you all know best?" he said. The five looked at each other, none willing to speak up. "How about Placid Airs, or maybe Gander's Hush?"

"Gander's Hush," said one, and the others nodded. "Although I only know the first section."

"Well, if you know that part, the rest isn't so hard," said Patch. "How about I start, and you join me when you think you're ready?"

They agreed, and Patch began to play. Gander's Hush was made of three elements, and while the melody was the most obvious to an untrained ear, there were two deeper parts that changed gradually, with a slow rhythm. He built those up first, and then began the melody. It was a familiar tune—it formed the basis of a popular lullaby and was quickly recognized by many in the chamber.

The trainees began to play too, and people quickly fell silent and listened. Gander's Hush had a sorrowful component in its melody, but it was one that changed as the Song went on, turning from sorrow to triumph. It took your heart by the hand and acknowledged the sadness within you, before holding you tightly and showing you that things would be better soon.

Patch looked to the toddlers and saw that each now had thumb firmly in mouth, watching him and the trainee Pipers play. Wren was smiling at him. As time passed, the toddlers fell asleep, then the trainees dropped off too. Even so, Patch's Pipe was not the only one he could hear. Through the entrance to the chamber came the echoes of other Pipes. All were playing Gander's Hush for the people of Tiviscan, to let them find some comfort in dreams.

Patch woke to the steady thrum of the Battle Horns. He opened his eyes, seeing Erner crouching beside him, gesturing for him to follow. Erner gently woke Wren too, and the three of them went out to the corridor, away from the sleeping citizens.

"I wanted to see how you were both getting on down here," said Erner. "I would have come last night, but . . ." He yawned. "Sorry. Only got a couple of hours' sleep. I was helping Virtus Stone."

"With the tests for magical persuasion?" said Wren. "How many did you find?"

"Just two," said Erner. "To add to the three Custodians who held knives to the throats of the Council. Both of the new finds were Castle Guards."

"What's been done with them?" asked Patch.

"Safely imprisoned," said Erner. "Until we can figure out how to help them."

"Did they try to fight when they were revealed?" asked Wren.

"No," said Erner. "Both were horrified and denied it with such sincerity that it made me doubt we'd got the right people. But the three Custodians had been just the same, once they'd dropped their knives. They really seemed unaware of the things they'd done."

"A horrible thought," said Wren. "A greater curse than being turned into a rat, I reckon."

"Alia seems certain they can be cured," said Erner, before changing the subject. "A young trainee told me about the Gander's Hush you started, Patch. The older trainees in the other chambers joined in! It worked wonders, they said."

"Well, it was obvious really," said Patch. "It was Wren's suggestion, but I should have thought of it earlier."

Erner slapped him on the shoulder, a little harder than strictly necessary. "Sometimes the things that seem most obvious in hindsight are actually the hardest to think of, Patch."

"And how is Barver coping up there?" asked Wren.

"He's frustrated," said Erner. "The Hamelyn Piper's army will reach us within the next few hours. He wants to join with our forces in the initial attack, but he's been ordered to stay in the refectory with the griffins and Underath. There'd be a risk of them getting in the way of the Songs of the Battle Horns, apparently."

"So now we just wait . . . ," said Patch.

Erner nodded. "When they reach us, the Hamelyn Piper will make his demands, and for a couple of hours we'll let him think he has the upper hand. Then our army will *strike*, sallying out of the Castle under the protection of the Battle Horns." He smiled, but it was a nervous one. "I should be getting back, though. Stay safe, my friends."

"Good luck," said Wren. When Erner was out of sight,

she turned to Patch and smiled. "Although we won't be staying safe, will we . . . ?"

Patch was torn. He wanted to see the Hamelyn Piper's defeat firsthand just as much as Wren, but he knew how guilty he would feel at breaking his word to Alia.

In the end, though, there was no question of what he'd do. "No," he said to Wren. "We won't."

29
The Siege Begins

Erner walked up the stairway from the stores and headed to the Keep. There he stood outside and waited. Rundel had gone to meet with the Pipers of the Keep, the skilled players who specialized in the huge Battle Horns. It was ten minutes before he emerged from the Keep gate.

"I hope I didn't keep you waiting too long," said Rundel. "You saw Patch and Wren?"

"I did," said Erner. "They're anxious, but well. And you? Are your concerns soothed?"

Rundel gave a brisk nod. "I spoke with the Pipers of the Keep," he said. "They're a select few—twelve of the best. They have absolute confidence in the new capabilities of the Battle Horns, even though they've not yet tested them to the full limits of their additional power. We have to trust their judgement. Now Lord Drevis wishes me to join the Council on the parapet above the Castle Gate, and you'll be with me."

"What for?" said Erner.

"To watch the approach of the Hamelyn Piper's forces," said Rundel. "They'll come into view within the hour."

Lord Cobb was surly. "I don't see the point of this," he said, frowning at Lord Drevis. "We should pay him no attention at all. *That* would get under his skin."

All four remaining members of the Council were there on the parapet, along with Virtus Stone and Erner and six Castle Guards.

"We must show defiance," said Lord Drevis. "Our presence here makes it clear that we're not panicking, but it's a careful balance. Appearing too confident could raise suspicions."

Lady Rumsey laughed. "If you're saying we should seem nervous, Lord Drevis, I don't think that's going to be difficult." She nodded to the distance, where the ten-thousand-strong army of the Hamelyn Piper was visible on the plains about three miles away. Above them dragons soared, letting loose with bursts of flame.

Closer and closer they came, finally taking position half a mile from the Castle. The dragons continued on, making their camp in the forest below the cliffs. A single dragon remained with the mercenaries.

Lord Winkless squinted. "Is that General Kasterkan?" he said.

"No," said Lord Cobb. "Kasterkan flew on to his camp. *That* one is just a lowly private. You can tell from their battle harnesses."

The Song of the Battle Horns grew steadily in volume and complexity, the shield it created visible as a shimmer in the air that extended a little beyond the Castle walls. A dozen dragons began to lazily circle the Castle at a distance, all to add to the Hamelyn Piper's show of strength.

Within the mercenary camp, the remaining dragon took to the air. It approached, and on its back was the Hamelyn Piper in his black armor.

"So the dragon army has loaned him one of their number, as transport," said Rundel.

The dragon landed just outside the limit of the Battle Horns' shield, and the Hamelyn Piper dismounted, holding a white flag. He called out, without using the "thunder" voice that Patch and Wren had told Erner about. "Lord Drevis! I see you there, and you can see the forces that I've brought and the power that I wield! Will you and the Council join me here and speak with me face to face, where we can be more frank in our words? I think you know why I've come."

Erner glanced at Rundel and could see a look of disdain

there. The Hamelyn Piper knew the flag of truce would be respected by the Pipers, but there seemed little chance that the Council would be granted the same safety in return.

"We will not," called Lord Drevis. "Your business here is illegitimate. Yes, I see your forces, but the loyalty of your army is bought, not earned. As for the dragons . . . the last time they came to this Castle, it was to secure your *execution*. Whatever bargain you may have struck with them, be in no doubt—they owe you no allegiance! You shall fail, Piper of Hamelyn. As you have *always* failed."

Erner couldn't help but smile at that, an insult that would surely burn deep in the Hamelyn Piper's heart.

"Strange that you ignore the evidence of your own eyes," said the Hamelyn Piper. "The dragons give me their full support. My army is unwavering in its allegiance. Your Castle is small and weaker than you could ever believe. Besides, Lord Drevis, it's not you I speak to now: it is every other soul behind those *perilously* thin walls." And now he *did* use the thunder voice, the rumble quickly spreading, echoing around the Castle courtyard. *"Send out the Pipers' Council! Expel them! Do that, and none of you shall be harmed."*

He waited.

"*No?*" he said. "*So be it. You need time to decide, perhaps! But first I'll give you a glimpse of the fate that awaits you all.*"

The dragon lowered itself for the Hamelyn Piper to climb onto it again and took to the air. As the Black Knight reached his army, a canvas covering was pulled away from what had seemed to be a simple wagon. The same thing happened along the front ranks of the army, perhaps ten times in all.

But they were not wagons. They were *catapults*. Already loaded.

"He's going to test our defenses!" cried Lord Drevis. "Clear the parapet! Sound the warning!"

They descended quickly to the courtyard as warning signals blew, and the great Battle Horns grew even louder.

Those sheltering in the stores hadn't been lacking in news of the Hamelyn Piper's army. The deepest notes of the Battle Horns were a constant reminder of peril, but the reports that filtered down to them had left everyone in a permanent state of anxiety that even Songs of Peace wouldn't calm.

When the news came that the army had reached them at last, Patch thought his nerves had been stretched to their limit. To hear that General Kasterkan himself was leading the dragon forces was bad enough, but then the worst of all had come. The Hamelyn Piper had spoken in his thunderous voice, the sound easily reaching the underground stores. Patch and Wren had heard that voice before, so at least they had some level of readiness. For the people with them, it was an entirely new horror.

"Brace yourselves!" came a shout from the corridors; everyone put hands over heads and hugged children closer. The shuddering of the explosions was greater than Patch had expected. For an instant he felt like he was back in the sewers of Skamos as the city above him was annihilated.

And then the noise settled. The pulsing rhythm of the Battle Horns continued and was a great comfort. "The Battle Horns have held up," he whispered to Wren.

The terrified whimpers and sobs weren't just restricted to the children now, and fearful faces looked to each other, hardly daring to believe that the assault was over. At last a call came down the corridors: "All clear! All clear!"

But then the sound of thunder rose yet again, echoing around them, resolving into that dread voice: "*Send out the Council,*" said the thunder. "*Or face destruction! You have until dawn.*"

"Dawn," muttered Wren. "He's hoping that people are scared enough to reconsider their loyalties."

"Nonsense," said Patch. "They'd never turn against the Council." But as he looked at the shaken faces around him, he had to wonder—eventually, surely, everyone had a breaking point.

"Come on, then," said Wren.

"What?" said Patch.

"We've waited long enough," she said. "Our forces will attack soon, and I'm not going to miss anything." Without waiting for a reply, she headed out of the chamber. Patch followed her up the steps that led out of the stores.

As they emerged into the bright courtyard, he was surprised to find it empty. He'd expected a throng of Pipers and soldiers preparing for the attack on the Hamelyn Piper's army. Then he saw that there were dragons slowly circling the Castle and understood—the dragons were far beyond the official range of the Battle Horns, but close enough to see what was going on within the Castle walls.

They crossed to the refectory entrance and went inside. There, the griffins lay curled up, but awake and patient. Barver was on all fours, fussing with his harness packs. It took a moment before he noticed them, and then he grinned.

"Hello!" he called. He went back to adjusting one of the straps. "Can't quite get this *comfortable*," he complained, lifting up his wing with a grimace.

"Let me," said Wren, and she went over to help.

"The first wave goes out soon," said Barver. "I have to be ready for the second wave, if it's needed—when the mercenaries know that the balance of power is against them, but they're fighting all the same. That's when we hit them with something spectacular! Underath riding Alkeran, filling the sky with fireballs! And little old me, breathing fire to singe their backsides!"

"What about Alia?" said Wren as she undid a strap and pulled it tighter. "Will she be on your back?"

"She wasn't sure," said Barver. He frowned. "Um, speaking of Alia..."

"Oh, don't worry," said Wren, fastening the strap again. "We'll keep out of her sight. She'll not have any idea we're up here. But we can't stay stuck down in the stores, not with all this excitement going on." She stepped back. "There!" she said. "How's that?"

"I'm sure it's *fine*," said Alia, stepping through the door with Rundel. "Unlike your promises, I see."

Patch looked away guiltily, but Wren wasn't cowed. "I'm not going to hide, Alia," she said. "I've listened to the Hamelyn Piper threaten me and everyone I know with a horrible death. I want to see him *lose*. Consider it payment for what I did in Gossamer Valley."

It was Alia's turn to look away. "Nothing could ever repay that, Wren."

Wren strode across and hugged her. "So let us stay and be useful. *Please*. We're certain to win! The Castle is safe!"

"We *are* certain to win, or so Lord Drevis believes," said Alia. "And if the Battle Horns are all they're cracked up to be, the Castle is in no danger. But I look at you now, and I feel *sick* at the thought of anything happening to you..."

"I'll see they behave themselves," said Rundel. He put a hand on Alia's shoulder, and she nodded. "Alia, I know how Wren and Patch must feel, and so do you. We've waited over ten years for this day. I wouldn't miss it for the *world*."

30
THE TABLES TURN

They stood on the battlements looking out at the enemy camp—Patch, Wren, Rundel, and Erner.

All around the Castle walls, members of the Castle Guard were spaced twenty feet apart, keeping close watch for activity. There was no way the Castle defenders would be caught by surprise, whatever the enemy tried.

Patch's eyes were sore, because he'd hardly blinked since they came up here. His gaze was fixed on one thing: the small dark figure of the Black Knight, moving from a command tent to his dragon and flying to the dragon camp and back, his armor glinting in the low sun.

Rundel Stone too was watching the Hamelyn Piper. "I wish I'd recovered in full so I could join the assault," he said. He clenched his right hand—the part of him most badly affected by his poisoning. "Underath's potion improved my hand, but I still struggle with it. I yearn to venture out and teach the villain a long overdue lesson. I wanted to be the one who claps irons on him at last."

"You think he'll be taken alive?" said Patch.

It was Wren who gave a sour laugh. "The most important thing to the Hamelyn Piper is his own life," she said. "If it was a choice between a famous death or the shame of capture, he'd choose capture. After doing everything he could to escape, of course."

"He won't have *escape* in mind until it's too late," said Rundel. "Although our task here is to watch him to make sure of it. If he attempts to fly off on his dragon, the Battle Horns can pluck him from the sky."

Patch was amazed. "They can do that?"

"So I'm told," said Rundel. "The Battle Horns are powerful. If you look there, above the gate, you'll see a Piper of the Keep." They looked to where he gestured. The Piper in question wore bright red robes with a white sash. "She will signal the orders for the Battle Horns during the assault."

At that, Patch noticed the Piper of the Keep shift her stance, from feet together to feet apart. A very slight adjustment, yet the Song of the Horns changed in rhythm almost at once.

Rundel's smile vanished. "That's the signal," he said,

looking behind to the courtyard. "Our troops will take the fight to the enemy, while the Horns give them protection!"

Soldiers began to stream out of the East Hall doors and the other places they'd been hiding from the watchful eyes of the dragons. At their head, Patch noted, was Tobias.

The Piper of the Keep raised one arm out to the side, and the Song of the Horns changed again, growing faster. The Castle Gates began to open.

"Look," said Rundel. "The enemy has noticed at last." Patch could see activity build in the mercenary camp. The Hamelyn Piper stood on his front line, facing the Castle.

"More dragons are taking wing," said Erner. Previously only half a dozen or so had been in the air at a time, but now Patch could see at least twenty rise up.

The forces of Tiviscan were pushing out through the Gates like sand flowing through the neck of an hourglass. The Piper of the Keep raised her other arm, and the true power of the Battle Horns began to make itself known. The shield it had been maintaining around the Castle shimmered and extended out. Patch looked to his side and could see the dragons moving back, clearly wary of its expanding reach.

The last of Tiviscan's attack forces were beyond the Gates now, arranging themselves into formation. The instant they were in position, the Piper of the Keep swung her arms to the front, then up. The Song of the Battle Horns deepened; Patch felt the vibrations in his bones, layer upon layer of driving rhythm. He expected the army to begin to march forward cautiously, but instead they *charged*, the Song pushing ahead of them.

The Hamelyn Piper's soldiers loosed arrows, but the Song tossed them aside. He ordered catapults to fire, but even those terrifying spheres were useless, exploding harmlessly in the air.

The charge of Tiviscan's defenders halted, and they took a new formation with archers at the front. It was *their* turn to fire, and there was chaos for a moment in the front lines of the Hamelyn Piper's army; they pulled back fifty yards, out of archer range.

Rundel looked to the Piper of the Keep. "Any moment now," he said. "And she will unleash the full might. The enemy is eager to engage, because they believe their numbers will still make the difference. They believe they can *win*. If they knew the truth, they would have already fled."

Patch saw that Rundel Stone seemed troubled, and it unnerved him. But before he could think it through, the Piper of the Keep raised her arms above her head, then cast them suddenly down by her sides. The Song of the Horns seemed to split into two, the higher-pitched elements taking a much faster tempo while the deep bass added several new melodies. Patch could feel every part of him tremble in sympathy to the notes from his skin to his liver, and he was suddenly afraid.

Not even when the Hamelyn Piper had played the Obsidiac Organ had he felt such power in Song.

And when the sound ramped up in sudden, shocking volume, Patch flinched, almost throwing himself to the walkway on which he stood—but he kept his footing and watched in horror as the distant air appeared to *sharpen* somehow and burst forward into the massed soldiers of the Hamelyn Piper.

Patch watched as human forms were tossed up from where they stood, like leaves in a storm.

He looked to Erner and Wren and saw the same shock on their faces.

The Piper of the Keep changed her signal repeatedly, and the terrible Song withdrew, then advanced once more, scything into a different part of the enemy. Back it came, and this time remained poised as the Piper of the Keep stayed still.

The enemy pulled back another hundred yards but formed up again in attack lines. The Hamelyn Piper mounted the back of his dragon, and Patch saw how Rundel tensed, alert to the possibility that he would desert his forces. But no: the dragon pulled back its head and released a great spout of flame into the sky. They were holding their ground. There was no sign of the mercenaries' resolve fragmenting.

Rundel bowed his head. "We could have attacked them just with the Songs," he said. "But putting our troops out there made the enemy think that this was a battle, not a *slaughter*. It kept them close and made them *vulnerable*." He looked to the Piper of the Keep once again, expectant. The Piper began to move, her signals rapid, and the Battle Horns grew even more terrifying—attack after attack, the range increasing with each strike. The dragons too were forced to move farther away as the vicious Song lashed out toward them as well.

No army could stand up to this kind of power, Patch realized. The Black Knight's troops were being decimated. Victory was assured, and it should have felt like triumph, but all Patch felt was a deep and growing horror.

Then he heard something like a *scream* from behind him. He turned to look, but saw nothing. Something about the noise struck him as familiar, something he couldn't place, but when the scream came again Rundel and Erner both turned as well.

It had come from the Keep. The sound was harsh, making Patch think of undesirable harmonics—the squeal of Pipes carelessly played with overblowing. He placed it, then: the kind of thing he'd heard on newly made Pipes that had been mistakenly carved with small irregularities, or which had become distorted in the curing process, particularly when cracks had appeared—

The scream came again, louder than before.

"No!" cried Rundel. He yelled to the Piper of the Keep: "Silence it! *End the Song!*"

The Piper of the Keep signaled frantically, but it was too late. Patch looked out to the distant Song as it seemed to draw in on itself, thrashing uncontrolled, before snapping back toward its origin.

Patch flung himself down, as they all did, the Song shrieking above them, the shimmering air reaching the top of the Keep. There the ends of the great Battle Horns shattered with an appalling cacophony, the explosion tracking down the wall of the Keep as the largest of the Horns tore itself apart, ripping a long wound through the Keep's stonework all the way to the ground.

Pieces of Horn and stone blasted through the air, the shrapnel of the Song's disastrous end. Even though they were far from the blast, Patch felt an impact on his arm that left his hand numb. As they stood, he saw blood drip from a small wound on Rundel's neck. Erner had a cut above his eye.

"Look!" cried Wren, pointing to fallen figures of the Castle Guard along the top of the eastern wall. They'd been closest to the blast and had suffered its full force. Their colleagues were rushing to their aid.

"Come on!" said Rundel. "They need all the help they can get!"

He hurried toward the watchtower at the southeast corner, and they all followed. Patch glanced out at the battlefield and saw their own troops trying to fall back, undefended now, the Battle Pipers desperately attempting to create Shielding Songs as they ran. The Hamelyn Piper's forces were advancing, their archers letting loose at will.

Patch reached the watchtower a moment after the others. He ran along the wall, passing the least wounded, who were still able to walk. The top of the wall nearest the Keep had been significantly damaged, leaving a breach. Castle Guards came from the far side to aid the fallen beyond the gap.

Soon they reached the worst of the injuries. One of the Guards had his hand clamped to his jaw, blood pouring between his teeth.

"Erner!" said Rundel. "Do what you can to slow the loss of blood. I suggest the Song of Salia. Wren—stay with him and help. Patch—with me." On he went, Patch close behind. The next injury was worse, the soldier's leg red and raw under the knee. Blood flowed freely, and Patch couldn't bring himself to look too closely, fearing that bone protruded. He felt faint for a moment but drew deep and shook the feeling gone.

Rundel crouched by the man and studied the wound, then looked to the next injured soldier, whose head was drenched red. "Patch, you must stay here and stop the blood loss if we're to save his life."

"But I don't know the Song of Salia . . . ," said Patch.

Rundel shook his head. "It wouldn't be enough here anyway," he said. "A Song isn't always the best way to use your hands . . . watch!" He showed Patch what to do, clasping the wound to stem the flow. Patch held as tightly as he could, trying not to think about what he gripped beneath his fingers. "I must see to the next guard," said Rundel. "I'll return as soon as I can." He looked to the courtyard and caught sight of Alia—she, Underath, and Alkeran had emerged from the refectory. "We need the griffins!" shouted Rundel. "Carry the wounded down to where we can treat them!"

"Rundel, what happened?" cried Alia. "What about those outside?"

What about Tobias? Patch thought, for surely that was foremost in Alia's mind.

"The Battle Horns tore themselves apart," yelled Rundel. "We're defenseless until our troops fall back—you and Underath must fight until they're here!"

Fight? thought Patch. *Fight what?*

And then he looked over the wall and saw. The dragons had seen the disaster that had befallen Tiviscan. Several dozen of them approached now, breathing fire as they came. "We will," cried Alia. "And you'd better keep those children safe, Rundel. You'd *better*."

Underath mounted Alkeran's back, and together they rose above the courtyard. The Sorcerer conjured a ball of light at his fingertips, hurling it toward the dragons. It split into two, then doubled again, too bright to look at in the fading daylight. Alia stood where she was, purple sparks flowing over her hands. She reached to the sky and drew lightning from thin air, its tendrils spreading out.

For now, the dragons backed away.

Barver and the rest of the griffins were in the air, helping take the injured down from the walls. Barver came to Patch first, but Rundel waved to him.

"Over here," ordered Rundel. "I need to work more on Patch's patient before it'll be safe to move him. This one can go now."

Barver went to Rundel, carefully picking up the injured Guard before flying down. To Patch's right, the Guard that Wren and Erner had been helping was taken by Merta.

Rundel came to Patch and took out his Pipe, playing a Song Patch didn't know. "My hand still lets me down," said Rundel, shaking his weak right hand in frustration. "It cramps quickly, but I can play well enough. Just."

Well enough may have been how Rundel described it, but his playing was intricate and precise. Patch could feel the pulsing of blood in the wound under his fingers slowing down and reaching a steady beat.

He looked to the Castle Gates, where the soldiers and Pipers were still streaming back through, desperately fleeing the battlefield. Pipers—both Custodian and Battle—played Shielding Songs that were beginning to overlap. It would take time, but soon it would create protection that, while far weaker than the Songs of the Battle Horns, still provided a reasonable level of defense to the Castle. He could see Lord Drevis and Tobias at the Gates, urging their troops on. What he couldn't see was how many more remained outside or how close the enemy forces were.

Then thunder rolled across the Castle, and Patch felt his blood chill. Even Rundel was put off his playing for a moment as the Black Knight's laughter filled the air.

"*You actually thought you were going to win . . . ,*" said the thunder. "*And now you think you were unlucky.*" Laughter again. "*You fear you pushed the Horns too far. But did you? Was the work flawed, or was there treachery?*"

Patch and Rundel shared a wary look: those they had found under a spell of magical persuasion . . . whether controlled by Quarastus or the Hamelyn Piper, any one of them could have sabotaged the new Battle Horns.

"*You have nothing left,*" said the thunder. "*People of Tiviscan, your Council has failed you. But I am a man of my word, even after such a merciless attack on my troops. I told you I would give you until dawn, and I honor that pledge. But if the Council is not handed over . . . you will all perish.*"

As the thunder faded, the Castle Gates began to close. Beyond the breach of the collapsed wall, the last of the injured on that side were being gathered up by the griffins. On this side, closer to the watchtower, Wren and Erner were helping another of the injured Guard. Everything was lit brightly by the lightning and fireballs that Alia and Underath were sustaining to keep the dragons at bay.

Rundel stopped playing and called to the griffins. "This one is ready to move," he cried.

"I'll return as quickly as I can," called Merta as she flew down with her charge held delicately in her grasp, heading to the north wall where all the injured had been taken.

Rundel took a knife from his belt and cut a strip from his Custodian robes, wrapping it around the patient's wound. "You may release your grip," he told Patch, pulling the material tight as Patch let go. Rundel nodded. "Good. I must keep the Song close, though, so I'll descend with Merta. Give Erner and Wren assistance with their final patient."

Patch nodded, stepping back as Merta returned. The griffin perched carefully on the narrow wall-walk. She gathered the injured Guard as Rundel climbed onto her back, then she flew off.

Patch looked at his hands, drenched in blood, and felt overwhelmed with hopelessness. Above him, the sorcery of Alia and Underath lit up the sky, but their magic would do little to hold back the Hamelyn Piper's forces once the villain chose to press his advantage. The Shielding Songs of the Pipers would succumb quickly to the kind of onslaught that was now inevitable.

From outside the walls, the battle cries of the enemy filled the air.

"Come *on*, Patch," Wren called to him. He looked and saw her and Erner with the Guard between them, arms around their shoulders for support, the three already limping to the watchtower. He started moving toward them.

But another sound came, even louder than the roar of the battle cries—a sound like the bones of a *giant* breaking. Pipers and soldiers in the courtyard started running. Patch turned as the huge sound grew, and he saw it.

The Keep.

At its base, cracks were spreading through the stone, great chunks falling from the gaping scar the Battle Horns had left. It was already *leaning*, he could see, figures on the ground scrabbling to get away from it before . . .

It began to topple, crumbling at the base as it did, pitching over toward the eastern wall. Toward *him*.

He ran and saw the horror on Wren and Erner's faces ahead as the noise behind him grew ever louder. He felt the impact, felt stone shift under his feet, the top of the wall giving way. In an instant he was tumbling, *falling*.

Above him, he could see Wren against the lightning and fire in the sky, reaching out over the battlements, her mouth wide as she screamed his name.

Below, at the base of the cliffs of Tiviscan Castle, death waited.

31
No Way Back

Patch tumbled, losing sight of Wren on the battlements. He saw dragons flying just above the forest ahead and the rocks below getting ever closer...

When a dark shape loomed above him he closed his eyes, thinking it would be a *dragon* that ended his life and not the ground after all. The breath was knocked out of him as he was plucked from the air.

"Got you!" cried Barver.

Patch opened his eyes. He was dangling from Barver's feet, and they were plunging downward at a terrifying rate, the ground coming up awfully fast. Barver barely managed to pull out of his dive, speeding away from the cliff face and over the trees.

"Be ready to grab my harness when I throw you," yelled Barver.

"Wait, what?" said Patch, but Barver was already flinging him over his shoulder.

Patch slammed into Barver's back, grabbing the harness for dear life. He sat up, facing the wrong way, and was shocked to see Wren sitting there.

"Thought I might be able to help!" she cried. "Now turn around and anchor your feet!"

Patch did so, putting his feet under the harness straps. "We're secure!" called Wren, and Barver banked suddenly. The nearest dragons had been slow to spot them, but there was no question now that they were closing in. As Barver turned, Patch's heart sank—there were already dragons between them and Tiviscan.

"Hold tight!" cried Barver, climbing then diving as two dragons came at them from the front. He outmaneuvered the larger creatures, zipping between them and battling to keep his speed up. Patch looked back and saw that the dragons were still on their tail. Ahead, a dozen more were turning toward them.

Barver was heading north, away from both the Castle and the dragon camp. There was no clear path to get back within Tiviscan's walls. "I can't shake them off!" he cried.

"How do we get around them?" said Wren.

Patch felt an idea brewing in his mind—a desperate one, certainly, but it was all he had. "We don't," he said. "We go *up*. Barver, do you hear me? Go up, where it's too cold for them to follow . . ."

"You'll both freeze!" yelled Barver.

"Trust me!" Patch shouted. He leaned over and unbuckled the flap of one of Barver's harness packs, pulling out a coat from among the warm clothing stashed there. He handed it to Wren.

"Watch out!" cried Barver, jerking suddenly right as a jet of fire shot past them, a dragon darting up from below. He dived down to pick up more speed, skimming over the tops of the trees and making Patch very grateful that he wasn't still dangling from Barver's feet.

Patch reached to the harness pack again, pulling out a second coat and a scarf, other items falling free in his haste. Wren had her coat on already, and Patch hurriedly shoved his arms through the sleeves of his own.

Barver snuck a glance back. "That won't be enough," he said, but now the dragons were closing from all sides.

"I can play a Heating Song," yelled Patch. "It'll be plenty." *I hope*, he said to himself. "Now go!"

Up they went, Barver straining hard to maintain speed, his passengers clinging on for dear life. There was a ring of dragons closing in on them from below. Bursts of flame came, uncomfortably close, but the air was starting to chill already as they reached the higher windways.

Patch took his Pipe from his pocket and built a Heating Song. His fingers started to go numb in the freezing wind, but he managed to get the basic elements of the Song in place and could feel the glow of warmth spread out.

"It's working!" shouted Wren.

The dragons weren't wasting their breath on fire now as they began to struggle with the altitude.

The air was thinning, and Patch suddenly feared that he wouldn't have the breath to spare on his Piping. The cold began to get truly *brutal*, and Patch sped up his Song to increase the heat it provided. He began to feel light-headed. This was as fast as he could go, he knew, yet the cold was quickly working its way in; the feeling in his feet already gone.

Barver cried out from the sheer effort, but then he looked down and cheered as the dragons below broke away one by one, their flight stuttering.

"Too much for them!" he yelled, leveling out. He looked to Patch and Wren. "Once we're far enough away, I can circle around, then dive back to the Castle."

Patch broke off playing his Heating Song. "We're not going back," he said.

"*What?*" cried Wren. "You mean we just *abandon* everyone in Tiviscan? They need all the help they can get!"

Patch shook his head. "We're not abandoning anyone."

"So you have a plan?" asked Barver.

"I think so," said Patch. "Half a plan, at any rate. But I think it can work. More than that: I think it can defeat the Hamelyn Piper."

"What is it?" asked Barver.

"*Monsters,*" he said.

Tiviscan was fifty miles away by the time they landed on a grassy hill to the northeast. Barver had dropped to a less brutal altitude once the Castle disappeared over the horizon and they were far beyond the sight of any dragon. Patch and Wren fell from Barver's back when they touched down, their feet numb and their joints stiff.

"Let's n-never do that again," said Wren. "My f-feet may never forgive me."

Barver breathed flame on a large rock until it glowed, giving Patch and Wren much needed warmth. It was a few minutes before they stopped shivering.

"Come on, then," said Barver. "Tell us."

Patch had put off explaining his idea until now, wanting time to think it through and make sure it wasn't absolutely crazy.

He told them.

"That is absolutely *crazy*," said Wren.

"I've tried to think of other ways," said Patch. "They're all much worse. Barver?"

Barver shrugged. "It does sound pretty desperate," he said. "Which is exactly what we are. So I say we try it."

"Well, a bad plan is better than no plan," said Wren. "Isn't that a famous saying?"

"No," said Patch. "Nobody has *ever* said that. Also, there's one big problem with it."

"Just one?" said Wren.

"My plan deals with the mercenaries, but not the dragons," said Patch.

Barver scratched his muzzle, deep in thought. After a minute he widened his eyes. "There is *one* thing I can think of. Timing will be pretty tight, though." He looked to the setting sun. "How long until dawn?"

"About nine hours," said Wren.

"Should be enough," he said.

"Enough for what?" asked Patch.

"*Onions*," said Barver, and he explained what he meant.

Once he finished, Patch stared at him. "And I thought *my* plan was crazy."

"Monsters and onions," said Wren. "Two crazy plans are better than one! And if that isn't a famous saying, it *should* be."

Back in the air, their first task was to locate Massarken.

Even though Lar-Sennen had said the Guardian could always find it, Patch wished he'd asked *how*. In the end, though, he needn't have worried. When he simply closed his eyes and thought of the island, he immediately had a strong sensation of where to go. "That way!" he cried, pointing, and Barver turned.

It wasn't long before they were over the sea. The sun had almost set, and the sky was growing dark. Below them was sparse cloud, but eventually a great swirl of sea fog came into view.

"That's it!" said Patch.

Down they went until they were surrounded by fog and flying only tens of feet above the ocean. "We're almost at the island, so take it slow," said Patch. "I think we have to find the bay where we left—that's where the entrance is. We mustn't get too close, or we'll fly headlong into the barrier."

On they went in silence, the ocean mercifully calm.

"I don't like this," said Barver. "If I smack my face into that barrier I'll be *very* annoyed."

"Agreed," said Wren.

"Close enough!" cried Patch suddenly. He could almost *see* where the barrier was, even though the fog meant visibility was less than a hundred feet in any direction. "Turn to the right," he said. "We'll follow it around. I'll know when to stop." Soon he sensed they were in the right place. "Circle here and watch out for the tentacle." He spoke to the island then: "Massarken, I command you! Open the way!"

They could hear the churn of water from nearby. Out of the fog loomed the great tentacle, unfurling enough to give them a platform to land on.

Patch dismounted. "I'll meet you here," he said. "Four hours, you reckon?"

"We'll be at the mercy of the air currents, but four hours

is my best guess," said Barver. He frowned, working out the times in his head. "For my part of the plan to work, we need to be back at Tiviscan well before dawn."

"Good luck," said Patch.

"You too!" said both Wren and Barver, and they took to the air once more.

Patch made his bracelet light up, then hurried along the tentacle, wary of the fog around him. He reminded himself that he was the Guardian of Massarken—if anyone should feel safe here, it was him. But there was something about walking along a giant tentacle in dimly lit fog that made a person feel uneasy.

He could sense the moment when he crossed through the barrier. The fog ahead of him thinned, and the rocky bay came into view. He reached the beach and hurried to the boulder, finding the Soul Bottle right where Alia had left it. As he put it around his neck the familiar glowing shape of Lar-Sennen appeared nearby. The Sorcerer's expression was blank at first, as if he'd been caught in a doze; then his eyes snapped wide, and he frowned.

"Back so soon?" said the ghost. "Did it not go well?"

"I *am* back," said Patch. "And it did *not* go well. I need your help."

"Of course!" said Lar-Sennen. "What exactly can I do?"

"*Well*," said Patch. "I need to borrow some cockatrices..."

32

A Cunning Plan

Four hours later, Patch was standing on the vast tentacle again, waiting for Barver in the soft glow of light from his bracelet. At his feet were six securely tied burlap sacks.

He wondered again if his plan stood any chance at all. It had popped into his mind all at once as they'd fled from the dragons outside Tiviscan.

I'm the Guardian of an island of monsters, he'd thought. *Surely some of those monsters can come to our aid!*

But what did he think the monsters could do? Tear people apart, like the devil-birds? Even if Patch had been able to stomach the idea, Lar-Sennen would surely never sanction such a thing. Besides, unleashing the devil-birds could have proved catastrophic, with no way to make sure they only attacked the Hamelyn Piper's forces. And imagine the difficulty catching them afterwards—perhaps letting some escape into the wild!

So it was a *no* to the devil-birds. Cockatrices, on the other hand...

When Patch told him his plan, Lar-Sennen agreed at once.

"A good choice," said the ghost. "Even a single cockatrice would leave anyone within fifty yards paralyzed with fear, while those farther away would flee screaming from terrible things that are only in their imaginations! And if I'm honest, a change of scene might do them good. Of all the creatures on the island, the cockatrices are the most pitiful."

Pitiful seemed a strange word to use, thought Patch, given the terror just *one* of the little beasts had managed to cause him. "How so?" he asked.

"They get very little stimulation on the island," said Lar-Sennen. "It tends to make them unhappy. We should choose the most miserable ones we can find—it would be such a *treat* for them!" He said this with a wide smile, even though the "treat" meant delivering *absolute horror* to as many mercenaries as possible.

And so Lar-Sennen guided him to the six most dejected cockatrices they could find. Wearing the Guardian's bracelet meant Patch was now protected from their fear-inducing magic; one by one he caught them and put them in sacks he'd collected from the wheelhouse. Once in a sack, each bird made a brief fuss before becoming utterly still.

There had been a few additional details of his plan that he and Lar-Sennen thrashed out, but then the time had come to leave the Soul Bottle back on the boulder and bid Lar-Sennen farewell again.

Patch had returned to the tentacle, hoping that Barver's mission had been just as successful.

There was no fog now—Patch had ordered the island to stop it so that Barver could find him more easily. As he waited, the only sound was the ocean water lapping against the mighty tentacle. Eventually he heard a distant call echoing in the night, and a minute later Barver touched down with Wren on his back, two barrels hanging from his sides.

Patch strode over to Barver and tied the sacks to his harness. "No difficulties, then?" he said.

"We made good time," said Barver. "The barrels were easy to find, although Wren had to wrestle them out of the pantry on her own. The kitchen doors were too small for me."

"So these are the famous cockatrices?" said Wren.

"They are," said Patch. "Six of them! Lar-Sennen thinks a trip away from the island will do them good." He patted one of the barrels. "And these are the onions..." He thought back to when Barver had eaten them before, in the mansion of Ural Casimir—which was where Barver and Wren had just flown to collect them. "Are you sure this can work?"

Barver nodded. "I'm nowhere near as sensitive to hedge-beet as dragons are, and you saw what happened to me—a massive fiery burp! For a dragon it would be ten times worse, at least. Even a tiny amount of these onions would give dragons terrible stomach cramps, but I bet it would be far more dramatic than that! I'd guess they would have severe incendiary incontinence, which means . . ."

"We can guess what it means," said Wren.

"Uncontrollable fire!" said Barver. "From both ends!"

Wren raised an eyebrow. "I *said* we can guess."

"Won't they be able to taste the hedge-beet?" said Patch. "I mean, if it's such a big problem for dragons, can't they tell it a mile off?"

Barver grinned. "Normally, yes!" he said. "If you added hedge-beet to food, any dragon would know just from the smell, and the bitter taste would be unmistakable. But these onions are different. Pickled in hedge-beet vinegar, and the onions themselves don't even have a *hint* of hedge-beet's flavor in them. Tobias said the onions are made sweeter by the vinegar, but they must also soak up whatever turns the intestines of a dragon inside out . . ." He grinned. "I tasted an onion on its own to make sure, and I still couldn't have spotted the hedge-beet."

Patch stepped back, suddenly nervous of either of Barver's ends. "You tasted an onion?"

"Don't worry, I spat it straight out!" said Barver. "Even

then my stomach was a little iffy a few minutes later. So, yes, the onions are perfect. We've poured away the bitter vinegar, so all I need to do is add the contents of the barrels to the Pestleken."

"That's the special cooking pot, right?" said Patch.

Barver nodded. He'd explained all of this before they'd separated: a dragon army, Barver had told them, always eats at dawn before battle, as tribute to the Gods of Fire and Scale. The meal is cooked in a large cauldron called the Pestleken. The whole camp gets a portion—and all must eat.

"But how do you plan to do it?" said Patch. "There's no way you can just sneak in unseen . . ."

Barver raised an eyebrow. "You asked us to trust you about the cockatrices, so the least you can do is trust me about the onions."

"That's fair enough," said Patch, and he climbed onto Barver's back behind Wren. As they flew off, the tentacle sank below the water, and Massarken shrouded itself in fog once more.

They landed well to the east of the dragon camp, Barver flying close to the ground wherever possible.

With the light of his bracelet, Patch removed the sacks

from Barver's harness and began to unpick the knots holding them closed.

Wren glared at him. "What are you doing?" she said. "I'm not keen on being reduced to a terrified wreck."

"Ah, good point," said Patch. "You should become a crow before I open these so the cockatrices can't affect you just as they don't affect Barver. As Guardian I'll be immune."

Wren shape-shifted to a crow and Patch opened the sacks, taking out the six cockatrices within. They were a sorry bunch, it had to be said—their feathers thinning and ragged in places, nothing like the healthy specimen who'd ambushed Patch.

All six seemed drowsy, and Barver was unimpressed. "I'm not sure these creatures will inspire anything more than pity," he said.

"Don't worry," said Patch. "Lar-Sennen was certain they'll perk up when the sun rises and they sense prey. But it's crucial that the dragons have been dealt with by then. They're immune to the cockatrices too, and if they just fly in and stop it the way you did with me, Barver, the whole plan comes crashing down."

"So how do we get this lot into position near the mercenaries?" cawed Wren, nodding at the cockatrices.

"My first plan was for me to creep close to the enemy lines," said Patch. "Place the birds one by one in thickets near their camp. That should be all we need to do. They'll stay hidden until daylight."

"That sounds very risky," said Barver. "You could easily be seen."

Patch nodded. "I did come up with a better idea," he said. "It relies on you doing most of the work, Wren."

Wren hopped in excitement. "Sounds good," she cawed. "What is it?"

"The Song of the Shepherd," said Patch. "One of the tools of the Arable Pipers. It makes animals follow a herd leader. That'll be you."

"A long way to walk," observed Barver.

Patch shook his head. "Lar-Sennen said cockatrices can fly farther than you'd think. Make sure you don't get too far ahead of them, Wren, that's all. Get to the edge of the forest, close to the enemy. They're solitary animals, so when you release them from the Song they should naturally spread out, finding a hiding spot where they'll sleep until dawn. If any mercenaries see you from a distance, they shouldn't think anything of it—just some birds in the forest." He took his Pipe from his pocket and started to play, and soon the Song was complete. The cockatrices were all watching Patch, almost in a trance. "Wren, you need to turn around three times for this part," he said. "That's what makes them see you as the leader. To release them, you just do the same thing again when you're ready."

She nodded and made three turns. All six birds looked to her, docile and with only the occasional cluck.

Happy with the result, Patch let the Song fade. How long the effect would last depended on the intelligence of the animal in question. It had no effect at all on humans, for example, whereas sheep would dutifully follow the leader for many hours. Patch suspected that cockatrices were smarter than they looked, but that still gave Wren plenty of time.

"You can go now," he said to her. "Good luck!" Even in her crow form, he could tell that she was nervous, but she took to the air. The cockatrices followed.

Barver and Patch watched anxiously as the curious little group flew southwest. There was so much that could go wrong, but as soon as they were out of sight there was nothing that Patch or Barver could do to help.

"Right, then, *onion boy*," Patch said. "Time for *your* crazy idea."

"Okay," said Barver. "But I need you to do one thing first."

"What?" said Patch.

Barver untied the barrels from his sides and set them on the ground before rummaging in a harness pack. He held up something metal, like two large knives. He squeezed them together, and Patch realized it was a small pair of shears. "I didn't want to mention it until Wren had gone, because she really wouldn't have liked it."

"And I will?" said Patch.

"Oh, you won't like it either," said Barver. "I want you to cut off my feathers. Every last one."

33
Plucked and Shorn

Barver had been right. Patch *really* didn't like it. Neither of them did—every time the shears closed and another feather was cut, they both winced.

"You're sure it doesn't hurt?" said Patch.

"Just keep going," said Barver, but he looked rather distressed. "Wings next, I think."

So far, Patch had removed the feathers from Barver's face and neck, his glowing bracelet invaluable to let him see what he was doing. The shriveled little ones around his muzzle hadn't been a problem, as they were kept in check by Barver's fire. The rest, though . . . Patch had never fully appreciated how many there were. As he cut them away, Barver quickly stopped looking like himself. His dragon-like features became more obvious, and his muzzle, being a strange mixture of beak and snout, seemed even more conspicuous than usual.

Barver routinely kept most of his underwing feathers trimmed, but the top of his wings had a few regions that he retained for improved loft.

Patch hesitated as he reached for the first of them. "Are you absolutely *sure* you want me to keep going?" he said.

Barver gave a sad nod. "It could make flying tricky," he said. "But there's no other way. I'm confident I can sneak my way to the Pestleken, but I have to look as dragon-like as possible."

"Couldn't someone still recognize you?" said Patch, wincing as he cut one of the larger flight feathers. "What if you bump into Kasterkan?"

"I'll make sure to avoid *him*," said Barver. "As for anyone else . . . dragons never pay much attention to a dracogriff, Patch, certainly not a lower one like me. They just see the feathers and the strangeness, not the face." He reached into a harness pack and produced a long white strip of cloth. "Speaking of which . . ."

"Bandages?" said Patch.

"My face is just a little *too* strange," said Barver. He wrapped the cloth around his upper muzzle, leaving a gap for his nostrils.

It took Patch another twenty minutes to finish clipping away the feathers on Barver's wings and torso, but at last he was done. "That's that," he said. "What if someone asks your name?"

"Uh ... Varber?" suggested Barver. "Varber Konkerpoople?"

"You could at least put *some* thought into it," said Patch, exasperated.

"Dekkit Glinker, then," said Barver. "Used to be a protector in the Eastern Sea."

"Friend of yours?"

"Goodness, no," said Barver. "Grumpy dragon, kept borrowing money he never repaid. Died in a freak laundry accident. Always liked his name, though. So, how do I look?" He pushed out his chest and tried to appear dignified.

Patch took in the view of his unrecognizable friend, featherless and with a bandaged face. "Um ... yes," he said at last, because he had no idea how else to reply.

Barver set about fixing the barrels to his sides again, but just as he finished they both heard the crunch of heavy steps approaching through the forest. "Quick," Barver whispered. "Under my wing! Someone's coming!"

Patch commanded his bracelet to cease its mysterious light and dived under Barver's right wing just as two dragon soldiers emerged from the trees to his left.

"Hold, stranger!" said one soldier—male, a good three feet taller than Barver. The other soldier was an even bigger female.

"Uh ... hello," said Barver.

"I *thought* I could hear something in this direction," said the male soldier. "And here you are! Name and rank!"

"The name's Dekkit Glinker," said Barver, grateful now for Patch's foresight. "Unranked, sir. Part of Provisions, sir. Bringing some specialist ingredients for the morning Pestleken, to ensure the Gods look favorably on us today."

"You're cutting it fine," said the female soldier, and even though she seemed rather surly, Barver felt a great deal of relief that his story had been believed—so far, at least.

"Difficult journey?" she said, gesturing to the bandages.

"You could say that," said Barver.

"So what are you doing out here?" she said.

Barver paused, his mind blank. "I was just, um . . ."

But the male soldier supplied an answer. "Hunting, by the look of it!" he said, disapproval in his voice. He gestured to Barver's feathers, scattered on the ground.

"Hunting, yes!" said Barver. "That's *exactly* what I was doing."

"I suppose we can't blame you," said the female soldier. "We've been on ground patrol for three hours, and my stomach could do with a top off. But everything's far too small to be worth catching! You've certainly had better luck . . ." She pushed the feathers around with her foot, examining them. "What in all the skies did you find?"

"Yes, what *did* I find?" said Barver, thinking fast. "A very unusual bird. Some kind of really big pigeon probably. More feathers than meat. Never seen the like before. I would have saved you some if I'd known you were coming."

The female soldier strolled around to Barver's right, and Barver lowered his wing a little more to make sure Patch's feet were hidden—he was painfully aware of what would happen if his friend was discovered. Their plan would be in tatters, and they would both be taken as spies.

She was eyeing him as if only really seeing him for the first time. There was pity written clearly on her face. "No offense," she said. "But you look like you need a good meal more than we do!"

The male soldier laughed. "Yes, you're a scrawny one, aren't you, Dekkit? I can see why you work with Provisions, can't imagine you in a fight. You should take to the air and bring your cargo to the Pestleken!"

Barver felt his throat go dry. With the dragons on both sides, Patch had no chance of sneaking off, and no way to hide if Barver tried to fly. "Uh, I banged up my wing a bit on the way here," he said. "I'll walk, I think."

The female nodded. "I *thought* you'd done yourself an injury," she said, looking at the awkward way he was holding his right wing. "We'll escort you back, give you some company."

Barver forced himself to smile. "Oh, that'd be *great*," he said. "That'd be just *great*."

Humans have a *smell*.

Some are much worse than others, of course, but even with the cleanest human it was a smell that dragons could usually detect quite easily. So far, however, Patch's odor hadn't given him away. Barver presumed it was the slight odor of onions from the barrels that was masking him. That, and maybe the nervous sweat that Barver was producing in copious amounts. He didn't imagine that under his wing was a pleasant place to be right now.

They'd reached the edge of the dragon camp after fifteen minutes or so, where regularly spaced lanterns gave out plenty of light. At first Barver could feel that Patch was bent low under his wing, trying to walk without revealing his presence. Then he felt Patch grip his harness, looping his arms and legs inside the straps and holding tight to Barver's side. The added weight made Barver walk a little lopsided, but at least he no longer had to worry about Patch's feet being visible.

Most of the dragon army still slept, and he saw no sign of Kasterkan. Even so, there were plenty of eyes watching him as he made his slow, limping way along. He felt a deep dread that at any moment one of them would leap up and cry "Human!" and all would be lost. He could feel Patch shift his position now and again, which was the only sign that his friend hadn't suffocated.

The soldiers accompanied him all the way to a large tent—the cooking area where the Pestleken was being prepared. "There you go," said the female soldier. "Here at last."

"Thank you both," said Barver.

"Just doing our duty," she said.

"Although some extra helpings wouldn't go to waste, eh?" said the male with a wink, and off the pair went.

Barver stepped inside the tent. There were six dragons, and in the middle of the tent was an enormous iron cauldron sitting over a fire. The air was filled with the smell of roasted meat and spices. The liquid in the cauldron bubbled furiously.

Two of the dragons were hunched low, breathing fire at the base to boost the heat. Creating the Pestleken was a holy ritual and had a long list of necessary steps. Two of the other dragons were running between the cauldron and a huge leather-bound tome, gathering ingredients and adding them while reciting the required prayers.

Of the final two dragons, one was standing by a table piled high with a green plant that Barver identified as hill-parsley, a foraged herb that was fiddly to prepare. The dragon was wincing at the moment, as the sixth dragon was yelling *"Hurry up, you waste of space"* in his ear.

The sixth dragon, Barver knew, was Old Tisker, who had been in charge of the camp meals when Barver had traveled with the dragon army, the last time they'd besieged Tiviscan. There weren't any good things Barver could say about Tisker, a short-tempered bully—so intent on his outburst that he'd not even noticed Barver's arrival.

In the corner of the tent was a shrine to the Gods of Fire and Scale, a gold cage containing an urn of sand from the Dragon Territories and various effigies of the Great Gods themselves.

Making sure he stood with his right wing to the side of the tent to eliminate any risk of Patch being seen, Barver hurried to untie the barrels. He had a quick glance at Patch, who looked bewildered, frightened, and sweaty. "It's going to be okay," whispered Barver. "I'll be as quick as I can."

Patch gave a thumbs-up.

"What's this?" came the irritated voice of Tisker.

Barver turned slowly. He was wary that Tisker might recognize him and make trouble, but he saw no hint of recognition in Tisker's eyes.

"Out with it, boy!" said Tisker. He sniffed one of the barrels. "What do you have? Onions?"

"I was sent to deliver ingredients for the Pestleken," said Barver. "An auspicious gift, sir. For good luck on this important day."

Tisker shook his head and sighed. "Why am I always the last to hear of these things?"

"It's come all the way from the Burning Temple, sir," said Barver. "Blessed by the High Priestess herself!" He turned to the shrine in the corner and made the Sign of the Flame with his hand. All the dragons in the Pestleken stopped what they were doing and did the same—even Tisker.

It was a bold lie—the blessing of the High Priestess was one of the highest honors the Burning Temple could have bestowed on them—but the look on everyone's face showed him that the lie had worked like a charm. The dragons seemed awestruck.

"Well, get them in the pot, then!" snapped Tisker. "The final stages must be completed; we don't have long!" Two of the assistants took a barrel each and opened them, pouring the onions into the cauldron and stirring the contents with huge spoons.

One of them took a great sniff, then brought the vast spoon they were using out of the stew, raising it to their mouth. Barver's eyes widened as the assistant prepared to have a taste...

There was a loud *thwack* and the spoon was dropped. Tisker lowered the long stick he'd used to hit the assistant's hand.

"Didn't your parents teach you?" said Tisker. "The Gods have the first taste, you fool, right before sunrise." He pointed to the shrine.

The assistant lowered his head. "I just wanted to try it. It smells incredible."

"Of course it smells incredible!" said Tisker. "Blessed by the Burning Temple!" He puffed up his chest with smug pride. "This will be a truly great Pestleken," he said. "I can feel it in my gizzard."

As Tisker and his underlings continued with the preparation, Barver could tell that nobody was paying him any attention. "I'll, um, get these empty barrels out of the way," he said, and when there was no reply he took the barrels and headed back out of the tent.

Sometimes being ignored had its advantages.

He raised his wing enough to see Patch. "Mission accomplished," he whispered. "All we can do now is get out of sight and wait."

34
Monsters and Onions

Barver and Patch hid among supply crates stored at the edge of camp, on the upward slope of a hillock. There were so many crates that it was clear the dragons had come prepared for a long siege. With the Battle Horns out of the picture, though, a far quicker resolution was inevitable. If the monsters-and-onions plan came to nothing, the catapults would soon decide things. What little protection Tiviscan could muster wouldn't be able to stand up to the terrifying exploding spheres. If Barver's assessment had been right, the dragons were here to make sure that Tiviscan was destroyed. Even if the Pipers' Council surrendered themselves to the Hamelyn Piper or told him the truth about Quarastus, it would change nothing.

Below, Patch could see the lanterns of the dragon camp, looking fainter now as dawn drew near.

In the distance, the windows and ramparts of Tiviscan were dark. The sound of Piping drifted through the morning air, Shielding Songs being maintained by the Battle Pipers. Patch had a good look at the damage caused by the collapse of the Keep. The top of the eastern wall of the Castle was in ruins.

As the sun crept above the horizon, a bell was rung nearby. The soldiers of the dragon camp stirred, making their way to the tent where the ritual meal was being served from the Pestleken.

"Well, here goes," whispered Barver.

Patch was too nervous to speak. As he watched the dragons queue up, he felt a hand on his shoulder and whimpered in terror.

"It's only me," whispered Wren. "Did it go okay?"

"So far," said Patch. "You?"

"All good," she said. "The cockatrices looked exhausted when I hid them, though. I don't think they'd flown that far in a long time."

"Well, let's hope they don't decide to have a rest," said Patch.

"What happened to your *feathers*?" Wren said to Barver, shocked.

"I had to look as much like a dragon as I could," said Barver. "They'll grow back, don't worry."

"They'd better . . . ," she said. "I think we should move on. This equipment dump goes all the way up the hill, and at the top is an enormous catapult. There's nobody crewing it yet, but there probably will be soon. If we can get to the other side of the hill, it's a clear path into the forest."

They wove carefully among the crates. At the top of the hill they crouched among tarpaulin-covered piles that were taller even than Barver. Beyond the piles was the vast catapult.

"Look!" said Barver, pointing to the southwest.

Something was flying toward them. They worked their way farther back in among the tarpaulins. Patch put his hand on the nearest covering. Whatever was underneath felt smooth. The Hamelyn Piper's dragon landed next to the catapult, and the villain dismounted. Patch, Wren, and Barver all tensed. The dragon hurried down the hill toward the Pestleken tent.

The Hamelyn Piper looked at the great weapon and smiled, nodding to himself in satisfaction. He wore an ornate belt around his waist; Patch could see a small dagger there, a sailor's spyglass, and what looked like a pair of red manacles. He glanced at Wren. "Are those . . . ?" he began, but she nodded at once. The same magic-draining manacles she'd told him about.

Another dragon landed, and Patch immediately felt his hackles rise as he recognized General Kasterkan. He shared a look with Barver and Wren, all three of them feeling the same sense of loathing toward the dragon who'd destroyed Skamos.

"Good work," the Hamelyn Piper said to Kasterkan, patting the impressive frame of the catapult. "They'll be suitably terrified just seeing it here!"

"Indeed," said Kasterkan. "I hope Filkess is serving your needs well?"

"Of course," said the Hamelyn Piper. "Although as soon as the bell rang, he was a little *too* keen to get over here for your dawn meal."

"It is a requirement of the Gods," said Kasterkan. "Those of highest rank get to eat first, and it was delicious! But it won't be long before the meal is complete, and then we're ready to begin." He looked to the Castle. "I assume they'll be stubborn." He seemed to relish the prospect. "Their shielding magic looks more effective than I would have expected. It doesn't seem like they're going to give in to your demands quite yet."

"The shielding is no match for us," said the Hamelyn Piper. "They'll surrender the members of the Council soon enough, and once I'm done with them . . . you can do whatever you like to Tiviscan."

And there it was—confirmation that the Hamelyn Piper's promise to leave everyone else unharmed was worthless. Even though it had come as no surprise, Patch found himself clenching his fists in anger. The dragons, meanwhile, were clearly intent on the destruction of Tiviscan, as Barver had suspected.

"Did you know that would happen to their Battle Horns?" asked Kasterkan. "Your forces took many casualties when the Horns played their Songs. I had no idea Songs could be so destructive! I was concerned that you'd underestimated their strength." He belched briefly. "Pardon me," he said, rubbing his chest.

"I knew what the Horns were capable of," said the Hamelyn Piper. "I also knew what would happen if they were played to their full power. You shouldn't doubt me."

"No, I . . . ," said Kasterkan, pausing to belch again. He winced, both hands around his stomach, and then a vast jet of flame shot from his mouth. Kasterkan looked shocked, as did the Hamelyn Piper.

Shouts came from the dragon camp; Kasterkan and the Hamelyn Piper both turned to look down the hill, staring in disbelief. Although Patch couldn't see what was happening, it was obvious from the sounds that reached them in their hiding place—warning cries, panicked yells, and the roars of uncontrolled flame.

"Stay at your posts!" yelled Kasterkan to his troops before clutching his belly and moaning in pain. "The Gods . . . ," he moaned. "The Gods must be displeased!" He leaned over and his tail came up. Patch could hardly watch as flames burst from underneath, engulfing the front of the catapult for a good five seconds.

The Hamelyn Piper looked on in horror. "Go!" he yelled. "Get away from the shot!"

Kasterkan, his stomach gurgling loud enough for Patch to hear, stumbled down the hill. The Hamelyn Piper whistled up a Song, creating a cold wind that extinguished the burning parts of the catapult. He turned and looked at the dragon camp again, his face filled with rage.

They could hear wails of despair now and occasional screams. The dragons were in disarray, a dozen already abandoning the battlefield—flying north, leaving trails of unnatural flame behind them. If the rest thought the Gods were displeased, as their general did, surely they would *all* flee.

Barver, Patch, and Wren grinned at each other, ecstatic at what was happening—Operation Onions was a huge success!

"It's up to the cockatrices now," whispered Wren.

With the sun above the horizon, Patch tightly crossed his fingers, hoping that the waking cockatrices would sense their prey sooner rather than later. He suddenly feared that the Hamelyn Piper wouldn't wait to see if the Council surrendered—he might just use his thunder voice to order all their catapults to fire.

And with that thought, Patch remembered the Hamelyn

Piper's words when Kasterkan had set the catapult alight: *Get away from the shot*. He placed his hand on the tarpaulin beside him, feeling the smooth curve of the surface underneath, and a terrible notion occurred to him. He found the tarpaulin's edge and glanced underneath.

His blood ran cold.

"Um . . . Barver, Wren . . . ?" he whispered. "Do you two realize what all *this* is?" He pulled the tarpaulin edge back, and their eyes went wide when they saw. They were hiding among piles of ammunition. *Explosive spheres*.

"It's a good thing Kasterkan's bum was pointed away from us," whispered Barver. "The whole lot might've gone up."

"Death by fart . . . ," said Wren, but the shock on her face was soon replaced by a smile as she caught sight of something else. "Do you see what I'm seeing?"

Patch and Barver both looked.

From their hiding place they had a very slim view of the Hamelyn Piper's forces in front of the Castle, but they could see movement. At first Patch feared that the army was preparing an attack in response to the disaster afflicting the dragons, but as he watched he could tell there was no *organization* involved in what they were doing. Instead, the movement was haphazard and rushed. It was *panic*, and there was surely only one explanation.

"*Monsters*," Barver said, slapping Patch and Wren on the back, winding them both.

The Hamelyn Piper had seen it too, the villain's focus now entirely on his own mercenary troops, even as the sound of flame and anguish still came from the nearby dragons. He took the spyglass from his belt and raised it to his eye, then cried out: "No!"

He cried out the same word again, but this time in his thunder voice, and the sound of his anger filled the air and echoed across the forest. All the while, his mercenary troops were stampeding away from their camp in utter chaos.

Patch could see people on the still-standing parts of the eastern wall of the Castle. The griffins were there too, watching the Hamelyn Piper face defeat at last. More than defeat—*humiliation*.

But as Patch wondered what the Hamelyn Piper might do now, he heard another voice, and his blood froze yet again: "Things not going quite as you planned?"

The Hamelyn Piper turned to look behind him. Patch couldn't see the person who'd spoken, but he'd known at once who the voice belonged to.

"You . . . ?" said the Hamelyn Piper.

"You don't recognize me?" said the voice. "After all we've been through together." From the charred far end of the catapult, the speaker came into view.

It was Lord Pewter. *Quarastus*. Walking slowly, leaning on his staff.

He stopped by the catapult and *changed*. Wren had told

Patch all about his true nature—stick-thin, clinging to life—and that Lord Pewter was merely one of his disguises.

Yet Patch almost gasped as he saw Pewter become someone else before his eyes, shorter in height and slightly plump, his beard lengthening.

The Hamelyn Piper said nothing.

"Is that better?" said Quarastus, smiling. "The face you knew for so long! The face you trusted so *completely*. You really didn't know who I was!"

"I knew you were *Quarastus*," said the Hamelyn Piper. "But not that you were one of the Pipers' Council."

"You began to suspect, though," said Quarastus.

"Not until after my attempt at taking control with the Obsidiac Organ," said the Hamelyn Piper. "When the Council devoted so much to capturing me, it seemed *desperate*. That's when I realized. I admit I suspected Drevis, not Pewter."

Quarastus smiled. "Ah, yes, why would anyone suspect harmless old Lord Pewter?" He grinned. "Enough, though. For ten years I was your teacher. I found you as a lost and lonely child and gave you *hope*. I trained you. I thought we'd become *friends*."

"So did I, for a while," said the Hamelyn Piper. Patch was shocked to hear *anguish* in his voice. "Yet all that time you never trusted me enough to show me your true self."

"You betrayed me," said Quarastus. He bowed his head,

sorrowful. "And you complain about a lack of trust? But look at us! I have been discovered at last and had to flee the Castle. And your forces are scattered to the winds. Yet we can still be victorious! I don't know how Drevis has beaten you, but if we join forces now we can still bring our plans to fruition."

"So you have the amulet, then?" said the Hamelyn Piper.

"I know where it is," said Quarastus. "When armor and amulet combine, our victory is assured."

"You would forgive me?" said the Hamelyn Piper. Patch's mouth gaped wide as he saw the Black Knight's face, wet with tears. He was *crying*. "I stole the obsidiac. All your years of planning, and I betrayed you . . ."

"You wanted the armor for yourself," said Quarastus. "I understand. Perhaps I'm the only person in the world who *could* understand. So, yes, I forgive you. All you have to do is take my hand." He reached out. "Please," he said. "Join me. We can rule a new world, together."

The Hamelyn Piper seemed to waver, but then he strode forward and took the hand of Quarastus, and the two men embraced.

But Patch could see Quarastus grip the head of his staff and pull. Metal glinted in the morning sun. Patch saw the careful placement of the blade midway down the back of the Black Knight's armor and gasped as the knife was driven home. The Hamelyn Piper's legs buckled. He fell to his knees, clutching the legs of Quarastus, who sneered with pleasure. "My turn for a spot of *betrayal*," said Quarastus, his expression smug. "The armor was protecting you. It would deflect whatever attack I tried to use, whether magical or brute force. So I had to get close! You are not immortal, not without the amulet. And I know where the *weaknesses* are, the places a blade can penetrate its protection. And I know *your* weaknesses too. Still a lost and lonely child, after all this time."

The Hamelyn Piper tried to stand. He backed away, half-crouched, the hilt of the knife out of reach of his grasping hand.

"Oh, don't look at me like that," said Quarastus. "You would have betrayed me again as soon as you knew the amulet's location. And if..." He suddenly stopped speaking and looked down. Clamped to his feet were the red manacles the Hamelyn Piper had carried. Quarastus stepped away from the catapult, but the chain of the manacles was looped around a supporting strut, trapping him. He kneeled and pulled at the chain with his hands, to no avail. He stared, his eyes wide with rage.

The Hamelyn Piper managed to seize the hilt of the knife and pull it from his back with a cry of pain. "You'll wish you'd kept hold of this," he said. "It would have given you a chance to take *those* off." He grinned, but was clearly weak from his wound. "Can you feel your magic ebb?" he said. "It's all that keeps you alive, I know that. The manacles drain your power, and with it your *life*."

With a sneer, Quarastus reached to a pocket and took out a small bundle of dried herbs, breaking it in two. When nothing happened, the sneer fell away, replaced with abject horror.

"Oh *dear*," said the Hamelyn Piper. "The manacles drain the power of *braids* too." He smiled. "I know all about the curious knots you use, storing magic. I've used the same trick myself, paying Sorcerers to create useful little spells." He limped toward the pile of catapult spheres, perilously close to where Patch, Wren, and Barver were hiding.

Barver and Wren shrank back, but Patch stayed where he was—he *had* to watch, even at the risk of being seen.

"Feeling weak, Quarastus?" the Hamelyn Piper called. His movement toward the spheres was slow, each step wrenching an agonized grunt from him.

The ancient Sorcerer was growing more gaunt by the second. With eyes that spoke of cruelty and malice, he glared at the Hamelyn Piper. "I could ask you the same question. You'll die very soon, but not me . . . I'll *fade* and grow so thin that these manacles will slip from my feet. And when they do, my magic will start to return."

At the ammunition pile, the Hamelyn Piper cut into a tarpaulin with the blood-covered knife, revealing the sphere beneath. He plunged the blade into the sphere's gray surface, opening a gouge from which black powder began to pour. It was so close to Patch that he could smell the sharp odor of sulfur.

The Hamelyn Piper dropped the knife and held cupped hands under the flow, filling them before making his slow hobbled way back toward Quarastus, letting the black powder pour between his fingers, creating a line stretching back to the sphere. Patch could see another line beside it—a dark wet line of the Hamelyn Piper's blood.

Quarastus watched in horror. "What, you think you can scare me?" he said. "You expect me to tell you where the amulet is, is that it?"

The Hamelyn Piper said nothing, taking each slow step carefully, watching the flow of black powder from his hands.

"I'll outlive you!" cried Quarastus, wrenching at the manacle chain. "I'll strip the armor from your corpse!"

The Hamelyn Piper stayed silent. At last, ten feet from Quarastus, he stopped and fell. With great effort he sat up and took a fire steel and flint from a small pouch in his belt. With the flint in one hand and the fire steel in the other, he held his hands ready to strike sparks.

"You wouldn't dare," cried Quarastus. "You're *bluffing*. You'd die too—and you'll never find the amulet if you kill me."

The Hamelyn Piper, his breathing difficult, smiled. "I'm not so sure I couldn't," he said. "I came here to make you tell me where the amulet was, yes . . . but the closer I got, the more I *felt* it. This *space* in the armor where the amulet fits, it called out. And I heard a reply!" He looked toward Tiviscan Castle. "You kept it close, all this time."

The sudden shock on the Sorcerer's face gave him away. "I thought so," said the Black Knight, nodding. He started to cough, and when he finished he spat blood onto the grass. "Your knife went deep," he said. "It's time to end this." He raised his hand to strike the fire steel.

"Please, no!" cried Quarastus. "I can save your life if you just free me! I *promise*!"

"Goodbye, teacher," said the Hamelyn Piper. "You taught me well."

The hand came down, the sparks hitting home. The trail of black powder erupted into smoke and flame, working its way back toward the damaged sphere.

Patch felt panic surge through him. He'd thought the same as Quarastus—that the Hamelyn Piper wasn't really going to *do* it and kill them both. He turned to Barver, but Barver was already taking action, grabbing Wren and Patch and slamming them on his back before leaping into the air, flying desperately toward Tiviscan.

Patch turned to look behind them. The burning powder reached the sphere and erupted into a vast plume of smoke and fire, rushing toward them. Barver adjusted his position to put his body between the blast and his passengers just as an even greater explosion came, the entirety of the stockpile going up at once. It struck with such force that Patch couldn't breathe. Smoke engulfed them, and Patch felt himself torn from Barver's back, hurtling onward as he was plunged into darkness.

35

VICTORY?

All Patch knew was that he was *falling* again.

Engulfed in the chaos of noise, smoke, and dust from the explosion, he screamed Barver's and Wren's names as he plummeted, even though the dust choked him.

He was *still* screaming when he had the wind knocked right out of him, and only when they emerged from the dust cloud could he even see who his savior was.

It was Wintel. "Don't talk," the griffin told him as he spluttered and coughed, trying to thank her. She brought him to the top of the Castle's eastern wall, and there were Alia, Tobias, Rundel, and Lord Drevis.

Wintel took off again immediately, flying back out to the devastation.

Alia kneeled beside Patch as he struggled to breathe,

unable to stop coughing. "*Slowly,*" she said. "Breathe slowly. You're safe."

"Wren . . . ," he managed at last. "Barver . . ."

"All the griffins are out there, looking," said Alia. "They took to the air just before the explosion. We'd been watching the Hamelyn Piper but had no idea you were even there until Barver suddenly flew up with both of you on his back."

Patch stood and looked out toward the dragon camp. He could see all five of the griffins, flying close to the dust cloud, and the thought hit him hard: *nobody caught Wren.*

His legs gave way and he slumped down, but only a moment later he saw a small black shape flying toward them and realized nobody had *needed* to catch her. She had become a crow and flown to the Castle herself.

She perched on his shoulder, and together they waited anxiously for news of Barver while watching the rapid retreat of the mercenary army.

"Was this *you?*" Tobias said to them, astonished. "The dragons? The mercenaries?"

Patch nodded. "Team effort," he said. He didn't quite have the breath yet to explain—nor did he *want* to, until their friend was found.

When Barver appeared at last, several minutes after the explosion, he could barely keep in the air. He landed just outside Tiviscan town and seemed to collapse, lying utterly still. Wren and the griffins flew over to him, and by the time Patch got there Wren had taken human form again.

Barver's eyes were closed. Gaverry was holding him, sobbing; he was so much larger than his son, it made Barver seem especially fragile. The other griffins looked at Barver in shock. Stripped of feathers, and his flesh still seeming to smoke, they feared the worst.

Patch reached out and touched Barver's underside, scorched by the explosion. The heat from it was almost painful. "He took the brunt of it," he said, looking to Wren. "We'd both be dead if he hadn't."

"His feathers...," said Merta, horrified.

"He told me to cut them off," said Patch. "So he would look more like a dragon, and we could sneak into their camp and..."

But at that moment Barver opened his eyes. He looked to Wren and then Patch and smiled weakly. "We made it, then," he said. He saw his father's face above him. "I might just lie here for a bit, Dad," he said. "I hurt all over." His eyes closed as he slipped into unconsciousness again.

Gaverry wrapped his great wings around his son, enclosing him completely.

"Let me examine him," said Merta after a moment. Gaverry opened his wings. Patch and Wren stepped back to give Merta space, and soon she told them that Barver had broken no bones and suffered no severe injury that she could find. "We'll nurse him here until he wakes and is ready to move," she said, and Gaverry nodded in silent gratitude.

Patch caught sight of the statue of Erbo Monash, with its trough and hand pump, in the central square of the town. *Water*, he said to himself, thinking of the heat emanating from Barver. He set off at a run, a little unsteady. Spotting a wooden bucket lying abandoned on the roadside, he grabbed it on his way. The hand pump took a dozen strokes before the water gushed out, but the bucket was soon filled and he hurried back.

"Good thinking," Merta told him, dabbing the water carefully on Barver.

Alia and Tobias were there too. "We were watching when Quarastus made his appearance," said Alia. "It was difficult to see exactly what happened, but you were right there . . . Why did the Hamelyn Piper do it? Killing them *both*?"

Patch explained about Quarastus stabbing the Hamelyn Piper, only to find the red manacles clapped around his ankles. "There was so much blood . . . ," he said. "I think the Hamelyn Piper was moments from death."

"He couldn't have his victory," said Wren. "So he wasn't going to let Quarastus win either."

Merta had used all the water he'd brought, so Patch took the bucket and turned to go back to the statue to refill it. For a moment he looked out at the plains of Tiviscan, where the Black Knight's mercenary forces had camped. The mercenaries were fragmented and distant now, fleeing the scene in scrappy clusters. In their panic they'd left behind equipment, weapons, and even some of their horses, and Patch knew that they would always believe they'd encountered the most horrifying monsters in existence—creatures that no description could possibly do justice to—instead of half a dozen slightly ragged oversized chickens.

The thought made him gasp.

"Oh!" he said to Wren. "The cockatrices!"

Wren's eyes widened. They looked out into the plains until they spotted a small group of mercenaries, kneeling motionless about half a mile away—those who'd been closest to a cockatrice as it had started to hunt. There would be five other such groups, Patch knew—one for each of the cockatrices they'd released.

Those unlucky few were still paralyzed, caught in a trap of indescribable terror. Much longer, and their hearts would give out, ready for the cockatrices to feed. But the siege was over—just because they were mercenaries didn't warrant letting them die. "You should take Cramber and Wintel," said Patch. "Go as a crow. If I go with you I'll slow you down."

"I'll grab some sacks," said Wren, and she went to fetch the two young griffins.

"Are you going to explain any of this?" Alia said to Patch. "Wait . . . did you say *cockatrices*?"

Patch smiled, but he realized that it wasn't just Alia and Tobias waiting to hear what he said. More and more people had come out of the Castle, and now he was surrounded by faces eager for his response. "Monsters and onions," he said. Those around him raised confused eyebrows, but they would have to wait. "I'll explain later. Right now I want to get more water for Barver."

"We can get someone else to fetch water, Patch," said Tobias, but Patch shook his head.

"I'd rather do it myself," he said. "If that's okay."

He made four more trips before Alia forced him to rest, and—of course—give the explanations everyone was desperate for. When Wren, Cramber, and Wintel came back, carrying six well-tied sacks, Patch was telling the tale of how their plan had come about.

Everyone listened enrapt as he described the final confrontation between Quarastus and the Hamelyn Piper. They cheered when the tale ended; they cheered even harder when Barver woke again.

Patch and Wren ran to him, and the three hugged. No words were necessary.

As morning became afternoon, clouds stifled the early warmth of the sun, a chill breeze coming across the plains. Underath and Alkeran had been searching in the area around the explosion, looking for what was left of Quarastus and the Hamelyn Piper—Underath not willing to take their demise for granted. When they came back from their search, it had apparently been fruitful, although Alia refused to tell Patch the gruesome details.

The dragons and mercenaries were long gone. Of the Hamelyn Piper's troops, the only ones left were those who'd been captives of the cockatrices and those too injured to flee the waves of terror that had swept through them all. They had been securely locked in the Castle dungeons.

The soldiers and Battle Pipers ventured out into the remnants of the mercenary and dragon camps, hunting the remaining explosive spheres and destroying them from a safe distance. The whole of Tiviscan, it seemed, gathered to witness the spectacle. Food had been brought to the town's outskirts, and fires lit to roast meats and cook flatbreads as the celebrations truly began.

Whenever a cache of spheres was found and prepared for destruction, the sounding of horns gave notice. Then a volley of fire-arrows would trigger the great boom of another explosion.

And even though Patch, Wren, and Barver would jump at every one of the blasts, they cheered and applauded along with everyone else. It was, Patch noted, *far* better to watch that kind of thing from a distance.

There was a particularly large explosion from the farthest end of the mercenary camp, which brought a roar of approval from the crowd. This one had been triggered by Underath, with a pleasing display of colored sparks falling from the air.

"Best one so far," said Wren. She took a bite from the chunk of roast pork she was eating and offered some to Barver. Although he'd recovered enough to get up and move around, he'd not eaten anything yet, and that worried her. "Hungry?"

"Not really," said Barver. "Thirsty, though. I could do with some water."

Patch laughed. "I can handle that," he said. He picked up the empty bucket and set off for the town square again. With the celebrations in full flow, the town itself was deserted. Patch saw a solitary figure slowly crossing the Castle courtyard, wearing a hooded coat that would surely become far too warm once the cloud cover broke and the sun came out again.

As he filled the bucket and started to make his way back, Patch let himself dream about what the future held. His training in Healing Songs could begin soon, he hoped, once he'd found someone to take over as Guardian of Massarken. He would offer it to Wren first; he reckoned she would think Alia was the better choice, but she deserved first dibs.

He spotted Wren and Barver and gave them a wave, but they didn't see him and were still too far away to hear him above the bustle of the crowd, even if he shouted.

And then a curious thing happened. The noise of the crowd fell away, though he could see everyone still talking. He stopped and set down his full bucket and gave his ears a tug. They *had* been ringing, he realized, ever since the huge explosion, so it had presumably affected his hearing. He snapped his fingers, but was surprised that he could hear it perfectly.

Frowning, he picked up his bucket and started walking again. Wren and Barver, he saw, were definitely looking toward him. He waved, but they didn't wave back.

"What *is* going on?" he muttered. Then he walked into something *hard* and stumbled backward, clutching his stinging nose.

For a moment he thought there was nothing there, but then he saw a slight shimmer. He reached out a hand and found it, hard and unyielding—some kind of *barrier*. Ahead, Alia, Tobias, and Lord Drevis were rushing toward him, Wren and Barver close behind. A line of Pipers and soldiers was gesturing to the rest of the crowd, keeping them back.

Wren was mouthing something, but he couldn't hear; she used Merisax instead. *Behind you*, she signed. She was staring past Patch, and so were the others. Patch turned slowly. He could see the extent of the barrier, creating a dome a few hundred feet across that seemed to be centered on the statue of Erbo Monash. By the statue stood the person he'd seen before, in the hooded coat. The figure was behaving strangely, scooping water out of the trough and running a hand over the ornate stonework.

Patch's blood went cold. The hood of the coat had been lowered, and Patch could see the man's face. It was a face he knew, but he could also see the slight glint of shining *black* around the base of the man's neck.

The armor of the Hamelyn Piper himself.

36
Not Quite Dead

"How?" said Patch. He looked to the worried faces on the other side of the barrier. "*How?*"

Stay right where you are, Wren signed with Merisax, but Patch found himself walking toward the figure, bewildered and enraged. He stopped as he drew near, setting down the bucket that had still been in his grasp.

The Hamelyn Piper stepped back from the statue and removed his coat, revealing his armor in full. Only then did he sense Patch's presence—he turned around suddenly, ready to defend himself. When he saw Patch, though, any urgency vanished. Although they'd faced each other once before, Patch had been wearing the Iron Mask then; as far as the Hamelyn Piper was concerned, he was just another boy.

The Black Knight dismissively turned back to the statue. "You *died*," said Patch. "You were caught in the middle of that explosion . . ."

"Yet here I am," said the Hamelyn Piper. He looked weak, his face glistening in sweat, a smear of blood across one cheek. He started to rap his knuckles on the base of the statue.

Patch knew he had to do *something*. He slowly took his Pipe from his coat, but it hadn't even reached his lips by the time the Hamelyn Piper turned around again.

"I wouldn't do that if I were you," said the Black Knight with a cold smile. "You Tiviscan trainees, such empty-headed courage! I'm inclined to kill you where you stand."

"Is that the kind of ruler you plan to be?" said Patch.

The Hamelyn Piper's smile faded. "Cast your Pipe aside, and you'll not be harmed."

Patch didn't move, staring back defiantly. The Hamelyn Piper began to whistle, building a Battle Song. "Okay, okay!" said Patch. He threw his Pipe to the side, but the Hamelyn Piper released the Song anyway. Patch flinched, his hands coming up to protect himself, but the Song was well aimed—it struck his discarded Pipe, shattering it and sending the pieces flying.

"Don't test me, lad," said the Hamelyn Piper. He took several steps away from the statue, and Patch could see how slow and delicate his movement was. The man was clearly in pain, and he swayed slightly in a manner that suggested he could collapse at any moment.

"You *are* dying," said Patch.

"I am," said the Hamelyn Piper, angst written on his face. "The magic of the armor protects me well, but it has its limits. It excels at defending against a direct, forceful assault, like the explosion—even Quarastus hadn't fully understood its capabilities. The knife's blade, however, went slow and deep. Without a miracle, I'll be dead within the hour." The angst fell away, all an act; he grinned. "But I know a miracle is coming. Just as I knew I'd survive the explosion."

He started to whistle again and built another Battle Song. When it was ready, he launched it at the statue, destroying it. "I wonder how long that's been here," he said. "Centuries, do you think?" He walked over to the plinth, rummaging among fragments of stone before pulling his hand back. He held a folded piece of cloth. "Behold!" he said. "The miracle!" He peeled back the cloth and took out what was inside—a jewel the size of his palm, a golden gem roughly carved, held within a silver rune-inscribed ring with eight metal spurs radiating out like the points of a compass.

It was the same shape as the hollow in the chest of his armor.

"*Vivificantem*," said Patch. "The Life-Giver."

The Hamelyn Piper looked at him in surprise. "You know its name?"

"I know all about the armor," said Patch. "And the amulet that completes it. And I know you're just another tyrant—arrogant, cruel, and greedy."

The Hamelyn Piper sneered, then placed the amulet in his armor. There was a solid *click* as he pushed it home. "And *immortal*," he said. "You neglected to mention that."

The amulet glowed softly at first, then brightened. Tendrils of that golden light began to spread from his chest. Glowing lines moved along the armor, swirls of dense pattern making their slow way outwards. Even so, his breathing was still ragged and his movements cautious.

"You're not immortal *yet*," said Patch.

The Hamelyn Piper gave an appreciative nod. "Observant, aren't you?" he said. "The amulet's power must saturate the armor. When it reaches my fingertips, I cannot be killed." He pointed to the crowd beyond the barrier and laughed. "Look at them!"

Patch looked. Alia was sending a stream of purple light toward the barrier, joined by Underath, his magic green. The two magical flows joined in one place high on the barrier's surface, forming a bright region ten feet across.

"The Sorcerer there . . . ," said the Black Knight. "Two of them, indeed. They try to create a point of weakness—but even if they succeed, anyone passing through it will be left incapacitated, unable to put up any kind of fight." He grinned. "Even if they forced an *army* inside, it would be as useless as an army of *mannequins*."

Patch began to sign to his friends, warning them, although surely Alia—an expert in Shielding Songs and barriers—already knew.

It was Wren who replied.

We're coming, she signed. *Distract him.*

Patch thought quickly and moved closer to the Hamelyn Piper. "You held my friend prisoner," he said. "The girl who stole the piece of your armor. You told her you'd foreseen your victory in a *dream*."

"A friend of yours, eh?" said the Hamelyn Piper. "She spoke the truth. I have always been blessed with such dreams, and I saw this very moment—wearing an armor of obsidiac, the power of *Vivificantem* coursing through me. As you see, the dream came true, as I knew it would. And so I knew I couldn't be killed."

Patch saw that the griffins were flying in a tight circle high above the dome of the barrier. "There was something you wouldn't tell her," he said.

"Go on," said the Black Knight.

"She asked why Hamelyn was chosen to suffer."

The Hamelyn Piper laughed and nodded. "Another prophetic dream," he said. "It showed me the children of Hamelyn. A voice came, saying: 'Watch them as they run and play. One of them is all that can defeat you. Without him, your victory is certain.' The moment I woke, I knew what I would do—get rid of the children of Hamelyn so that nothing could stop me. And so Hamelyn was chosen, and I began at last to enact the *story* I'd prepared—a tale that would capture the imagination of all who heard it, and thus spread throughout the world." He looked at the armor's glowing lines as they crept along his arms. "And those dreams have served me well. My victory is here at last, as they foretold."

"But one of the children of Hamelyn lived," said Patch. "A lame boy, who couldn't keep up with the others."

"The child who survived was no threat to me," said the Hamelyn Piper.

"You think being lame makes someone harmless?" scoffed Patch.

The Hamelyn Piper laughed. "I'm not a fool," he said. "There are plenty of fighters among my mercenaries who kill just as effectively as their colleagues, even though they lack an arm, a leg, an eye. There was another reason I knew the child was not the one. You think me a monster, and I admit I felt the urge to have the child killed all the same, but I resisted."

"How *noble* of you," said Patch.

The Hamelyn Piper laughed at Patch's sarcasm. "Watch your mouth, boy. Killing *you* becomes more tempting with every word you utter. I paid well to have the town watched in case other children had been missed. But there were no others."

Above them, the griffins flew faster; the bright glow of Alia and Underath's magic was almost blinding to look at.

"Someone told me about prophecies once," said Patch. "Dangerous things. Tend to cause endless trouble. I learned firsthand that they're never as simple as they sound."

The Hamelyn Piper scowled. "What are you saying, boy?"

"How can you be so foolish?"

The scowl became a glare. "You'll regret speaking to me like that."

The glare was intimidating, and Patch's mouth felt utterly dry, but he kept going. *Distract him*, Wren had said, and that was exactly what he would do. "Are you sure that the dream meant the *children*? Perhaps a parent was there too, unnoticed by you as they played with them? Maybe a fletcher, who fashioned the arrow that'll pierce your eye an instant before your immortality comes?"

There was, for the briefest of moments, a look of concern on the Hamelyn Piper's face. "I know the meaning of my own dreams, boy!" he said.

Patch realized that the man had never even *considered* another interpretation. "There can be any number of ways," he said. "For all you know, the wood for this *bucket* might have been cut down near Hamelyn by someone you didn't notice in the dream."

"So kill me with the bucket, then," sneered the Black Knight. "But you'd better hurry, because the time is almost here." He raised his arms, showing off the patterns of golden light now at his wrists. Movement from above caught his eye, and Patch looked too. Beyond the circling griffins, a shape was plunging toward them.

The Hamelyn Piper was unfazed. "Interesting," he said. "They think breaking through at speed might work."

A moment later, the shape collided with the barrier, precisely where the bright magic of Alia and Underath was focused. The shape almost stopped, as if it had hit molasses—but slowly, slowly, the glowing part of the barrier bulged down around it like molten glass.

"Painful!" said the Hamelyn Piper as sparks fell from the bulge. "It's almost hard to watch."

The bulge stretched more and more, until with a wrenching sound it finally gave way. The shape broke through the barrier—the hole behind it sealing at once—and landed thirty feet from them.

Patch looked in horror at the unmoving shape of Gaverry, curled into a smoldering ball, his wings wrapped unnaturally around his front.

Sparks still fell from the barrier above, and when they landed on Gaverry his feathers were visibly scorched.

The Hamelyn Piper shook his head and turned to Patch. The golden pattern was at the base of his fingers now. "I will be your king," he said. "For all time."

Behind him, Gaverry opened his wings, and from within stood Barver, his face filled with rage. He opened his mouth and for an instant Patch wondered what he would say.

But there was only fire.

There was terror on the face of the Hamelyn Piper, but as the fire kept coming the terror fell away. The obsidiac armor took on an orange glow, but Patch could see that the man's *skin* was glowing too, a deep and dreadful red as a wide grin spread across his inhuman face. After thirty seconds of the most brutal heat Barver could summon, his flame was depleted. The dracogriff looked despairingly at Patch.

The Hamelyn Piper raised his hand, and the pattern was visible as white lines over the orange glow of the armor. It was only halfway along the fingers, but it had been enough to protect him.

He began to laugh. The laughter deepened and became thunderous as his expression grew wilder, his eyes frenzied. The sound was overwhelming, a crushing mixture of malevolence and triumph.

Despairing, Patch backed away, his foot knocking against the bucket of water; suddenly he remembered the lesson Lord Winkless gave the trainee Pipers every year, heating pieces of glass and crystal to demonstrate how they were flaked for use in Pipe glazing.

It was all he had left. Patch took up the bucket and flung the water out toward the Hamelyn Piper.

Steam flashed. Like hot glass dropped into cold water, the armor shattered explosively.

37

A Final Breath

Barver flinched as shards of obsidiac peppered him. Most bounced off his tough hide, but some pierced the skin of his wings.

The Hamelyn Piper, screaming, crumpled to the ground. Barver moved closer. Little of the obsidiac armor was still intact, leaving behind the heat-twisted metal framework that wrapped around him like a cage. The moment the armor's protection had disappeared, the accumulated power of Barver's fire had taken a horrific toll—the man's flesh was charred beyond recognition.

Yet he was still alive. His eyes were wide with pain and rage as his screams continued.

Barver looked down at him and felt a pity he'd not expected. The screams began to subside.

The Hamelyn Piper's eyes met his. "My dream...," said the evil Piper. "*My dream...*"

And with one final tremor passing through his body, the Hamelyn Piper was no more.

Above, the air rippled as the barrier started to dissipate, its creator dead.

Barver looked to Patch, who stood fifteen feet away, his hands gripping the top of the bucket, holding it in front of him—an instinctive action, to shield himself.

Long black shards of obsidiac were impaled in the bucket's base: *dozens* of them.

Patch met his eyes and smiled, and Barver had only the briefest moment to think how badly those shards would have hurt his friend if the wood of the bucket hadn't stopped them, before the realization came. His face had been protected, yes. But what of the rest?

As Patch's arms came down and the bucket fell from his grasp, Barver could already see the myriad black marks that dotted Patch's clothing, marks that *spread* as blood began to soak through the material—first on his legs, then his chest. Every part of him, it seemed, was bleeding. Patch looked at his friend, and his eyes filled with fear.

"Barver...," he said as he began to fall.

Barver was with him in an instant. He caught him and laid him on the ground, cradling his head. "Help us!" he cried to the others, who were rushing toward them now that the barrier had gone. "*Help us.*"

Alia and Wren reached them first. Wren gasped in horror and kneeled at Patch's side, taking his hand. Patch's breathing was shallow and rapid. He locked eyes with Wren and then with Barver; his mouth opened and closed, his lip trembling.

"*Hold on*, Patch," said Wren. She stared at the black shards that had pierced him and the sheer amount of blood pouring from his wounds. She looked to Alia. "Please...," she said, but there was no hope in Alia's eyes, only powerlessness.

She looked to Tobias, and Tobias gave the slightest shake of his head, his face gray, his eyes wet.

Wren turned to Underath then, the Sorcerer who had survived having his heart torn from his chest, but Underath couldn't even meet her gaze.

"*Please*...," said Wren again.

Barver moaned in despair, tears streaming down his face. "Can nothing be done?" he cried. "*Can nothing be done?* The helsterhogs! Fetch a helsterhog, and—"

Rundel Stone placed a hand on his shoulder. "Barver...," he said. There were tears running down *his* face too. The Cold Heart of Justice was crying. Beside him, Erner watched in anguish.

And Barver could feel the truth hitting home, as could

Wren. Patch's injuries were so severe that nothing *could* be done. Nothing except to comfort their dying friend.

Patch tensed for a moment, and then his body went limp. His eyes closed as his breathing weakened, and his head fell to one side.

He was slipping away.

Barver wanted to roar, to take to the skies and rage at whatever God or Gods he could blame for such an atrocity. But seeing Wren's distraught face, he put his arm around her. They held each other, trembling with grief.

"Step aside," came a voice. "*Step aside!*"

Barver and Wren looked up as the gathered crowd parted and revealed a disheveled griffin, shuffling forward with blackened feathers. It was Barver's father.

Gaverry put his hand on Barver's shoulder.

"Dad . . . ," said Barver. "I . . ." He stopped, unable to speak.

"My son," said Gaverry, moving his hand to Barver's cheek, wiping a tear. "There is one way."

38
ONE LAST HOPE

"Do you think it could work?" whispered Wren as they watched the three griffins argue.

"I just don't know...," said Barver. Earlier, when Alia had explained her plan to break through the Hamelyn Piper's barrier—with Barver wrapped in his father's wings—she'd sounded completely confident, even though she admitted the chances of it working were remote. Yet Barver hadn't doubted her for a second.

Now his father sounded just as confident, but Barver was *filled* with doubt.

They had cleared the area around Patch while Tobias played the Song of Last Hope, the most difficult of all Healing Songs. It was a Song that slowed down all processes in the body of the subject to the point that the heart hardly beat and almost no breaths were taken—a form of hibernation, almost.

All it could do was buy some time in cases where other methods of healing might help.

There is one way, his father had said, but when Gaverry had explained what he meant, Barver had expected the other senior griffins—Alkeran and Merta—to dismiss it out of hand. Gaverry had lived in isolation for so long, and when Barver had talked with him on Massarken his thoughts had often been so *confused* . . . Barver assumed this was just another delusion.

But they hadn't dismissed it. Instead, they set Tobias to work while the three of them stepped away and spoke in private, their words often heated.

Gaverry's idea was to use the same ancient magic that had bonded Alkeran and Underath—a *pairing*, something that was only possible between griffin and human. That was how Underath had lived, even with his heart removed; it was how Alkeran had survived being submerged until he was dredged up from the sea by fishing nets.

Gaverry had volunteered to be the one who would attempt to pair with Patch. The question the griffins now argued over was simple:

Given Patch's condition, was it too late?

At last they returned to the group that remained by Patch's deathly still form.

"We've discussed Gaverry's proposal," Merta told them. "We think it can work, but the danger is great." She gestured for Gaverry to continue.

"A pairing between human and griffin is a mysterious form of magic," he said. "At its core is one requirement—both must be ready to give up their life so the other can live. Without that, the pairing will fail. If it fails, death for both is the result. That is why it's so rarely attempted."

"But Patch is so close to death," said Barver, his voice catching as he said it. "He's not even conscious. How can it possibly work?"

"We can't be certain it will," said Gaverry. "We don't know if it's ever been done this way before, but that is the risk we take."

"Then it should be *me* taking that risk, not you," said Barver.

"A pairing can only happen between a human and a griffin," said Gaverry. "That is simply how things are." He took his son's hands. "Your friend deserves life," he said. "And I believe I can save him. I know you would take my place if you could, Barver, but let me do this. All the years I was chained on that island, I only ever hoped for a chance to show how much you mean to me."

"You could die," said Barver.

"I'm prepared to give up my life for your friend," said Gaverry. "As long as your friend would do the same, then the pairing can work. *Would* he do the same? Would he give up his own life to save the life of someone he hardly knows—just because I'm your father?"

Barver looked at Patch's still form and then turned to Wren. She gave him a fragile smile, and he smiled back. "Absolutely," said Barver.

"Then there's no reason to fear," said Gaverry.

Alkeran knew the Ritual of Pairing better than any of them, having researched it in detail to bond him and Underath, and so he took charge of the preparations.

Underath and Alia were sent to gather various branches from the forest and began to weave them in the style of a simple shelter while Gaverry lay down, his head beside Patch's.

"Those are branches of what griffins call The Four Watchers," said Alkeran. "Rowan, elder, hawthorn, and hazel. The cage they're building must fit over the human and griffin being paired."

Barver looked at Patch, his heart in agony. The Song of Last Hope meant that Patch's body had the stillness of death. The black shards of obsidiac that pierced him from his chest to his legs hadn't been removed, Tobias insisting that the risk to Patch was too great unless the pairing was a success. Barver found it unbearable to see.

When the cage was ready, Alkeran lit a bundle of herbs on the ground between Patch and Gaverry, then set the cage over them. He kneeled, placing one hand on Gaverry's head and the other on Patch's. He chanted under his breath as the smoke filled the cage and seeped through the tightly woven branches.

Time passed. Two minutes. Ten.

The cage was removed, and Barver gasped. "He's stopped breathing," he cried, pointing at his father. He went to go to him, but Alkeran and Merta held him back.

"Barver, wait!" said Alkeran. "You *must* wait. This is expected—his body takes the rhythm of Patch's."

In turmoil, Barver stayed where he was and watched. After what felt like an eternity, his father's chest rose again, almost too slowly to see.

And at the same time, something astonishing happened: the black obsidiac shards that protruded so hideously from Patch's flesh suddenly fell away, dropping to the grass.

Underath picked up one of the shards and pulled at a hole in Patch's trousers where the obsidiac had pierced him. The skin was uninjured now. Underath held the shard up and looked at it, and Barver could see that the shard hadn't simply been pushed out of Patch's flesh as he'd first assumed. Instead, one end was flat and smooth, as if the portion that had impaled him had simply melted away.

"Fascinating," said Underath, enthralled.

Alia tore open Patch's tunic, revealing his torso—which was now entirely unharmed. She picked up another of the obsidiac shards, and it too was flat along one end. She frowned, then shared a look with Underath. "You don't think . . . ," Alia began, but then Wren shrieked and pointed.

"He's breathing," she said, tears pouring. "Patch is *breathing.*"

39

THE DISPERSAL

It took a week before Patch and Gaverry regained consciousness.

They'd been moved into the Castle and kept together in a small hall on the western side that had been turned into an improvised infirmary.

Wren and Barver spent most of their time there, watching the two patients as they made slow progress, but the signs were all positive. There was gradual but reliable improvement day after day.

At last Barver's father woke, and Barver spent the long night talking to him. Then, while Wren ate breakfast in the refectory, Alia came to tell her that Patch had woken too. "He asked for you and Barver," said Alia. "When he saw Barver asleep next to him, he told me to let him rest and fetch you quietly."

Wren hurried over, and there was Barver snoring away beside his sleeping father.

Patch was sitting up in his makeshift bed. Wren sat and gave him a long hug.

"You look rested," she said. "I feared you'd be plagued with nightmares."

"Only good dreams, thankfully," said Patch. "Most of all, I dreamed of my mother smiling down at me. It's my only memory of her, and I always feel happy when I wake with that in my head."

They spoke of simple things for a while before the conversation turned to the Hamelyn Piper and Patch's own brush with death.

"Alia told me what Gaverry did," said Patch. "It's a lot to take in. Is Barver okay?"

"He is," said Wren. "It's certainly not a day we'll ever forget!"

"The Black Knight is really dead," said Patch. "I still can't quite believe it. The Hamelyn Piper, gone forever. And Quarastus. At least, I *hope* Quarastus is dead . . ."

"He is," said Wren. "Underath found the manacles, with, um, *contents*. He and Alia had ways to be certain it was really Quarastus, although Alia won't tell me the details."

"A world without the Hamelyn Piper!" said Patch. "Has the news reached beyond Tiviscan? Do people know?"

"Of course!" said Wren. "I think the celebrations will last

weeks. You talked with him, though . . . just before Gaverry and Barver broke through the barrier. We couldn't hear any of it. What did he say?"

Patch thought for a moment and frowned. "I'm hazy on what happened," he said. "I think I just tried to keep him talking and distract him like you asked. I can't quite remember."

"It's to be expected," said Wren. "You've only just woken. Your memories will come back soon."

Patch nodded, but then he had a glint in his eye. "I *did* ask him about the dream he told you about," said Patch. "Where he'd seen his future. He talked about the one thing capable of stopping him . . . and about why he chose Hamelyn."

"And?" said Wren, desperate to hear what it was. "Did he tell you?"

"Yes," he said. "He dreamed of the children of Hamelyn, and the dream told him that one of them was all that could defeat him. That was why he chose the town. A child of Hamelyn was the only thing in his way, so he decided they all had to go."

Wren scowled. "A whole town loses its children because of prophetic dreams. It's sickening."

"I told him it could mean anything," said Patch. "A parent he'd not noticed in the dream, who crafted an arrow that would kill him, or cut down the wood that made the bucket at my feet, or . . ." His eyes widened. "The bucket? That would be madness. It can't have been . . . Can it?"

"No," said Wren. "I'm sure we could make *anything* seem to fit if we tried hard enough. Patch, sometimes dreams are just dreams." But then a sudden thought struck her. "You grew up in Praze-by-Desten, didn't you?"

"With my grandparents, yes," said Patch. "From when I was two."

"And before that?"

"My parents had always lived nearby, before they died," said Patch. "When I went to Tiviscan it was the first time I'd even left the area." He gave her a strange look. "Why are you asking?"

"Just . . . something occurred to me. I wondered if . . ."

Patch smiled sadly. "I'm not a child of Hamelyn, Wren. Like you said, sometimes dreams are just dreams."

After Wren left him, the thought of the dream nagged at her. Patch's first suggestion of the bucket was nonsense, yes, but she couldn't leave it at that. There was so much in the Hamelyn Piper's dreams that *had* come true. He'd seen himself wearing the armor, with the amulet . . .

It had to mean something, she thought.

She sought out Rundel Stone. Her suspicions were vague,

but she had a very specific question for him. She spotted him crossing the courtyard and ran over.

"Virtus Stone!" she said.

"Wren!" said Rundel. "How can I help you?"

"The rats of Patterfall," she said. "Something always puzzled me about the way you got rid of them."

"The Song of Dispersal?" said Rundel.

"That was the same Song the Hamelyn Piper used against the children."

Rundel's expression saddened at once. "Yes," he said.

"Why did you use it in Patterfall?" said Wren. "I know you made a promise to the people of Hamelyn to bring back their children. Then you found out they'd been killed using the Dispersal, not kidnapped." There was real pain on his face, and Wren felt guilty asking him about it. But she had to. "Using the Dispersal against the rats . . . didn't it bring all those bad memories back? Why not use a different Song?"

Rundel nodded slowly. "The Dispersal is a Song of Execution," he said. "The very thought of it struck fear into people—the prisoner's body is reduced to its smallest components, scattered across a thousand miles."

"That's horrible," said Wren.

"But is it?" said Rundel. "Compared to any other form of execution? You see, the Song of Dispersal is instantaneous. There's no pain, Wren. Before Patterfall, I'd used it several times—once to put down an injured fox I found in the forests near Juniper Point. Painless and quick."

"So with the rats, you saw it as a mercy?"

"Not only that," said Rundel. "You wonder why I would use a Song that reminded me of the children of Hamelyn? I used it precisely *because* it reminded me. My promise to bring them home could never be fulfilled, but even so . . . I swore I would never forget them." He gave her an appraising look. "Why do you ask, Wren? Something's on your mind."

"I knew the rats of Patterfall well," she said. "I was one of them, after all—their leader! But I led them to destruction, and the guilt has stayed with me. Sometimes I would see a rat and I would think I *recognized* it—a ghost of a rat from Patterfall. This happened when we went to save Erner from the Pirate King. It happened again in the sewers of Skamos."

"Guilt is a powerful thing, Wren," he said. "You saw rats similar to those you knew, and guilt did the rest."

"I'm not so sure," said Wren. "What if I truly did see them? You said the Dispersal reduces things to their smallest components and scatters them across a thousand miles. But for a pack of rats, might the smallest components be *the rats themselves*? And if I really *did* see rats from Patterfall, I started to wonder if . . ." She stopped, unable to speak the impossible thought she'd had.

But when Rundel Stone's eyes widened, she knew the same impossible thought had just occurred to him.

With Patch and Gaverry recovered, Wintel and Cramber decided it was time to set off for home. Underath and Alkeran too bade them all farewell and headed back to their own castle.

Merta stayed to help Gaverry get used to being free after his long imprisonment. They ventured out on a trip, supposedly to get away from the bustle of Tiviscan for a few days, and from the noise of the ongoing repair work to the Castle walls and Keep.

Wren, however, knew the truth about where they'd gone. Three days later she knocked on Patch's door. Like her, he'd been given an unoccupied room in the Pipers' Quarters.

"Hi," said Patch when he opened the door. "I was going to the refectory to get something to eat. Are you hungry?"

"Actually, we wanted to have a word," said Wren.

"We?" said Patch. He leaned through the doorway to see Rundel, Erner, Alia, and Tobias in the narrow corridor. "What's up?"

"I was doing a bit of investigating," said Wren. She told him her idea, that the "ghost" rats she'd seen hadn't been ghosts at all, and what that might mean for the Song of Dispersal.

"You think the rats weren't killed?" said Patch. "They just . . . ended up far away?"

"Not exactly," said Wren. "Alia's been looking into it."

"Yes, with the help of Lord Winkless," said Alia. "The Song breaks the target down into its smallest components. That's how it works—in theory, little more than specks of dust remain, spread over a thousand miles. Lord Winkless studied the Song carefully and believes it would mostly work as expected, even on a pack of rats."

"Mostly?" said Patch.

"Of a few thousand rats, several dozen could survive," said Alia. "Finding themselves very far from where they started, but unharmed."

"Interesting," said Patch. "But . . ." He looked at them all and frowned. "What aren't you telling me?"

Alia nodded to Rundel, who turned and shouted up the corridor: "You can send them through now!"

"Send who through?" said Patch, bewildered.

"Merta and Gaverry's trip wasn't just to get away for a while," Wren told him. "They'd gone to Praze-by-Desten, to your grandparents. Rundel went with them."

"Home?" said Patch. "Does that mean . . . ?" He grinned and stepped out into the corridor. There, he saw them approaching—it was the first time he'd laid eyes on them in almost two years. He ran and hugged them both until they winced. "I've got so much to tell you!" he said. Then he saw the anxious looks on their faces. "What is it?"

"Don't be angry with us," said his grandmother. They both glanced at Rundel, as if for confirmation.

"You have to tell him," said Rundel.

His grandparents nodded.

"We love you, Patch," said his grandfather. "We always have, and we always will."

His grandmother took a deep breath before she spoke again. "It was a month after our daughter and her husband died in a landslide in Southern Praze," she started, and Patch noted that it was a very strange way for them to talk about his mum and dad. "We found a little boy, wandering lost in the forest near our home. Two years old, we reckoned. We went to the village constables, and they tried to find out who your parents were, but . . ."

"*My* parents?" said Patch. "I . . . I was the boy?"

"Nobody knew where you'd come from," said his grandfather. "Or whose child you were. You didn't talk, not for a long time. And even then you didn't seem to remember what had happened."

"No . . . ," said Patch.

"We didn't tell you any of this," said his grandmother. "We didn't see any need to upset you, but now . . ."

"Now?" said Patch, getting angry. "*Now?* What are you talking about?"

Then Wren was beside him, taking his hand. "You were found the morning after the children of Hamelyn vanished, Patch," she said. "Don't you see? One hundred and thirty children fell victim to the Song of Dispersal. But not all of them became dust."

He shook his head, tears in his eyes. "I don't understand..."

He felt panic rising within him, the walls of the corridor closing in. He pulled his hand from Wren's and walked away from his grandparents, pushing past Alia and Tobias.

Rundel caught him by the arm and crouched, looking at him eye to eye. "Patch Brightwater!" he said, the sternness in his voice startling Patch out of his panic. But then Rundel's tone changed, to gentle sympathy. "The Hamelyn Piper's dream was *true*," he said. "He dreamed that a child of Hamelyn would stop him. There was no trick to it. The child of Hamelyn was you all along."

40

In Hamelyn Town

As Rundel Stone walked along the streets of Hamelyn, Patch could see the respect the citizens had for the Virtus Piper. Yet there was also sorrow when they looked at him.

Merta and Barver had brought them here. For Barver's father, the flight to Praze-by-Desten had been more than enough to exhaust him. While it would still be months before Barver's feathers had regrown, he'd found that his flying wasn't as badly impacted as he'd feared, as long as he stayed at a reasonable altitude.

Barver carried Patch, Wren, and Erner, while Patch's grandparents rode on Merta with Rundel. Merta opted to remain outside the town walls, not wanting to intrude on what she considered a very personal matter, and Barver decided to stay with her.

"There's no need," said Patch. "I'd rather you were with me."

But Barver had insisted. "I'll see you soon enough," he'd said. "I'd be too much of a distraction."

Some of the citizens nodded to Rundel, and he nodded back, but none approached him. "I try to come here every year or two," he said. "The people know me well enough, and they leave me to mourn in my own way." He turned to Patch. "Do you have any sense of recognition?"

"None," said Patch. He still only half-believed any of this. "When the tale of the Hamelyn Piper is told, there's always mention of a lame boy," said Rundel. "A boy who survived because he couldn't keep up with the other children. But some parts of the tale weren't quite true. To protect those whose lives were torn apart, we changed some details." Far ahead on the street, a fair-haired woman stood outside a flower seller's shop, arranging bunches of tulips on a small display cart. Rundel smiled when he saw her and continued with his tale. "The child who survived was actually a girl, eleven years old. She was not lame. She fell as the children danced toward Koppen Hill. Her leg broken, she tried to dance on, but soon she couldn't go any farther."

The woman didn't see them approach, but when Patch saw her face he thought of his mother, and the dreams of her that he'd had for as long as he could remember. She certainly wasn't old enough to be his mother, though—she was only twenty or so.

"Enneleyn?" called Rundel as they neared.

For some reason, the name struck Patch as familiar. She looked at Rundel quizzically, and then she looked at Patch. Her eyes went back to Rundel, then to Patch once more, and suddenly she gasped and dropped the flowers she was holding. Her hands flew to her mouth in shock. Her eyes filled with tears, and so did Patch's—because he finally knew. He finally understood.

All that time, it had not been his mother he'd dreamed of. As Enneleyn embraced Patch, Rundel lowered his voice and spoke to the rest of them. "Forever after, that poor girl was devastated with guilt. You see, she'd danced with her little brother—just under two years old and very precious to her. Her brother was taken by the Hamelyn Piper, and she'd not been able to protect him."

Wren looked at Enneleyn and Patch, both sobbing as they held each other. She could barely see them really, her own eyes brimming with tears.

"I promised her," said Rundel Stone. "I promised I would do everything I could to bring her brother home." His voice was breaking with emotion.

Along the street, the citizens saw what happened, and they knew that Rundel Stone had finally kept that promise.

A child of Hamelyn had returned.

Barver, Wren, and Erner sat with Patch by the River Weser, enjoying the evening sunshine as they watched ducks paddle near the bank.

Patch was thoroughly exhausted. It had been a very long day, and an emotional one. He'd met his sister . . . and his parents, and had been terrified that they wouldn't like him or that he wouldn't like them. He found it very strange to be called by the name he'd been born with—*Jakob*—although his sister Enneleyn tended to call him *Patch* to put him at ease. He would get used to it, he thought, whichever they settled on.

His grandparents had been just as anxious—afraid that now he had his "real" family, he would decide he no longer needed them. In the end, they'd laughed together and talked of the littlest things and the biggest, and all their fears proved groundless.

But Patch found he needed time away from them to begin to process all that had happened. So he'd sought out Wren, Barver, and Erner, and they'd headed beyond the town walls to the riverside.

"Do you think there could be others?" said Wren. They had some bread, and she threw crumbs to the eager ducks. "Other children who survived the Dispersal?"

"It's possible," said Erner. "Rundel plans to search for

children who mysteriously appeared on that day, too young to talk or maybe with their memories gone. He seemed quite hopeful about the prospect."

"It feels so strange that we can be hopeful again," said Wren. "The Hamelyn Piper is gone. We can finally look to the future and not be afraid."

"And what does the future hold for you, Wren?" said Barver. "Will you become Alia's apprentice soon?"

"Not right away," smiled Wren. "Alia's considering whether to become the permanent Guardian of Massarken."

She nodded to Patch and smiled; he'd made his offer before they'd left for Hamelyn, and as he'd expected Wren had declined. *Visiting* the island sounded exciting to her, but actually taking responsibility for it had far less appeal. "In the meantime, she wants me to start my training with her in Gemspar as soon as I can. I'll be going home to see my parents for a while first, though." She stretched out on the grass, enjoying the sun. "And maybe I'll find some new shapes to change into . . . What about you, Barver?"

"Dad plans on doing some traveling," said Barver. "I'll go with him and keep him safe. I also want to visit my little cousin Kerna." Barver had received a letter from his aunt and uncle, who were trying to establish a new home for the refugees from Skamos—both dragon and human—on one of the uninhabited Islands of the Eastern Sea. "I look forward to telling them all about Kasterkan's humiliation.

The thought of him setting that catapult on fire will always make me smile!"

"Has there been any news from the Dragon Territories?" asked Patch.

"Just rumors," said Barver. "Support for Kasterkan has plummeted now that everyone thinks he made the Gods angry, so there's a chance the Dragon Triumvirate might return to power. Maybe *everything* Kasterkan did will be reconsidered and they'll rebuild Skamos just as it was, for humans and dragons to share. Although that's probably just wishful thinking..."

"I think we're all allowed a bit of that, Barver," said Wren. "And what are your plans, Erner?"

"Virtus Stone is going to end my apprenticeship when we return to Tiviscan," said Erner. Barver looked outraged, but Erner smiled. "That means I'm being promoted," he said. "To a full Custodian Piper—an apprentice no more! And you, Patch? I suppose you'll be going back to your training at Tiviscan?"

But Patch's answer shocked them all.

"No," he said self-consciously. "You see...well, I can't Pipe anymore."

They stared at him. "*What?*" said Barver.

"I've lost my gift," said Patch. "The moment I woke up beside Gaverry, I could feel something was wrong—I just *knew* it. Alia said it sometimes happens that way—trauma can make a Piper lose their gift. And almost dying certainly counts as trauma..."

"Why didn't you say anything?" said Erner.

"It didn't seem all that important at the time," he said. "Not compared to everything else. Now I don't know what to feel."

"Surely it'll return?" said Wren, distraught.

"Apparently not," he said. "When it's gone, it's gone—like a Sorcerer losing their magic. Alia was stunned when I told her. She fetched Rundel, and they made me try to play all kinds of Songs. I could remember everything I've ever learned, but the notes I play on a Pipe are just notes now. There's no magic at all."

"What are you going to do?" said Barver.

"You can still be Guardian of Massarken, if you want," said Wren.

Patch gave a deep, sorrowful sigh. "We both know that Alia's the best choice for that, Wren," he said. "I thought back to the days after I ran away from Tiviscan and joined traveling bands. It wasn't such a bad life. Maybe I could become a musician. At least that way I'll still have music around me—I don't think I could bear it if I didn't." He took a Pipe from his pocket and put his fingers to the holes, exercising them.

"Wait," said Erner. "Isn't that Rundel's Pipe?"

Patch nodded. "He wanted me to have it as a keepsake," he said. "He's going to design a new Pipe for himself, one that he can play more easily with his weakened right hand." He frowned. "It was so *strange* the way Alia and Rundel kept making me try to play Songs, long after it was obvious I'd lost my gift. It was like they refused to believe it. I even got the feeling that Alia expected my Piping to be *stronger*, somehow. It was peculiar."

Wren thought back to the sight of the obsidiac shards melting away where they'd touched Patch's skin, as if Patch had *absorbed* them somehow. She remembered the look on Alia's face and understood why Alia had been expecting something extraordinary. Surely all that obsidiac couldn't just have *vanished* without leaving some kind of effect?

"Go on, then," she said, wondering if, just maybe . . . "Play something for the ducks. Play the Dance!"

Patch raised a disapproving eyebrow. "It won't work," he said. "Without a Piper's gift, it's no more magical than if it was you or my grandparents playing. And the Dance is forbidden, remember?"

"Surely if you're not a Piper anymore, there's nothing wrong with playing it?" said Barver.

"I suppose that's true," said Patch. "Nevertheless, the Dance did send me to the dungeons of Tiviscan. I'd rather pick something from happier times! See if you recognize this, Wren."

And so Patch Brightwater took up the Pipe and began to play.

Wren recognized the melody at once. It was the Lift, the Song Patch had played in Marwheel Abbey with the newly glazed Pipe that he'd carved himself. It was bright and cheerful, and she remembered the little ant that Patch had played for.

Perhaps Wren had been expecting a miracle—for Patch's Piping gift to flood back stronger than ever. But it wasn't to be. The curious way that Pipes kept each layer of music going while the Piper focused on another part of the Song simply didn't happen. Instead, only the notes that Patch was actually playing could be heard.

And as Patch had warned, the notes had no magical effect at all. It was just music.

Even so, it was *beautiful* music. It filled Wren with a sense of joy and peace as she sat with her truest friends on a stunning day. The ducks feasted on their bread crumbs, their gentle quacking adding to the blissful mood.

It was one of those rare perfect moments that Wren wished would stretch on and on. There was nowhere else she'd rather be.

All too soon, Patch stopped and set the Pipe down. "See?" he said. "Nothing. No magic, not anymore."

"Oh, I wouldn't say that," said Wren, the beauty of the music still filling her heart. "I wouldn't say that at all."

★   ★   ★

It wasn't until three months later, with winter around the corner, that Alia's suspicions about the obsidiac shards would bear fruit.

After a few weeks in Hamelyn, Patch and his grandparents returned to Praze-by-Desten, this time traveling by cart. They planned to move within a year, selling their cottage and finding a new home nearer Hamelyn to make it easier for Patch to spend time with all of his family.

His grandparents bought him a wooden flute, an instrument with vastly fewer finger holes than a Piper's Pipe and crucial if he was going to make a living as a musician.

As he practiced he would look to his bedroom wall, where he'd hung Rundel Stone's Pipe as a reminder of what he'd once been. He found it frustrating, though. He knew that eventually he'd be able to get a better sound from the flute than a Pipe, but the habits learned on a Pipe made playing a flute surprisingly difficult.

Yet he stuck to it, and gradually his flute playing improved.

Then one evening, he found himself missing his friends even more than he normally did. He knew he would see them again in a few short weeks—they'd made plans for Barver to come, and together they would drop in to Tiviscan to visit Erner.

After that, they would travel to Gemspar, where Wren had started training with Alia at last. From there, the four of them would set off to find Massarken in time for the next full moon, ready for Alia to take on the role of Guardian.

He looked forward to showing them how good a flute player he was becoming, yet the sight of Rundel's Pipe caused a wave of melancholy to sweep through him. He decided that the time had come to focus on mastering his new instrument, and to do that he needed to truly forget the old.

He took the Pipe down from its hook, intending to pack it away out of sight once and for all, but he gave in to the temptation of playing it one last time—and what better thing to play, he thought, than the Lift.

Yet this time, as his fingers moved and the notes of the melody came, he could tell at once that something was different. As he began to play a different part of the Lift, the melody kept playing in the Pipe on its own. He could feel the Song building, exactly as it should.

There were tears of joy in Patch's eyes as he thought of telling his friends.

And then, as if the return of his gift wasn't enough, the most *extraordinary* thing began to happen.

But that is a story for another day . . .

Acknowledgments

It was twenty-one years ago that I first thought of Patch and the world of the Pipers. It's been a long journey from there to this, the final Songs of Magic book—and I couldn't have done it without the help I've had along the way.

My thanks to my erstwhile agent Luigi Bonomi, who managed not to choke on his coffee when I told him how long the first draft of *A Darkness of Dragons* was. Thank you for your enthusiasm for the idea, and your guidance and patience as I wrangled it down to a more reasonable size.

Thanks, too, to all at Usborne who made me feel so welcome—Rebecca Hill, my editors Anne Finnis and Sarah Stewart, and Jacob Dow and the team. Without your hard work and help, these books would have been a shadow of what they became. I'm hugely grateful to George Ermos too, for his wonderful covers.

My love and thanks go to my wife Laura, and my children—especially to my son, who has read these books more times than anyone else in the world.

Last, my thanks go to Patch, Wren, and Barver, who had to wait for so long to make it out of my head and onto the page. I'll miss you!

As Wren learns to become a powerful shape-shifting Sorcerer, and Patch finds he has some surprising new talents, I know that Barver will always be there to keep an eye on things. And who knows—maybe one day we'll meet again.

About the Author

S.A. Patrick was born in Belfast. When he was a child, he wanted to write video games, become an author, and have magical powers. The first two came true. If he does ever get magical powers, he hopes people like dragons and griffins because there'll suddenly be a lot of them around.

He has had four previous books published as Seth Patrick. The Songs of Magic trilogy is his first endeavor for children.